UNDER A SEA OF RED FOAM

G. ELMER MUNSON

SEVERED PRESS
HOBART TASMANIA

UNDER A SEA OF RED FOAM

Copyright © 2017 G. Elmer Munson

WWW.SEVEREDPRESS.COM

ISBN: 978-1-925711-40-0

PART 1 - THE RED SEA
1

As Dinesh stared at the body lying at his feet, he struggled to accept that it had once been his brother. He could no longer recognize Singh; his head had been torn from his body and lay crushed a few feet down the passageway. As the movement of the sea rocked the ship back and forth, Singh's head rolled from side to side. It made a disgusting sloppy noise as it slapped against the bulkheads.

What remained of his torso had been turned inside out, his intestines spilled across the deck plates, his blood oozing down the hall. The only things left to identify Singh were his boots. Years ago, he had picked up a pair of snakeskin cowboy boots from a street vendor in Crete. He'd been so proud of them that he hardly ever took them off. They've had more sea time than most of the sailors on board.

If it hadn't been for the boots, Dinesh could have lied to himself. They were coated in red, but there was no mistaking. No one on board had boots like Singh.

"Dinesh," someone called. "Come on, we've got to get out of here."

Dinesh turned around and saw Viraj running towards him. His clothes were torn and his face was streaked with blood.

Fire erupted further down the passageway, the flames spreading up the wall and licking the insulation overhead. Dinesh looked back at his brother's boots and hesitated.

"Come *on* Dinesh," Viraj pleaded. "Singh would want you to get out while you could."

"I can't leave them," Dinesh said as he bent down and pulled both boots free. One of them had a chunk of flesh stuck inside. He shook the boot and the remains of Singh's foot fell to the deck. Dinesh stared at it until a ball of fire blew out a hatch nearby.

A body flew out of the remaining hole and landed in the burning passageway. It had been burned black, the skin gone, leaving a shell of a man no longer recognizable.

1

Dinesh turned and ran He followed Viraj down the passageway, still clinging to his brother's boots. "Where are we going?" he asked as they passed a line of hatches that led deeper into the ship.

"Got to get topside," Viraj said. "There's just too much smoke." He coughed into his hands as if for emphasis.

Dinesh slowed to a walk, shaking his head and trying to catch his breath in the sulfurous passageway.

"What are you doing?" Viraj asked.

"No," Dinesh said. "I'm not going back up there. Those pirates are everywhere. You want to mess with them?"

"It's not the pirates I'm worried about," Viraj said.

"I'm not going."

"You want to stay down here and burn to death?"

Viraj had a point, but Dinesh didn't like it. He hugged Singh's boots and looked back at the flames.

Dinesh and Singh had both been topside when the Somali pirates attacked. They both watched friends and shipmates fall to the deck, some dead quick, some thrashing in agony as they slowly bled out on the deck. Some of them screamed for Dinesh's help, but he could only run away. He felt like a coward, but he could not help them.

He didn't want to return topside. Regardless of what was there, he couldn't imagine facing the dead and dying, the ones who cried out for help only to watch him turn and run. He couldn't do it.

He looked down the passageway and wondered if anywhere was really safe.

It's not the pirates I'm worried about. Viraj's words hung like a poison threatening to choke the entire ship. While the pirates were attacking topside, something else had happened, something Dinesh couldn't explain. Across the ship, people started to die. Not by gunfire or rocket powered grenades, but in other, more horrible ways. Things happened to them, inhuman things, things like what had happened to Singh. For all Dinesh knew, he and Viraj were the only two left alive.

"No," he repeated. "I'm not going"

"Fine, then I'll see you in the next life." Viraj turned and ran five steps before the watertight door near him exploded inward. It crushed him against the bulkhead as a wave of seawater rushed into the passageway.

Dinesh turned to run, but within two steps his feet were swept out from beneath him. He fell backwards and hit his head on the steel deck as the saltwater carried him straight towards the inferno. He lost his grip on Singh's boots and they were carried away, somewhere deep into the bowels of the ship.

The bulkhead past the next ladder moved, metal bending inward under tremendous pressure. A moment later it gave way and the ship rocked sideways, water now pouring in from both directions.

Dinesh reached out and grabbed the ladder. He struggled to keep his fingers from slipping as the water rushed by. Past the new rupture, he could hear more metal giving way. It sounded like the ship was coming apart. As the passage filled up with water, steam compartment from the fires that raged below. Dinesh could barely breathe. Something crashed into his fingers, bounced off his head, and continued down the passage. Somehow he kept his grip.

The water continued to rise. The lower decks appeared to have filled up, and the ship listed heavily to port. As Dinesh lay clinging to the ladder with aching fingers, he felt his body going numb. Soon he would be completely under water.

Viraj was right.

Dinesh looked up and down the flooded passageway before pulling himself up the ladder. Two decks up, a few quick turns, and he would be topside. He had no idea what to expect, but there was really no other way.

He closed his eyes and climbed. He'd taken the ladder hundreds of times and could easily do it blind. He had to mentally pry his fingers off each step to get them to move to the next, but at least he was moving. He climbed without stopping, without thinking of whom and what he'd left behind. He tried to pull his feet under to push himself along, but the water rose too fast.

Dinesh reached the top of the ladder, just beating the rising flood waters. It followed up the next ladder, racing towards the upper decks to join the waiting Red Sea. The ship leaned even more to port. It listed so far from centerline, he wondered how it stayed upright. By the time he pulled himself through to the upper level, the angle was so sharp he couldn't even stand.

Dinesh crawled up the passage, away from the ladder and the rising flood. A left at the next junction led to the forward watertight door. That would bring him topside. When he reached the door, he was in shallow enough water to lean against the nearby bulkhead.

He brought his hand to the wheel, but before turning it he hesitated.

What's out there, he thought. It could be fire, it could be pirates, or it could be the piles of dead shipmates waiting for him just on the other side. *Waiting to judge me*, he thought. *Judge me for running.*

Or, it could be nothing more than the vast, empty Red Sea. That or something even worse.

An explosion from deep within the ship helped make up his mind. He spun the wheel in his hands, thankful that no water poured through the widening gap as he broke the seal. Once the cog had fully turned, he pulled the door open and stepped through to the night air beyond.

The dead lay everywhere. Sailors piled on top of pirates, neatly stacked against the superstructure so they would not slide into the sea, all reaching higher than Dinesh could see. There were at least ten piles.

Dinesh scanned the deck but could not find a single living person. He crawled to the closest pile and pulled a rifle from one of the sailor's hands. He checked the magazine; it was full. Not one shot had been fired.

Dinesh leaned back on the deck and stared at the scene surrounding him. He closed his eyes and wondered, *What did this? Who piled the bodies? And do I even want to know?*

From below, the scream of metal on metal made him jump to his feet. He fell to the side and rolled towards the sea, catching himself on a braided metal safety line.

The deck began to vibrate as the ship spun around, heading north. Dinesh could tell the direction from the stars; he'd learned how as a kid. He pulled himself from the edge and crawled towards the bridge, hoping to see a familiar face steering the ship back to Jeddah, their last port of call. Of course, the bridge was empty.

Dinesh stood to get a better look, leaning against the bulkhead for stability. Above, the Plexiglas windscreen had been melted away as the bridge beyond continued to burn. The charred remains of the piloting crew lay neatly piled by the quartermaster's plot, faces and uniforms burnt unrecognizable. Dinesh stepped back and tripped over an outstretched leg. He landed on something soft and rolled to the side, coming up to his knees.

He looked down and saw his friend Sanjay, or at least what remained of him. His now limbless torso had been gutted, his entrails scattered across the nonskid deck. The blackened space between his ribs hung empty. His eyes and mouth had locked open in a grotesque display of horror and pain.

Dinesh stood up and tried to run, his head spinning from the smoke and the scene. He opened his mouth and thought he could hear himself screaming, his voice echoing across the sea, perhaps reaching all the way to the Suez Canal. He continued to spin and scream until the blackness took over and he crashed to the deck.

For Dinesh, unconsciousness was bliss.

2

"Contact bears zero-six-four," Rodriguez said over the loudspeaker to the Control Room. "On the right, drawing right."

"Sonar, do you have course and speed?" Lieutenant Henry asked.

"Stand by." Rodriguez set down the microphone and slapped Seaman Parker in the back of the head. "Well, fucker?"

"What?" Parker asked as he rubbed his head and started to turn around.

Rodriguez slapped him again. "Keep your eyes on the contact," he said. He looked at the line of operators crowding the Sonar Room. "Can *anyone* tell me what this fucker is doing?"

"I got it, Supervisor," Petty Officer Santalino said from the far end of Sonar. He scribbled a solution onto a piece of paper and passed it to Rodriguez. "Send that in to Fire Control, that's dead-nuts right there."

"It better be," Rodriguez said as he slid open the door between Sonar and the Control Room. He passed the note to Chief Jacobs. "Chief, got a solution for you."

Jacobs looked at the paper and barked out a laugh. "You guys suck," he said. "This is why you need a Chief in Sonar."

"I think we're doing just fine without one," Rodriguez said as he slid the door closed.

"That guy's a dick," Santalino said.

"Tell me about it." Rodriguez grabbed a calculator and started running the numbers to see what he came up with on his own. Everything came out damn close to what Santalino had calculated.

"Supervisor, contact is changing course," Parker said.

"Show me." Rodriguez leaned in and watched the contact cut to the left at a sharp angle. He grabbed the microphone. "Control, contact has changed direction, now heading--" He slapped Parker on the back of the head once again.

"Uh, three-one-zero?" Parker said as he wrote notes on his display with a black grease pencil.

Rodriguez looked at the notes and punched a few keys on

his calculator. "Contact heading three-five-zero," he said before setting down the microphone.

The door slid open and Jacobs popped his head in. "What the fuck is wrong with you guys," he asked. "Are you all retarded?"

"Check your solution, Chief," Rodriguez said. "It works."

"Do we have a firing solution?" Lieutenant Henry asked over the loudspeaker.

"Come on, Chief," Rodriguez said. "Trust us." He glanced down at Parker's display. "He's speeding up, we're almost out of time."

"Fine," Jacobs said. "But I'm bringing this to the Captain if you fuck it up."

"Understood." Rodriguez smiled as Jacobs threw the door closed. "Prick."

"Dude, we're getting close," Santalino said. The display grew fuzzy as the noise from the contact began masking everything else.

"Control, we're seeing near-field effect."

"Stand by," Lieutenant Henry said. "Final bearing and shoot."

Jacobs came over the loudspeaker and said, "Firing, tube two, in three, two--"

The ship rocked as torpedo tube number two fired.

"Annapolis," Lieutenant Henry announced over the underwater communications microphone. "Target lock, hold you course three-five-zero, speed twelve knots, range twelve hundred yards. Over."

The system responded with a blast of sea noise before a human voice came across from the other submarine. "Roger, Alexandria, well played."

A cheer went up in the Control Room that could be heard through the walls into the Sonar Room. Rodriguez reached forward and rubbed each operator on the head. He couldn't contain the smile that consumed his face.

"Good job, Rodriguez," Santalino said as he held out his fist.

Rodriguez bumped it with his own fist and said, "Thanks to *you*."

The door slid open and Jacobs peered in. "Sonar!"

"Yes, Chief?"

"Good job." Jacobs slammed the door closed without another word.

Rodriguez looked at Santalino with his mouth hung open. He pointed at the door and asked, "Did you hear that shit?"

"You're on your way, brother," Santalino said with a smile.

"Fucking-a." Rodriguez leaned to the side and cracked his back. "Now who's getting me a cup of coffee?"

Before anyone could answer, a voice came over the general announcement circuit. *"Prepare to surface."*

Jacobs opened the door once again. "Suit up, Rodriguez," he said. "You're in the bridge." He closed the door without waiting for a response.

"Shit," Rodriguez said. "Never mind the coffee." He reached in a locker and grabbed his hat. "Santalino, you've got Sonar."

"Roger that." Santalino stood and walked to the back of the cramped room.

Rodriguez opened the forward door and headed to his bunk to grab his hat coat. *I hope I don't get stuck up there with fucking Brett again*, he thought as the submarine headed for the surface.

"So, dude, I'm like, dicking this chick and she's like, all into it, and we're like, all crazy and shit, and the door busts open, and it's her fucking *mom*, man, and she's like 'What the fuck?' and I'm like, 'What the fuck?' but the chick's like, 'Shit, man, don't stop the *deep dicking*,' so I just keep bangin' away, and so after a bit her mom gets all hot and shit, and next thing you know--"

"Stop," Rodriguez said with a sigh. "Just stop. I can see where this is going."

Seaman Brett paid no attention. He didn't even pause.

"--we're all banging away, and her mom's like, riding me, *screaming* 'Oh, I love the dick,' and then the door opens, *again*, and here comes the chick's dad, all pissed off and yellin' and shit, but, like, I just look at him and say, 'Fuck off,' and like, 'Wait your turn, old man,' and the mom starts howling and riding harder, and so dad pulls out his little dick and starts pulling it, but he can't get hard, right? So he just walks out, and he don't even like, come back and shit."

Brett stopped to catch his breath. He looked like he'd just run a marathon, his slack jaw sucking in great mouthfuls of the cool ocean air as he stared at the group huddled in the submarine's bridge. "It was awesome."

For a good thirty seconds, no one said anything. They all stared at Brett as he looked around with a ridiculous smile on his face. Eventually, Rodriguez was the one to break the silence.

"That's the stupidest story I've ever heard," he said. "What the fuck is wrong with you?"

"Nothin', man. Just passin' the time, you know?" Brett looked at Rodriguez, his eyes wide and eyebrow raised. He looked like he honestly couldn't understand Rodriguez's reaction.

"How about we pass the time in silence?" Rodriguez asked. "It's a nice night out. I'd like to enjoy some peace before we have to sink this hunk of shit."

"It's submerge, Rodriguez," Lieutenant Henry said from behind his binoculars. "We don't sink, we submerge."

"Come on, Lieutenant," Rodriguez asked. "Do we really have to listen to this mouth breather all night?"

"I'm not a mouth breather," Brett said.

"Oh yeah?" Rodriguez asked. "Then close your mouth."

Brett stared at Rodriguez without an ounce of comprehension. His lower lip continued to hang by his chin, a glisten of drool reflecting the soft glow of the moon above.

"Uh-huh."

"What?" Brett asked, shrugging his shoulders.

"He's right," Henry said. "You are a mouth breather."

"Aw, man," Brett whined, grabbing the night vision binoculars and strapping them on. He turned away and looked out over the ocean.

Rodriguez looked in the opposite direction. *There's nothing out here*, he thought as he scanned the horizon for a glimpse of light, a shadow moving against the sky, or pretty much anything. He looked back and watched the dark waters of the Red Sea churn, the submarine's wake stretching farther than he could see.

Rodriguez closed his eyes and took a deep breath. As much as he complained about it, he loved standing lookout at night. Even with an asshole like Henry and an idiot like Brett, it beat the hell out of the canned air stink of the submarine.

He had just begun to enjoy the peace when he heard a sound, like the light scrape of metal on metal. He let the air escape his lungs and opened his eyes. Brett had lit a cigarette.

"Christ, Brett, can't you go five minutes without lighting up?"

"Yeah," Brett said. He spit over the side and watched the water flow past. He took two quick, short drags of his cigarette and spit again before strapping the night vision goggles back to his face.

"Never mind." Rodriguez turned around, shook his head and wondered if his watch relief might be coming up early. He checked the time and sighed. "Zero-one-twenty-two," he said.

"Do you have to give us updates?" Lieutenant Henry asked. "We've still got a few more hours. I'd like to at least get *some* sleep."

"But Lieutenant Henry," Brett said as he turned around with the goggles still stuck to his face. "We're on watch. We can't sleep on watch."

The Lieutenant looked at Brett with no expression at all. After almost a full minute of silence, he pulled a lighter out of his pocket and flicked the flame in front of Brett's face.

"Aaah!" Brett screamed. He tore the night vision from his face and rubbed at his eyes. "Ow, Sir. That kinda hurt."

"I know. That was the point." Lieutenant Henry leaned back in the corner of the bridge compartment and closed his eyes.

Brett looked to Rodriguez as if for support. His eyes went wide and he pointed at the Lieutenant.

Rodriguez shrugged and turned away. He closed his eyes and took another deep breath, hoping for just a bit of silence.

Rodriguez saw it first. There was just a quick flash and then

10

it was gone. He kept his mouth shut and stared into the horizon, his eyes not leaving the spot, waiting for a repeat before he would open his mouth.

Once Lieutenant Henry fell asleep, he didn't like to be woken. If it turned out to be nothing, he would shit on Rodriguez for a week. Maybe longer.

Rodriguez squinted and stared, silently hoping he wouldn't see anything. *I just want this watch to be over.* As time passed, he grew less and less sure he was even looking in the same spot. *I'm just seeing things*, he thought. *Been up here too damn long.*

Then he saw it again; a flash of moonlight reflecting off something smooth, like glass or metal. He reached his arm out to wake the Lieutenant when a voice from the bridge box loudspeaker made them all jump.

"Bridge, Coordinator," Chief Jacobs said. "Do you have anything bearing one-two-zero?"

Rodriguez checked the compass; one-two-zero was just about right. "Shit," he whispered.

"What have you got, Rodriguez?" Lieutenant Henry asked, rubbing his eyes and leaning forward with his binoculars.

"Not sure, Sir. Thought I saw a flash out there."

"No lights?"

"No. Maybe derelict?"

"Could be," Lieutenant Henry said. "There's shit floating all over this place."

Brett moved in for a look, the nauseating stench of coffee, cigarettes, and halitosis overpowering the small bridge.

"Dude, can you back up a bit?" Rodriguez asked. "I mean, seriously."

"What?" Brett asked.

"Your breath stinks worse than my ass, Brett," the Lieutenant said. "And in the past day and a half I've taken three shits without showering."

"Aw, man." Brett cupped his hands in front of his face and breathed out through his mouth and in through his nose. After a few breaths, he dropped his hands. He blinked and stared at the other two men. "I don't smell nothin'."

Rodriguez turned back to Lieutenant Henry. "Sir, the

Coordinator?"

"Shit," the Lieutenant said as he grabbed the microphone. "Coordinator, bridge, we've got a visual down that bearing, no lights, possible derelict craft. Have radio attempt to contact." He dropped the microphone and turned to Rodriguez. "There, let them figure it out. Anything comes up, let me know." He leaned back in the corner and once again closed his eyes.

Rodriguez shook his head and turned back to the east, searching through his binoculars for a visual. He scanned the horizon for any other movement. He stopped as he caught a glimpse of something moving in the opposite direction of the ship. It disappeared as soon as it appeared, and in the unbroken darkness it would have to be something big. Or close. Or both.

It was a clear night, and the ocean was calm. *Nothing that big could have disappeared*, he thought, *not even at night*. He caught the glint of a reflection once again, but nothing else. He lowered his binoculars and stared at the bridge box. *Give me something*, he thought. *He should at least be on radar.*

A dark shape came into view, barely there but enough to track. Rodriguez looked through his binoculars and then back at the bridge box. *Fuck it.*

"Brett, call Sonar for me, would you?" Rodriguez asked as he grabbed the handset and held it up to his ear.

Brett picked up the microphone, *very* slowly bringing it up to his face, his hand already shaking.

"Dude, just call them."

"I don't wanna fuck it up."

"Then don't."

"But I haven't taken my communication test yet."

"Dude, seriously? Just fucking do it. Call Sonar and ask them to pick up. You can do that, can't you?"

Brett keyed the microphone. "Sonar, b-b-b-b-b-b-b-b-bridge," he stammered.

"Stop," Rodriguez said with his hand raised. "That's good enough." He waited a few seconds before a familiar voice came over the line.

"Sonar Supervisor," Petty Officer Santalino replied.

"Hey, it's Rodriguez."

"What the hell was that?"

"Fucking Brett," Rodriguez said.

"Shit, man, don't give that idiot the mike. What've you got up there?"

"Not much, that's why I'm calling. You got anything on Sonar?"

"What bearing?"

"We only have one contact, brainiac. I'm not getting any updates up here. See what they've got in Control."

"Yeah, all right. Hang on a sec."

The line went dead. Rodriguez stared out over the sea and tried to ignore Brett's nose picking. He closed his eyes until Santalino returned.

"Hey, Rodriguez?"

"Yeah?"

"Fire Control has him out at eighty thousand yards."

"Dude, I'm looking at it." Rodriguez stared at the distant contact, now close enough to maintain steady visual contact. "Tell them to fix their shit."

"The Coordinator's happy with it," Santalino said. "You want something done, ask the OOD. Who's up there?"

"Take a guess."

"Henry, the sleeping giant?"

"Who else?" Rodriguez said.

"So wake him up."

"Yeah, right."

"Pussy."

"Whatever," Rodriguez said. "Thanks anyway." He hung up the handset and looked back at the sleeping Lieutenant. He cleared his throat and spoke. "Officer of the Deck?"

One of Lieutenant Henry's bloodshot eyes cracked open and stared at Rodriguez. "What?"

"Sorry to wake you Sir, but Fire Control has this guy way farther than I can see him."

"And?"

"Well, I'd recommend a ranging maneuver," Rodriguez said. "There's no one else out here, we can find out how far this prick really is."

"Rodriguez, we're in the middle of the Red Sea. As soon as we clear the Gulf of Aden we're gonna dive this pig and be gone. I couldn't give two fucks what that fucker's doing or where he's going so long as he stays out of our way."

"Yeah, but--"

"Is he on the left?"

"Yes."

"Drawing left?"

"Well, maybe, yeah," Rodriguez said. "At least I think--"

"Then shut the fuck up," Lieutenant Henry said. "I'm going back to sleep, so try to keep your fucking mouth shut." He closed his eye and said no more.

Rodriguez turned and went back to his search. He scanned around, looking for something else to occupy the remainder of his watch. There was nothing else out there.

"Why you even care about this guy?" Brett asked. "He's far enough away. Don't seem to be doin' nothin'."

"I don't know," Rodriguez said. "Just seems odd, him being out there like that at night. It's sketchy."

"He can keep his sketchiness to himself for two more hours," Lieutenant Henry said with his eyes still closed. "Now seriously. Shut the fuck up."

"Roger that, Sir," Brett said. He strapped on his night vision goggles and turned back to starboard, leaving Rodriguez to stare at his mystery contact once again.

Rodriguez brought his binoculars to his eyes and looked down the contact's bearing. He saw nothing. "What the fuck?"

"What now?" Lieutenant Henry asked.

"Nothing, Sir," Rodriguez said. "Just can't seem to find our contact."

"Well, good. Maybe *now* I can get some sleep."

"But it was there just a minute ago--"

"Nope," the Lieutenant interrupted. "Not. Interested."

"Maybe he went home?" Brett suggested.

"We're miles from the nearest port" Rodriguez said. "Unless his home is Atlantis." He looked over at the bridge box and noticed the compass spinning wildly. He reached over and tapped on the glass but it didn't stop.

"Hey, what's up with the--" Rodriguez began. He stopped when he glanced up and saw the look on Brett's face.

His jaw hung down, his eyes bulged, and his nostrils flared in and out as he tried to speak. "Ah...ah...ah..." was all he could get out. He held up an arm and pointed behind Rodriguez.

"What?" Rodriguez turned and saw a hulking grey shape. A surface ship was closing in, towering over the submarine and moving fast. It listed badly to one side and glowed like it was on fire.

"Oh shit," Rodriguez whispered. He spun around, pushing Brett with one hand while grabbing the microphone with the other.

"Collision imminent, port side," he screamed before pushing the collision alarm and ducking down.

"What the fuck?" Lieutenant Henry yelled.

Brett let out a series of incoherent yelps as he stared at the closing ship.

Rodriguez reached up and grabbed them both, pulling them down into the sail seconds before the ship crashed into their submarine.

Below decks, all hell broke loose.

3

Until he woke to the sounds of screaming from below, Rodriguez didn't even realize he'd been unconscious. He opened his eyes and the submarine's bridge seemed to spin around him. He wiped his forehead and felt the sticky dampness of sweat and blood dripping from his hair.

Next to him, Lieutenant Henry had his hands on the bridge box and was trying to pull himself upright.

Brett lay on top of them both, his massive foul smelling body sprawled out and filling the small bridge. He was not moving.

Rodriguez reached over and tried to push him off. His hand sunk into soft flesh that moved like jelly. "Gross," he whispered, barely audible over the noise from below decks.

The general alarm rang throughout the submarine. Rodriguez could hear voices screaming as they ran down the Command Passageway.

"Goddamn it Brett, how did such a disgusting fat fuck ever get on board a submarine?" Lieutenant Henry asked. "Rodriguez, get this pig off me."

"Roger that." Rodriguez braced his back against the wall and put his foot against Brett's hip.

Lieutenant Henry grabbed one of Brett's arms and lifted it as best he could. "Ready? On three," he said. "One. Two. *Three*." The Lieutenant pushed up as Rodriguez kicked Brett to the side.

Brett rolled over just enough that they could both slip out and stand.

"Shit," Lieutenant Henry said, "that's one fat fuck."

Rodriguez stared up at the rusty wall of grey before him. The ship floated so close he could almost reach out and touch it. It was badly damaged. It listed at least forty degrees to port and oily black smoke poured from the main deck. No one seemed to be on board.

Lieutenant Henry was trying to contact someone on the radio. He didn't seem to be having any luck.

Rodriguez leaned his head back and yelled up to the ship.

"Hello! Anyone up there?"

"Look at that piece of shit," Lieutenant Henry said. "There's no one alive up there. I'm amazed that thing still floats." He spoke into the microphone one last time. "Control, bridge, damage report." There was no reply. He dropped it and kicked the bridge box. "*Fuck.*" He turned back to Rodriguez. "Nothing. This thing is dead"

"Should we go down?" Rodriguez asked.

"Shit, no. We're still on watch. Besides, it sounds like a warzone down there. We'd just get in the way." He looked up at the burning ship. "I do wish I knew what was going on though." He glanced at the ladder before shaking his head and leaning back against the bridge box.

A wave crashed against the side of the ship, turning the rusty bow around. It scraped along the submarine until it pointed north. It spun the submarine around until they were side by side.

Rodriguez looked along the ship's hull. About a quarter of the way down, he could make out the hull number D60 in mostly faded white print. "D60? Not one of ours."

"Certainly not," the Lieutenant said.

"Maybe local? Who around here has destroyers?"

"This is the Red Sea," Lieutenant Henry said. "Everyone passes through here. Have a look at the flag." As the ship spun to the side, much of the main deck became visible. Lieutenant Henry pointed to a small soiled flag hanging from high up in the superstructure. It was mostly white with a red cross splitting it into quarters. In the top left corner, horizontal stripes of orange, white, and green filled the quarter. A small circle sat in the center of the white stripe.

"What is that?" Rodriguez asked. "Iran?"

"No, India. We did an exercise with them on my last boat. They were a good group of guys. I can't imagine what the hell happened here."

"I don't know, and I don't think I *want* to know," Rodriguez said, shaking his head and backing away from the ship. He stepped on Brett's hand.

Brett woke up and jumped to a sitting position. He yelled, "Shit, man, my fucking *hand*." He shook his fingers and put them in his mouth.

"Sorry, dude."

"I think you broke one of my fingers."

"Which one?" Rodriguez asked. "Not the one you jam in your ass, I hope?"

"Very funny, dick head," Brett said. "No, not that one. This one." He held out his middle finger.

Rodriguez whipped his arm out and flicked Brett's finger.

"*Shit*." Brett pulled his hand back and held it against his stomach. He covered it with his other hand. "Ow, man. Not cool."

"Well, keep your stinking asshole finger away from me then," Rodriguez said.

"Can you two please shut the fuck up?" Lieutenant Henry pointed up to the deck of the Indian ship. "There's something moving up there."

Twisted deck lines and debris had collected along the safety rail, some of it hanging out over the sea. One section of line moved, as something under the mess shook it back and forth.

"What is that?" Brett asked.

"Shit, man. That's a *hand*." Rodriguez brought up his binoculars and peered at the moving pile.

A man's hand stuck out from under the line, shaking back and forth as if trying to reach from something.

"What do we do?" Brett asked.

"We do shit," Lieutenant Henry said. "Did your last boat come with a fucking extension ladder? We're not a fire truck."

Brett stopped talking and looked at his boots.

"Officer of the Deck?" a voice called from inside the submarine. "You guys okay up there?"

Rodriguez stepped over and looked down the ladder.

Lieutenant Jackson stared up at them, a clipboard in his hand and a cigarette burning in his mouth.

"Sir, are you smoking?" Rodriguez asked.

"Fuck you, Rodriguez," Lieutenant Jackson said. "New rule. When we get hit by a destroyer in the middle of fucking nowhere, we're allowed to smoke."

"You just make that up?" Lieutenant Henry asked. He

walked over to stand next to Rodriguez.

"Yep, sure did."

"Good enough for me," Lieutenant Henry said. "Smoke if you got 'em."

"Fucking-A" Brett said with a smile. He pulled out his pack of Marlboro Lights and held them out. The Lieutenant grabbed one, but Rodriguez shook his head.

"No way, man," he said. "I quit years ago. I'm not starting back up."

"Suit yourself," Brett said. He lit his cigarette and held the lighter out for Lieutenant Henry, who lit up and blew smoke in Rodriguez's face.

"Come on, Sir," Rodriguez coughed, waving his hand in front of his face.

"It's not my fault you're a fucking pussy."

"*Up ladder*," Lieutenant Jackson yelled from below. "Make a hole, people."

Rodriguez stepped to the side to make room.

Lieutenant Henry reached down and grabbed Lieutenant Jackson's outstretched hand, pulling him up to the bridge.

"Wow," Lieutenant Jackson said as he looked up at the destroyer. "That's one ugly-ass piece of shit."

"Tell me about it," Lieutenant Henry replied. "Inconsiderate too, running into us like that. Everyone okay down there?'"

"Yeah I guess, now that the flooding stopped." He continued to stare up at the destroyer. "Actually, I can't believe we're still floating," Lieutenant Jackson said. "I mean, that thing's fucking *huge*."

"Hey, Sir?" Rodriguez said. "Look." He lowered his binoculars and pointed to the mess along the railing. A man had crawled out from under the tangled lines. He was looking around with wide eyes as he scrambled to hang on.

Everyone in the bridge turned to look just as he fell into the ocean below.

"Shit," Lieutenant Henry said. "Grab the life ring."

Brett grabbed the orange ring and the tangle of coiled line and threw them both into the water.

They landed nowhere near the Indian sailor. His arms flailed at the otherwise calm surface as his head repeatedly dunked under the water.

"You fucking idiot, you threw the whole thing," Rodriguez said.

"Yeah?" replied Brett.

"How the fuck are we supposed to pull him up?" Lieutenant Henry asked. They all looked at the water. The balled-up line floated about ten feet from the hull of the submarine.

"Idiot," Lieutenant Jackson said. He slapped Brett on the back of the head for emphasis.

In the water, the sailor managed to grab hold of a mess of floating debris and wrapped his arms around it tight. It was enough to keep his head above water.

"So what, are we all going to stand here stroking ourselves while this guy drowns?" Lieutenant Jackson asked.

"Nope," Lieutenant Henry said as he turned to Rodriguez and clapped him on the back. "Looks like Diver Dan here gets to take a swim."

"Fuck." Rodriguez looked at the water. There was oil and debris and random shit floating everywhere from the crash. He let out an exaggerated sigh and glanced back at the ladder. "Can someone help me grab my shit?"

Rodriguez stood on the deck of the submarine, with Seaman New Guy standing nearby. He was huddled directly behind the sail, as if he could blend into the steel. Rodriguez looked at New Guy's uniform where his name had been scribbled out. His Chief had written "New Guy" with a black Sharpie and told him he wasn't allowed to use his real name until he completed his qualifications. After just a couple months on the submarine, he was already well behind schedule.

Rodriguez didn't even know New Guy's real name. The two stood there in awkward silence while waiting for instruction from the bridge. Any time spent with New Guy was awkward. The kid was weird, and he barely talked. Rodriguez was never so happy to hear Lieutenant Henry yelling at him.

"What, are you waiting for an invitation?" he called from the bridge. "He could have built his own raft and sailed to fucking India by now."

"Yes Sir," Rodriguez replied. "Right on it, Sir." He stared out over the water, looking for any sign of movement. He wanted to be sure there was no one -- or no *thing* -- out there before he jumped in after the guy. It was hard to see with all the debris. Rodriguez was a fast swimmer, but he didn't want to run into something faster.

He stepped towards the edge, the warm water licking his bare toes as the waves passed over the hull.

The Indian sailor was about fifty feet out. He had managed to grab the life ring but was not really moving.

If there was something out there, Rodriguez thought, *it would have found him first. Right?*

"God damn it, Rodriguez, get in the fucking water," Lieutenant Henry yelled.

"Yes Sir, fine, fuck it." Rodriguez sat down and pulled on his flippers. He stood, grabbed the line from the deck bag, tied it around his waist, and held the other end out to New Guy. "You ready, fuck stick?" he asked.

New Guy stepped closer."Yes, Petty Officer," he said without looking at Rodriguez. He appeared about as far from ready as humanly possible. His face lost all its color and his eyes had gone wide. He stared out at the open ocean like it could jump up and bite him.

"Did you really go to dive school?" Rodriguez asked.

"Yes, Petty Officer."

"Fucking cut that out, man." Rodriguez looked out at the Indian sailor and back at New Guy. "Look, New Guy, it's no big deal. I swim out, I swim back. Something happens, you pull us back. Cool?"

New Guy nodded and grabbed the rope.

Rodriguez pulled on his face mask. "Okay then. Watch for any problems. Just don't let go and I won't have to kick your ass when I get back."

Without waiting for a reply, he jammed his snorkel in his mouth, leaped off the side of the submarine, and splashed into

21

the warm water of the Red Sea. He popped his head above the surface and blew out water. As soon as he got his eyes on the lone sailor, he began to swim.

Half way there, Rodriguez paused. He could hear the sailor babbling something he couldn't understand. He wasn't sure what language Indians spoke, but it was nothing he'd heard before. He put his head back down and swam as fast as he could.

Stupid dive school, he thought. All *I wanted was to scam a trip to Florida instead of going on deployment.* He kept his eyes on the sailor as he swam. *Now look at me, rescuing some random bastard in the middle of nowhere.*

As Rodriguez got closer, the sailor began to splash around, screaming and waving at Rodriguez. Rodriguez pulled the snorkel out of his mouth.

"Hey, man, calm down," Rodriguez said.

The sailor only splashed more.

Rodriguez dove under the water and kicked the last ten feet, surfacing right behind the panicked sailor. He spit out his snorkel and said, "Calm down."

The man whirled around, splashing water in Rodriguez's face and losing his grip on the life ring. His head slipped under the water. His arms flailed around, splashing in all directions before grabbing the ring once again. His head popped up and he coughed and grabbed Rodriguez, pulling him close and trying to climb on top of him.

"Cut it out, man," Rodriguez yelled. "You're gonna pull us both under." He slipped behind, grabbed the guy around the waist, and tried to hold him still. The guy kept squirming around, his body shaking as he coughed. Water and vomit sprayed from his mouth.

Aw, man, he thought as chunky bile coated the surrounding water. *Gross.* Rodriguez held him as still as possible as he waved one hand in the air as high as he could. Within seconds he felt the line around his waist pull tight and they were on their way back to the submarine.

New Guy kept the line tight and steady, but he was pulling very slowly.

The Indian sailor calmed down once they started moving,

but Rodriguez kept looking around, watching the water and trying to avoid the debris from the crash. The Red Sea was thankfully calm. Nothing moved, but he'd still feel better once he got back topside.

As they moved closer to the submarine, Rodriguez saw that Petty Officer Cartwright was helping New Guy with the line. *Great*, he thought. *Fucking Cartwright*. He hated Cartwright; everyone did.

"Hey, prick," Cartwright yelled from the safety of the ship. "You catch yourself a sand nigger or what?"

"Fuck you, Cartwright." Rodriguez reached the ship and grabbed on to the rope ladder that hung over the edge. He climbed with one hand while dragging the Indian sailor with the other.

The sailor stopped struggling once he was out of the water. He went slack, becoming dead weight.

"Can you quit dicking around and give me a hand?" Rodriguez asked.

"No way, man," Cartwright said. "I don't know where he's been. He might have the sand fleas or some shit."

"You're a real asshole," Rodriguez said. "New Guy, give me a fucking hand."

"Yes, Petty Off--"

"*I said cut that shit*. Just because you're brand fucking new doesn't mean you have to act it."

"Sorry Petty Off--I mean, uh..."

"Just call him Rod," Cartwright said. "*Hot* Rod. Like as in the Hot Rod of cock that he *wishes* he had." He followed with an obnoxious laugh that consisted mostly of pointing and snorting.

"Rodriguez is fine," Rodriguez said to New Guy. "Now help me pull this guy out of the water." Between the two of them, they managed to get the Indian sailor up.

Cartwright stood to the side, still laughing to himself. "Hot Rod," he said with a chuckle.

"Why are you so interested in my dick?" Rodriguez asked.

"What?" Cartwright stopped laughing. "Fuck you, queer."

The Indian sailor flopped to the deck, flat on his back, staring up at the remains of his ship. He began to cry.

"Shit, man, are you okay?" Rodriguez asked.

"The guy's a pussy," Cartwright said.

"Shut the fuck up," Rodriguez said to Cartwright before turning back to the sailor. "Can you speak English?"

The Indian sailor stared up at the destroyer a moment longer before looking at Rodriguez and nodding.

"You speak English?" Rodriguez asked again.

"Yes, I speak English," the sailor said.

"Oh, Good," Rodriguez breathed. *Easier*, he thought, *so much easier*. "Are you hurt?"

"No, not really. A little, maybe." He looked back at his ship and then down at the water before closing his eyes. "I'm so tired."

"Is anyone else alive?" Rodriguez asked as he sat down on the deck. He pulled off his fins, snorkel, and mask and handed them to New Guy.

New Guy stowed them in the deck bag and walked back to hide near the sail.

"I don't think so," the sailor said. He opened his eyes and looked over at Rodriguez. "No."

Rodriguez looked up at the bridge.

Lieutenant Jackson stood alone, speaking to someone on the phone as he stared at the destroyer.

"What's your name?" Rodriguez asked.

"Dinesh."

"Well welcome aboard, Dinesh." He stuck out his hand and Dinesh shook it. "I'm Eric Rodriguez, and you're on board the USS Alexandria."

"Thank you," Dinesh said.

"Are you the crazy-ass drunken Arab who ran into us?" Cartwright asked.

"Shut up, Cartwright," Rodriguez said. "First off, he's Indian--"

"Indian?" Cartwright asked, a smile spreading across his face. "Dot or feather?" He laughed so hard at that he nearly fell over.

"You're an asshole," Rodriguez said. "Leave the guy alone."

Dinesh looked up at Cartwright with a raised eyebrow but he

24

did not answer.

"Oh, don't mind him," Rodriguez said. "He's just a dick."

"*You're* a dick," Cartwright said.

"Fucking cut the shit," Lieutenant Henry said from just behind the sail. Everyone turned in time to see him drop off the ladder and onto the deck. "You're both dicks."

"But Sir," Cartwright began.

"But nothing, fuckhead," Lieutenant Henry said. "Get your stinking ass back to the engine room. Come find me after watch, but not until you've had a shower."

Cartwright dropped his smile and lowered his face to his armpit. He took two sniffs and wrinkled his face.

"Yeah, that's right," the Lieutenant said. "You stink. Now get the fuck out of here."

"Yes Sir." Cartwright headed back towards the sail with his head down, eyes on the deck. When he stepped on the ladder, the rope stretched tight under his weight. As he brought his other foot up to climb, he stopped and hung in mid-air, cocking his ear and looking all around him. "What?" he asked.

"Fucking go," Lieutenant Henry yelled.

Cartwright ignored him. He continued to look at the surrounding water, his body hanging off the ladder as he leaned towards the sea.

Rodriguez stood and looked around. *What is that?* Something felt off, like the air around them had gone still; even the heat seemed to lift from around them.

Lieutenant Henry didn't seem to notice anything. He stood staring at Cartwright, his face a mixture of revulsion and anger.

Over by the sail, New Guy was staring at the deck without moving.

Rodriguez pressed his hands to his temples and tried to focus on the growing noise echoing in his head. He couldn't place the sounds, but they didn't stop. He looked down at Dinesh.

Dinesh had stopped moving and sat very still, his eyes open wide and staring at the destroyer. His mouth drooped slightly, a trail of spit and seawater clinging to his lower lip. When it fell, it bounced off his chin and broke apart into many droplets. They spread away like a fan, collecting colors prism before landing on the deck in front of Dinesh.

He feels it too, Rodriguez thought.

Behind him, Rodriguez heard Cartwright step back onto the deck, his feet scraping along on the rough surface of the submarine's hull. He looked out to the water, nodded, then stepped around the sail towards the front end of the ship.

As soon as Cartwright passed out of sight, a blast of heat hit Rodriguez in the face, the wind nearly blowing him off balance. He shook his head and looked back towards the sail. Cartwright was gone.

What the fuck was that? He glanced up at the destroyer and shuddered. He saw nothing move, but somehow it felt like everything around them moved.

Lieutenant Henry's voice brought everything back to normal. "'Bout time that fucker left," he said. He turned back towards Dinesh and stuck out his hand. "Sorry about that, sir." His voice was conversational, as if nothing had just happened. "Lieutenant Ramón Henry, United States Navy. Welcome aboard."

Dinesh rose slowly and shook his hand. "Dinesh. Thank you for finding me." He had lost the wide-eyed stare; he looked tired but relaxed.

"Glad to help. I've got the hatch coming open if you'd like to join us below." Lieutenant Henry stepped towards the aft escape hatch and stared at the deck. "We can get you some dry clothes and something to eat. Maybe if you're up to it you can tell us what happened." He kicked at the deck. "Should be any minute."

As if on cue, the hatch popped open with a hiss of hydraulics. Someone pushed it the rest of the way from below. A young squirrelly-looking guy popped his head up and looked around.

"All set, Sir," Seaman Bone said from the hatch. He reached down into the ship, brought up a metal bar, and fixed to the inside of the hatch. He grabbed it and pulled himself the rest of the way up.

"No wasting time down there," Lieutenant Jackson called

from the bridge. "We don't want any more flooding, so cut the shit and get everyone below."

Bone moved to the side as Lieutenant Henry stepped down into the hatch.

The Lieutenant paused on the top ladder rung. "Will you be okay to climb down?" he asked Dinesh.

"I think so, yes."

"Good. Then I suggest we get below."

4

Rodriguez walked down the Command Passageway heading towards the Sonar Room. Lieutenant Henry had taken Dinesh to the Ward Room, and he had made it clear that Rodriguez was not welcome.

Suits me fine, Rodriguez thought. *I don't want to hang out with those dicks anyway.* He knocked on the door, opened it, and said, "Request to enter Sonar?"

No one answered. The supervisor was not standing in his normal spot at the back of the room, so Rodriguez walked right in. He pulled the door closed behind him and walked past the row of computer stacks that were supposed to be monitored constantly.

Only one had a live body sitting in front of it. Petty Officer Harrison sat on his head behind the Basic Sonar Operator's stack, his bare ass in the air with a pair of headphones wrapped around his hips. He had his hands up to his ass cheeks and he moved them in and out. They flapped together like lips as he spoke.

"Petty Officer Rodriguez," Harrison's ass said, "I can't find my supervisor. Have you seen him?"

The sound of giggling came from the darkness. Rodriguez pulled out his flashlight and shined it in the corner where Seaman Parker sat hunched down on the floor, a metal trash can covering his head. It shook uncontrollably from his giggling.

"I can't see anything," Harrison's ass said. "I'm afraid I have too much hair in the way. Could you give me a haircut? Just a trim, perhaps?"

"*A trim,*" Parker squealed from beneath his trash can, followed by even more can-shaking laughter.

Harrison's ass sniffed the air. "Do you smell something?" it asked before Harrison could no longer hold back. He fell to the side, falling out of his chair and dropping to the floor with laughter.

Parker laughed so hard he beat his trash can against the wall and kicked his feet wildly along the floor.

Rodriguez shook his head. "You guys are fucking idiots," he said. He stepped over Parker's flailing legs and opened the door that led to the Control Room.

Santalino stood at the periscope talking with Chief Jacobs. He looked over when the door opened and practically jumped when he saw Rodriguez.

"Dude, what's the word topside?" Santalino asked.

"Nothing yet," Rodriguez replied. "You know you're fucktards are doing jack shit in there, right?" He jammed his thumb back towards the Sonar Room.

"Big deal. It's not like we're going anywhere."

"True, but it might be a good idea if Harrison puts his pants back on."

Santalino shook his head and sighed. "Fucking idiot."

"How are things down here?" Rodriguez asked.

"Not so bad, the flooding stopped pretty quick. It was mostly just in the engine room, so all the dirty nukes are back there cleaning up. No fire or anything."

"Anyone get hurt?"

"Not that I've heard," Santalino said as he glanced at the overhead. "What's really going on up there?"

"Nothing."

"Bullshit," Chief Jacobs interrupted. He pulled his eyes away from the periscope and stared at Rodriguez. "I just watched you pull some guy out of the water."

"Yeah, an Indian guy from the destroyer that hit us," Rodriguez said.

"Did he come on board?" Santalino asked.

Rodriguez nodded. "He's down with Lieutenant Henry. Guy seems okay, but who knows what happened to him. That destroyer has seen better days."

"It looks pretty damn jacked up," Jacobs said. He returned to the periscope and stared at the destroyer.

Rodriguez could see the image on the periscope monitor strapped to the top of the Fire Control consoles."I can't believe it's still floating," he said. "It's damn near sideways."

"Right. Well, I think it's finally sinking," Jacobs said.

"No shit?"

"Have a look." The Chief stepped back and held his hand out, signaling for Rodriguez to take over at the periscope.

Rodriguez stepped up, put his eye to the lens, and scanned the Indian ship. He looked down at the water line. Sure enough, it was sitting much lower in the water than when he had been topside.

"Shit," he said. "I think you're right, Chief." He stepped aside and turned the scope back over to Jacobs. "For their sake, I hope no one's still on board."

"Rodriguez," Lieutenant called from the Command Passageway. "Mess decks, now." He disappeared down the steps toward middle level.

"Looks like you're invited to the party after all," Santalino said.

"Lucky me," Rodriguez said as he headed after the Lieutenant.

###

Dinesh sat alone at the center table of the Alexandria's mess deck. He had been given a bowl of minestrone soup and two slices of bread. A cup of hot tea waited for him to finish his meal. He ate slowly, his eyes glancing around the small room with every bite. The ship had gone respectfully quiet, and that made him nervous.

Rodriguez stood off to the side, speaking with Lieutenant Henry and another officer Dinesh hadn't met. They spoke low, frequently glancing over to see if he had finished eating.

The new officer said something and waved Lieutenant Henry away.

The Lieutenant walked off, leaving Rodriguez in the corner, staring at the floor.

The officer walked towards Dinesh."Mr. Dinesh?"

"Just Dinesh, please."

"Very well, Mr. Dinesh. My name is Commander Barnes. I'm the Executive Officer here." He brought his hand up and adjusted his glasses. "I have a few questions about you and your ship, if you're up to it."

"Well--"

"Good," Commander Barnes interrupted. "What kind of cargo are you carrying?"

"Cargo?"

"That's right. And where were you heading when you crashed into us?"

"When did we crash--?"

"Mr. Dinesh," the Commander began, "if you're not feeling cooperative we can postpone this interview until later."

"What interview?" Dinesh asked. "What are you asking me?" He sat up straight, his face turned towards the unexpectedly harsh Executive Officer. A piece of ditalini pasta dropped from his spoon and splashed into his nearly empty bowl of soup. A few droplets landed on his shirt but he barely noticed. He set his spoon on the table.

"Let's be upfront, shall we?" Commander Barnes asked. "The ship out there is the INS Lahore."

"Yes, I'm stationed aboard the Lahore," Dinesh said.

"Uh-huh. The Lahore disappeared weeks ago during an anti-piracy patrol off the coast of Somalia. Ring any bells?"

"What? We were--"

"Where is the crew?" Commander Barnes asked. "What exactly happened to this destroyer, this once mighty ship of war, to leave it in such a condition?"

"I'm trying to tell you," Dinesh said. He moved to stand but Commander Barnes waved him down.

"You can stay seated," he said.

Dinesh slid back into his seat and stared at the Commander. "We were attacked."

"By whom?"

"By--" Dinesh began, but stopped. There was more damage than even the most heavily armed and well trained pirates could manage. He didn't even want to *think* about what had happened to his ship, its crew, and his brother. He didn't understand it, so he knew he couldn't explain it.

"Still with us, Mr. Dinesh?" Commander Barnes asked.

"Pirates," Dinesh replied. "We were attacked by pirates."

"That right? Pirates, huh? Where are they, where are these

pirates?" Commander Barnes folded his arms in front of his chest and stared at Dinesh. Neither of them spoke. No one came to the mess decks to break the silence. Dinesh felt like he could scream, but he would not give in. He kept quiet.

Commander Barnes finally spoke. "I think we have a lot more to talk about, Mr. Dinesh." He dropped his arms and took a step back. "Radio is trying to contact the Lahore's squadron as we speak. I don't know what you're hiding, but I hope you'll reconsider cooperating." He adjusted his glasses again and walked to the coffee maker. "Rodriguez?" he called as he poured himself a cup.

"Yes, Sir?" Rodriguez came around the corner and stood next to his Executive Officer. He glanced over at Dinesh but quickly dropped his eyes to the floor.

"Go tell Chief Falin we'll need an armed guard for Mr. Dinesh. He's not to leave the mess decks."

"Do you really think that's necessary?" Rodriguez asked.

Barnes shifted his gaze to Rodriguez without changing his expression at all.

Rodriguez quickly dropped his eyes and muttered, "Yes Sir." He stole another quick glance at Dinesh and shrugged his eyebrow as if to say "sorry" before heading off.

Dinesh stared at his cup of tea. He felt a chill move across the mess decks. He touched the mug; it had gone stone cold. The tea reacted to his touch, ripples moving out from the center and splashing over the edge. The air around him grew heavy; it felt like syrup, making it hard to breathe. His skin crawled and the hair on the back of his neck stood out against the well-starched collar of his borrowed US Navy coveralls. He shook his head and the air cleared.

What is happening?

Commander Barnes looked down at Dinesh, grunted, and crossed his arms again. He stood like a brick, not speaking. From what Dinesh could tell, the Commander was not even blinking. He stayed that way until a sailor walked onto the mess decks carrying a shotgun. Then, for the first time since he entered the mess decks, Commander Barnes smiled.

###

Rodriguez sat in Sonar, his boots kicked up on the console in front of him.

Harrison and Parker sat at the consoles on either side of Rodriguez. Harrison was chewing on sunflower seeds and Parker was doodling on a scrap of paper. Aside from an occasional glance, they were ignoring their displays.

I don't know, man," Rodriguez said. "I figure he's just some dude who got a shitty break. I don't know why the XO's busting his balls like that."

"Maybe he's a terrorist?" Santalino offered from the back of the room. He was sitting up on the workbench, hovering over a laptop and playing solitaire.

"Bullshit."

"No, seriously. Just because you pulled him out of the water don't mean he's a good guy. He could be one of the fucking pirates or something."

"An Indian pirate? Seriously?"

"Yeah, or maybe a *butt* pirate," Harrison added from his seat.

"Good one, bro," Parker added.

"Shut up, idiots," Santalino said without looking. "Why not, Rodriguez? It could happen." He sat up with a frown on his face. "Fuck."

"What?" Rodriguez asked.

"This fucking computer cheats," Santalino said as he slammed the laptop shut. He turned towards Rodriguez. "Look, all I'm sayin' is we don't know anything about this guy. With Poole missing and all--"

"Wait, what happened to Poole?" Rodriguez interrupted. He dropped his feet to the floor and swung his chair around to face Santalino.

"Fucker's gone, dude. Where you been?"

"Uh, swimming around pulling people out of the fucking ocean. You want to fill me in?"

"Nothing to fill in. He just vanished from the engine room. He was cleaning with the rest of the dirty nukes, then he climbed down in a bilge. No one's seen him since."

"No shit?"

"No shit. All they found was a pile of intestines and shit. Heard it was pretty nasty. That's why the XO has such a hard-on for this Indian guy. He thinks something fucked up's going on with that ship. Maybe there's more of 'em up there."

The door separating Sonar from the Control Room flew open and Chief Falin stuck his head in. His lower lip stuck out so far that the wad of tobacco stuffed in there nearly spilled out onto the floor. He looked back and forth between Rodriguez and Santalino and sniffed the air before looking over at Harrison and Parker. "Did one of you fuckers fart?"

"No Chief," Harrison said with a restrained smile.

"Not me," Parker said.

"Well it smells like cum and Vaseline in here." He turned to Santalino. "Sonar Supervisor, print me out a training report. We've got some new guy out here who needs to learn how to scrub the shitters." He spit into a paper cup and took a drink of his coffee. "I want that shit documented."

"Sure thing, Chief," Santalino said. He reached down and opened the laptop. The glow from the screen illuminated his face, showing the stubble that had grown over a couple days of not shaving.

"Shipmate," Chief Falin said. "In *my* Navy we shave every day."

Santalino reached up and rubbed his chin. It sounded like sandpaper. "Oh yeah, sorry Chief. I need a new razor. Mine got busted shaving Parker's mom's pussy." He clicked the mouse a couple times and the printer in front of the Chief spit out a sheet of paper.

"I bet," Chief Falin said. He glanced back at Parker. "I hear that shit's got bugs in it."

Harrison giggled in his chair, covering his mouth like a child.

"That's fucked up, man," Parker said from his seat. He didn't take his eyes off his doodles.

"Yeah, well unless you two dicks want a reeducation in the fine art of shitter scrubbing, I suggest you quit stroking each other and get back to work." Chief Falin grabbed the training report from the printer. "And Parker?"

"Yes Chief?"

"Fix your mom's pussy, would you?" he said. "That shit's busted." He stepped back and threw the door shut.

Harrison pointed at Parker and laughed, and soon Santalino had joined in.

Rodriguez just shook his head and smiled.

5

Dinesh sat at the Mess Decks table, his dishes long since cleared away by a young and disgruntled sailor named Seaman Edwards.

An armed guard stood by the front entrance at perfect attention. The door to the back had been shut and locked by Commander Barnes before he left the room. The only other door led to the galley.

Dinesh thought about asking for a fresh cup of tea, but Edwards was too busy wiping down anything that could be made shiny. That, and talking to himself.

"Fuckin' shit, fuckin' *bull*shit," he muttered as he scrubbed at the shiniest metal milk dispenser Dinesh had ever seen. "Can you believe I've got to wipe down the mess decks again?" Edwards turned toward the guard. "Ain't nobody used it but this guy." He jerked his thumb over towards Dinesh before turning back to the milk dispenser. He spat on the metal and rubbed it in with his rag.

"No talking to the foreigner," a voice called from behind the closed galley door. "He's not here to socialize."

"I'm not talkin' to *him*," Edwards said. "I'm talkin' to fuckin' Four Names."

"Well, *he's* not here to socialize either, so shut your trap."

"My name's not Four Names, dickhead," the guard said.

The door to the galley swung open as the voice from behind the door stuck his paper hat covered head out onto the Mess Decks. "What is this, fucking social hour?" he asked. "I told you to cut the shit."

"Sorry, Cairne," Edwards said. He dropped his head and scrubbed harder on the milk machine.

"What the fuck are you doing?" Cairne asked.

"Just cleaning up, like you said."

"You're gonna scrub right through to the milk." Cairne looked around the room. "Try scrubbing and waxing the fucking deck. It looks like someone took a dump on it, ate the shit, and then threw up on it." He disappeared back into the galley, pulling

36

the door closed behind him.

"Fucker," Edwards whispered, barely loud enough for Dinesh to hear. He dropped his rag on a table and walked to the back of the mess decks.

Dinesh looked back at Four Names. He stood at the doorway, still at attention and staring at Edwards with a look of disgust. He kept his shotgun cradled in his arm, the business end pointed at the deck. His name tag was sewn with letters so small Dinesh couldn't read them.

"Why do they call you Four Names?" Dinesh asked.

"'Cuz he's got Four Names," Edwards said from the back of the room. "Duh."

"What?" Dinesh asked.

"My parents--" Four Names began.

"His parents both had hyphenated last names, so Four Names here popped out with the wily and elusive double hyphen," Edwards interrupted. "Two names from each parent, four last names. Hence, Four Names." He stood up with a blue bucket in one hand and a green scouring pad in the other. "It was bound to happen. I think it's kinda like that double helix thing, but way stupider."

"Fuck you, dickhead," Four Names said. "You don't even know what a double helix is." He turned his head back to Dinesh. "My last name is Mendoza-Alphonso-Franklin-Pierce."

"Look at his fuckin' name tag," Edwards said. "Shit's so small you can't read it."

"Maybe you could read it if your eyes weren't full of jizz."

"I guess Four Names is easier to say, yes?" Dinesh asked.

"I guess," Four Names said with a shrug.

"Fuckin'-a it is," Edwards said. "It's either that or alphabet man, but that sounds too much like elephant man. Which would be funny if he was fat, but--"

The door to the galley flew open. Cairne stood there, his hand raised and mouth open as if he was about to start screaming, but the door bounced against the wall and swung back to slam shut.

Four Names and Edwards both burst out laughing.

A couple seconds later the door re-opened to reveal a red-faced Cairne.

"What the fuck are you two pricks laughing at?" he asked.

Edwards stopped laughing and looked up, but Four Names only laughed harder.

"What, you think this is funny?" Cairne asked. "Keep it up I'll have you down here scrubbing so close behind Edwards no one will be able to tell where your head ends and his ass begins."

Dinesh watched the exchange like he was watching a tennis match, his head flipping back and forth between Cairne and Four Names. When Edwards started to laugh again, Cairne turned a shade of red Dinesh had never seen on another man. By the time Cairne grabbed Edwards by the neck and started banging his head on a very shiny trash can, Dinesh felt like he might laugh right along.

Until he felt the room change.

The air grew heavy, like it had when Barnes had finished questioning him, but it felt more alive. He no longer heard the sound of Edwards' head on metal or Four Names' ceaseless laughter. Everything in the room slowed down. Cairne's arm barely crawled towards the trash can with Edwards' head in front. Dinesh could see the drool falling from Edwards' lip; he watched as sweat dripped from Cairne's strained, hairy arm.

Dinesh looked over at Four Names and knew that he felt it too.

Four Names was slowly raising his shotgun and dropping his smile as he stepped back, pressing his back against the wall. Something in the air between them shimmered. His eyes registered a terror that Dinesh could feel but not see.

Four Names' legs slowly moved up and out as his body slid along the wall. He hung in midair, the shotgun falling to the deck as his hands came up in a defensive shield. His cheeks rose and his brow furrowed. He squeezed his eyes shut and turned his head away, mouth opening to scream. Before he could make a sound, he was gone.

The world came back in a rush. Cairne dropped Edwards and spun around, yelling "What the fuck?" at the empty spot at the front of the mess decks. Where Four Names once stood, a charred mark ran along the wall. The shotgun lay discarded on the floor. Cairne turned to Dinesh with a snarl on his face. *"What did you do?"*

"I did nothing," Dinesh whispered without looking at Cairne. He couldn't tear his eyes off the burned spot on the wall.

"Yo, that's some voodoo shit right there," Edwards said. He scrambled to his feet and backed up to the locked door at the back of the mess decks. He grabbed at the handle, uselessly turning it over and over. "Get me the fuck outta here," he said. He looked down and stared at the lock even as he continued to turn the handle.

"You did this," Cairne continued. He took a few steps towards the spot where Four Names disappeared. "Just like Poole, you took him. Somehow, you did it."

"No, I didn't--"

"You lie!" Cairne reached down and grabbed the shotgun, bringing it up to his shoulder and turning towards Dinesh.

Dinesh flinched and raised his hands.

Cairne screamed and pulled the trigger.

The gun only clicked. Dinesh tried to keep his shaking body still while Cairne blinked and looked down at the gun.

"Uh, Cairne?" Edwards asked from the back of the room. He had stopped turning the door handle and instead stared at Cairne.

"Pfft," Cairne said with a shrug of his shoulders. "Fucking safety." He let the gun drop to his side. He looked at Dinesh and with shaking hands set the gun on the next table over. "What the fuck just happened?"

"Dude. Seriously." Edwards glanced down at the shotgun and then back at Cairne. His head tilted to the side and his mouth hung open.

"What's going on?" Cairne asked. He looked back at Dinesh. "What's happening here?"

Dinesh stared at the dark stain on the wall and whispered, "I don't know."

Rodriguez was sitting in the Electronics Space, staring at the wall. He was trying to simultaneously forget and figure out what the hell was going on. When Parker came running into the space, Rodriguez looked down and pretended to read a book.

"Dude, what's up with the Indian dude?" Parker asked.

"Why? What's up?"

"Dude, now fucking Four Names is missing, just like Poole."

"No shit?" Rodriguez asked.

"No shit. Cairne and Edwards were right fuckin' there. Saw the whole shit go down. Edwards said it was your boy pullin' some creepy voodoo shit, chanting with candles and all."

"Candles?" Rodriguez asked with one eyebrow raised.

"That's what Edwards says."

"Edwards is an idiot," Rodriguez said. "That's ridiculous."

"I don't know, man, but I ain't hanging nowhere near that guy. I only got six hundred and twenty-three days left on this pig before I'm outta here."

"Dude, that's almost two years."

"Closer to a year and a half," Parker said. He stuck his hands in his pocket and kicked a dust bunny under a power panel. "Sure beats the five fuckin' years I started with."

"Uh huh."

"Hey, you got any more Dr. Pepper?" Parker asked.

"What? No, sorry. So where'd Four Names go?"

"Dunno. Cairne said it was all like 'poof' and he just disappeared."

"Poof? Just like that?"

"No doubt."

"Sounds like bullshit."

"Shit be crazy 'round here," Parker said. "And you *know* this, man."

"Hey Rodriguez," Santalino called from behind Parker.

"Up here," Rodriguez said as he waved Parker to the side.

Parker stepped back and Rodriguez saw Santalino heading up to them in a hurry.

"Hey, you got any Dr. Pepper?" Parker asked.

"What?" Santalino asked. "No, man. I told you that shit already."

"Fuck, man," Parker said. "You sure? I got porn to trade."

"Keep that hairy old lady shit to yourself," Santalino said before turning to Rodriguez. "Dude, the XO is looking for you."

"Great," Rodriguez said with a sigh. "For what?"

"I don't know, but his bald head is so red it's practically glowing. You know it can't be good."

"Fuck." Rodriguez closed his book and stood up. "Guess I'd better find out what's up."

"Good luck," Santalino said.

"Yeah, better you than me," Parker added. "The XO, man. That guy sucks."

Tell me about it, Rodriguez thought as he headed down to berthing to drop off his book. *That guy sucks big time.*

Cartwright sat on the cold metal floor of the Engine Room staring at a power distribution panel. The smell of burning oil hung in the air, but he didn't notice it. After years of working around the power plant, he'd gotten used to the many sounds and smells, no matter how unpleasant. Other guys were wandering around sniffing the air, but Cartwright didn't care. He knew it'd all be over soon anyway.

"Dude, you smell that shit?" Adams asked. He stopped next to Cartwright and followed his line of sight to the power panel. "Hey man, what're you doing?" He tapped Cartwright on the shoulder. "Dude?"

"Don't fucking touch me," Cartwright growled without moving. His entire body tingled where Adams' finger had been.

"What?" Adams took a step back and looked back the way he came.

Cartwright didn't bother repeating himself. Adams didn't matter; no one did. He stared at the panel and thought about what he had to do.

Eventually Adams walked away without another word.

For Cartwright, it was time to think. For that, it was good to be alone.

###

Rodriguez headed down the ladder and through the hall towards the berthing area. It didn't look like he'd be sleeping anytime soon, but he wanted to drop off his book and grab his coffee cup. He cracked open the door and shined his flashlight inside to see if the coast was clear.

The passage through berthing stood empty. All the curtains were closed, and no half-naked men hung out in the passageway for him to brush past. *Good*, he thought. *I'm not in the mood to dodge man meat.*

He stepped in and closed the door softly behind him. His rack was all the way down at the end, the bottom of three racks. About halfway down the passage, an opening to the left led to another row of racks. This short hallway had a row of lights along the floor which illuminated the passages in both directions. Rodriguez shut off his flashlight and headed towards his rack.

He passed the opening to the left and glanced in that direction. The other side was as empty as the passageway he walked through. He continued to the end and knelt down to open his locker. He flipped on the light, and his coffee cup sat in front, right where it should be. He grabbed it and shoved his book behind his pillow, hoping to read a little later on.

Liquid sloshed around in the cup. He brought it up to his nose and sniffed. He couldn't remember the last time he'd filled it up, but he shrugged and took a sip anyway. *Still warm*, he thought. *Well, warmish*. He flipped the light off, closed his locker, and stood up. He heard a noise and instinctively backed against the wall and stood still.

At first he thought someone was climbing out of their rack, so he pressed his body against the wall to avoid being kicked. He waited a minute, peering into the darkness and searching for movement, but no one was there. He took a step towards the center hall and the soft glow from the floor.

He moved his head left and right as he walked, looking for a moving rack curtain, waiting for one to birth a naked sailor. The curtains all hung still. When he reached the center hall and looked to the right, a buzzing sound came from the lights. It started out low, but rapidly increased to a grating sound that felt like it pierced his brain. He brought his hands to his ears, but within seconds the buzzing stopped. All the lights went out along with the noise.

Rodriguez stopped and waited for them to return; they didn't. He brought his hand to his belt and felt along for his flashlight. When he pulled it out and twisted the handle, nothing happened. From behind him, he heard the noise again, like the rustle of fabric and the slide of a rack curtain along its metal frame. He spun around and squinted in the darkness, his arms out in front of him to feel if another person was there.

"Rod," a voice whispered behind him.

Rodriguez spun around again and hit his arm on a metal locker hanging on the wall. He dropped his coffee cup. "Shit," he whispered, grabbing his arm and looking across the short hall to the opposite row of racks. It was too dark to see, so he stopped and cocked his head to listen.

From his left, he heard the rustling again, followed by another whisper from the opposite passage.

"*Rod,*" the voice called again.

Rodriguez couldn't tell where it was coming from, but there was movement close by. He threw his arms up, trying not to punch anyone in the darkness, but his fingers only passed through air. He sidestepped to the left and felt along the row of racks.

On both sides of the aisle, all the curtains hung still.

"Who's there?" Rodriguez asked.

The voice whispered directly behind him.

"*Rod.*"

Rodriguez jumped at the sound, his skin tightening around his shaking body as his arms flew through the air towards the voice. The air in berthing had grown progressively warm. Rodriguez could smell the faint undertone of burning oil. All around him, the sound of movement and sliding curtains echoed in the dark empty passage.

"Who's there?" he yelled. He held his hands out and felt the surrounding curtains. Even though he could feel movement in the air, they were all still. He pulled a curtain aside and stuck his hand in. The rack was empty. He felt a hot breath of air in his face and smelled the stink of rotting garbage.

"*Rod!*" the voice called right in front of him.

Rodriguez jumped back and tripped on something that lay in the middle of the aisle. He landed hard on the floor, knocking his elbow on the edge of a rack and slamming his tailbone on the cold tile floor. Right next to him, a floor-level curtain slid open and more hot, fetid air poured over him. He coughed and ran his hand along the empty mattress.

Something in the cramped space moved next to him, something he could not touch. However, he could hear it and he could smell it; he knew it was there. It felt like it was reaching out for him. The pressure around him increased, quickly becoming so strong he could not stand up. Around him, all the curtains flew open and he heard the sound of bare feet upon the floor, but nothing physically touched him.

"Welcome to hell," the gravelly voice said in his ear. Rodriguez clenched his teeth and tried to stand but the oppressive force kept him down. The curtains moved open and closed, as if laughing at him as he struggled. From behind him, a soft glow returned, but not from the floor lights. A deep red glow made its way down the opposite passage towards the connecting hall.

As it lit the row of racks, Rodriguez could see that the curtains were in fact open. He saw bodies lying in them, the decayed corpses of sailors he knew, unmoving in the gloom. The glow was closer, moving up the opposite hall. Soon it would round the corner and find Rodriguez sitting on the deck, his ass frozen to the tile. In the rack in front of him, he could now see a body on its side, arms reaching out toward him.

He looked at the corpse and thought he could almost recognize the face. Dead fingers came within inches of grabbing Rodriguez's clothes. When the bony clutch caught his collar, Rodriguez opened his mouth to scream.

The door to berthing flew open before he could make a sound. The lights along the floor buzzed into life and a voice called to him from the glowing portal.

"Dude, you okay?" Warner stood in the doorway with a flashlight in his hand, illuminating the passageway. All around him, the curtains were closed.

Rodriguez felt along the floor and found his coffee cup sitting in a puddle of warmish liquid. "Yeah," he said. "Just spilled my coffee."

"You wanna shut your cake hole?" someone asked from inside a nearby rack.

"Yeah, man," another voice called. "Trying to sleep here."

Rodriguez grabbed a paper towel from his pocket and soaked up the spill as best he could before grabbing his cup and standing up. "Sorry," he whispered. He looked around once more before stepping over towards Warner. "Did you hear anything?" he asked.

"When?"

"You know, when you opened the door?"

Both men paused and stared at each other.

Warner tilted his head slightly and raised an eyebrow. "Dude, you fuckin' retarded or something?"

"Not funny, Warner. Just asking."

"Well, the XO's lookin' for you."

"No shit. That's where I was headed." Rodriguez walked past Warner and headed towards the Officer's Wardroom. It took all the willpower he had not to look back. *I don't know how the hell I'll ever sleep in there again*, he thought as he knocked on the closed Wardroom door.

6

"Mr. Dinesh, we'd appreciate it if you could tell us what happened to the Lahore." Lieutenant Silverstein spoke with his eyes closed. All the time. It drove Rodriguez crazy. The Lieutenant had been onboard for just over a year and the crew kept an ever-increasing pot of money for the first person who could catch him speaking with his eyes open. Even on the honor system, no one had yet been able to claim the prize.

"I already told you what happened," Dinesh said. "Many times." He sat by himself on one side of the Officer's Wardroom table, his head down and his hands resting in his lap.

Across the table from him sat Lieutenants Silverstein, Jackson, and Henry.

Cairne and Edwards stood behind them as close to the exit as they could get without becoming part of the door. They both fidgeted, their eyes locked on a spot on the carpet at their feet.

Rodriguez sat on a bench in the corner of the room. He kept his head down, only bringing it up from time to time to look at the clock.

At the head of the table, Commander Barnes sat with his hands folded neatly in front of him, his back so straight Rodriguez believed he must have had an iron rod jammed up his ass.

"What you've told us just doesn't pan out," Lieutenant Silverstein said. "We believe you're hiding something, and we'd like to know what that is."

"Why? What would I hide from you? We were attacked by pirates while transiting--"

"Yes, yes," Lieutenant Silverstein interrupted, his voice rising. "So you've told us. But pirates don't do the kinds of things I saw on board your ship." His face grew red and spit flew from his lips when he spoke. "We took a trip over there to look for survivors. What we found was body parts piled all over the deck, disemboweled men hanging from the superstructure, a burnt out shell where the engine room once was; does that sound like piracy to you?"

46

Dinesh glanced up while the Lieutenant spoke.

Rodriguez caught his eye and thought he saw fear; not fear of the men sitting in front of him, but fear of something else.

Dinesh broke eye contact and dropped his head back down to his chest. When Lieutenant Silverstein finished, he took a deep breath and let it out slowly.

"You want to know what did that?" he asked, still looking down.

"I want to know *who* did that, yes," Lieutenant Silverstein replied.

"No," Dinesh said, finally bringing his gaze up to meet the Lieutenant's. "There is no who. No human could do that. Something followed us from the island--"

"What island?" Lieutenant Henry interrupted.

Lieutenant Silverstein glanced over and frowned.

Lieutenant Henry shut his mouth and leaned back in his chair. Both men returned their attention to Dinesh.

"We found an island," Dinesh said.

"Congratulations, there are lots of islands in the Red Sea," Lieutenant Silverstein said.

"Yes, but not where we found this one."

"Where?"

"North of Dahlak, before Sudan. It's on no charts."

"Bullshit."

"No, no bullshit. It was there."

"Tell us about this island, Mr. Dinesh," the Captain said from the open door.

Everyone turned their heads at the sound of his voice, and the Lieutenants all moved to stand.

"Don't fucking stand, you butt sharks," he said. "Just pull your chairs in so I can get my fat ass past you."

The three Lieutenants scooted their chairs as far under the table as they could as the Captain slid past.

He walked up to the XO, who sat in the chair at the head of the table. "Do you mind?" he asked.

"Uh, no Sir," Commander Barnes said as he pushed the chair back and jumped to his feet. He stepped to the side and the Captain sat down, pulled a cigar out of his pocket and lit up.

"Smoke, Mr. Dinesh? Is it Mr. Dinesh or just Dinesh?"

"Just Dinesh, please."

"Fine. Smoke, Dinesh?"

"No, Captain, thank you."

"Right. As you can imagine, I'm pretty busy right now. Been trying to reach our squadron but for some reason we've got no satellite. No cell phones are working out here, either. If you wouldn't mind telling me what the fuck is going on, I'd greatly appreciate it."

Dinesh looked over at Rodriguez, who could only shrug his shoulders. He looked back at the Captain and said, "If you've lost radio contact, we're already on our way."

"On our way where?"

"To the island,' Dinesh said. "This is how it started..."

"We sailed into the Red Sea from Adan," Dinesh said. "That was a few weeks ago."

"Headed where?" the Captain asked.

"The east African coastline, to conduct anti-piracy operations. We were supposed to follow along Eritrea, turn around, and then head south to port in Mombasa."

"How far did you get?"

"I don't know." Dinesh looked at the Captain, paused, and dropped his eyes once again. "We lost radio contact somewhere north of Dahlak. No radio, no satellite, no mobile phones. We were so busy trying to figure out our communications problem that we didn't notice the island."

"You mean the mysterious island hidden in the middle of the Red Sea?" Lieutenant Silverstein asked.

"Yes," Dinesh said, ignoring the Lieutenant's sarcasm. "The air had gone foggy, and without our sensors we were sailing blind. We almost ran aground; we came so close to land."

"What did it look like?" Lieutenant Henry asked.

"What the fuck?" Lieutenant Silverstein asked. "Why are you humoring this guy?"

"Let him talk," the Captain said.

Lieutenant Silverstein closed his mouth and looked at his hands.

Lieutenant Henry looked from Lieutenant Silverstein to the Captain, then took a deep breath and asked his question again. "What did it look like?"

"A big rock," Dinesh said. "Nothing special, nothing that looked habitable. It was big, though. Really big. In the fog, we couldn't see the end in either direction."

"Did you investigate?" Lieutenant Henry asked.

"No. Our Captain ordered full reverse, and we brought the ship around just in time. Like I said, we almost ran aground."

"So what's this have to do with anything?" Lieutenant Silverstein asked.

"Something...happened while we were there."

"Like what?" the Captain asked.

"Well, I'm not really sure. Once we stopped the ship, we lost all power. Everything felt wrong. We all grew agitated, and it got worse when we heard sounds coming from the island."

"What kinds of sounds?" Lieutenant Jackson asked.

"Not human, not animal. Something different. I don't know how to describe it, but it made us all very uncomfortable. We floated there for what seemed like hours until our power was restored. The Captain ordered a full bell and we were on our way. We were in such a hurry to get out of there that we didn't see the pirates until it was too late."

"Again with the pirates," Lieutenant Silverstein began, but the Captain shot him a look and he shut his mouth.

"They were on us in minutes, out from Mitsiwa, maybe, I don't know for sure. They had machine guns and RPGs. By the time we'd armed up, half our security force was dead."

"So they weren't fucking around," the Captain said.

"No, Captain. No attempts at capture, no kidnapping, no negotiations. They showed no restraint."

"That doesn't sound like any pirates I've heard of," Lieutenant Jackson said.

I agree, but it was clear they were there to kill. Then maybe salvage whatever was left, not that there would have been much left." Dinesh cleared his throat before continuing. "We returned fire, but something went wrong." He coughed into his hand.

"Jackson, get him some water, would you?" the Captain asked.

Lieutenant Jackson looked like he'd been slapped, but he stood without complaint and walked out of the room.

"Take your time, Dinesh." The Captain turned his gaze to Lieutenant Silverstein and added, "There's no hurry."

"Thank you," Dinesh replied.

Lieutenant Jackson returned with a coffee cup filled with water and set it in front of Dinesh.

"Thank you," Dinesh said as the Lieutenant sat down.

Dinesh took a sip, leaned back, and rubbed the back of his neck. An audible crack of vertebrae echoed through the otherwise silent room. He took another sip and set the cup down.

"What went wrong?" the Captain asked.

"We fired at them, but no rounds hit. We rigged our fire hoses and sprayed their approaching Zodiacs, but they did not get wet. The water went right through them. When their rope ladders came up over the side, we tried to cut them with our knives, but the...the blades went right through them."

"Isn't that what you wanted to happen?" Lieutenant Henry asked.

"No, not like that. We cut nothing but air. We could see the ropes, but we could not touch them. When the first pirate climbed over the side, Sanjay shot him from not even five feet away. Somehow he missed. We all missed. We were powerless."

Lieutenant Silverstein let out a chuckle but said nothing.

"The first pirate held a dagger high above his head." Dinesh again looked up. His eyes scanned the faces of those in the room and he said, "I could see right through him."

"Say again?" Lieutenant Silverstein asked.

"It was like he wasn't even there. We all saw it. Soon more of them climbed over the side, men who shimmered in the sunlight and could not be shot. When the one with the dagger screamed and swung it towards us, Sanjay crumpled to the deck in a pool of blood. Soon our sailors were falling all around. We couldn't touch them, but they could. It was a slaughter."

"What did you do?" Lieutenant Henry asked.

"I turned and ran. We all did, at least the ones that still could."

"You gave up the ship?" Lieutenant Silverstein asked.

"How could we not? We couldn't even defend ourselves. We couldn't touch them, could barely see them. They were like ghosts." Dinesh stopped speaking and reached out for his cup of water. His hand shook as he picked it up, and some water splashed out onto the table. He drank the rest in one gulp.

"Did they follow?" Rodriguez asked. The Lieutenants all turned and looked at him, but the Captain held his hand out for their silence. Rodriguez glanced at the Captain, who nodded at him to continue. "I mean, if your weapons went right through them, could they...uh, I mean did they...pass through the walls?" He lowered his voice and dropped his head so his question was barely audible.

"No," Dinesh said. "They stayed on deck. We ran through the hatch and dogged it tight. Even though we knew it wouldn't help, half of us spread out in the passageway and aimed our weapons at the hatch. I guess it made us feel better, like we could actually protect ourselves. The other half of our group ran to the Control Room. I never saw them again."

"What did the pirates do?" Lieutenant Henry asked.

"For a while things were silent. We prepared to defend the hatch, but nothing happened. Then, they...they started to scream."

"Who, the pirates?" Lieutenant Silverstein asked.

"Yes." Dinesh picked up his cup and started to bring it to his mouth before realizing he'd already emptied it. He set it down too hard; the noise made Edwards jump partly out the door.

"Any of you buying this?" Lieutenant Silverstein asked. He looked around the room with disgust.

Lieutenants Henry and Jackson looked at him and each shrugged.

Cairne and Edwards both stood shaking in the doorway.

The Captain looked right at Dinesh. "What were they screaming about?" he asked.

"Shit, Captain--" Lieutenant Silverstein began as he slammed his hand on the table.

"Shit, Captain nothing," the Captain replied, his voice raised for the first time since he'd entered the room. "Let the man speak, unless you want to go back to that destroyer for an even closer look."

"Yes, Sir."

"I'm sorry, Dinesh," the Captain said. "Some members of my crew have no fucking patience."

"Thank you, Captain," Dinesh said.

"No problem. Would you like some more water?"

"Yes, please, if it's not too much trouble."

"Not at all. Silverstein, make yourself useful. And get a pitcher this time."

"Yes Sir," Lieutenant Silverstein muttered as he stood and pushed past Cairne and Edwards.

"Please, continue," the Captain said.

"Well, Sir, we weren't really sure. Pretty soon, the pirates were quiet. Then the overhead lights started to make a buzzing noise and the passage went dark. I heard voices all around me. I thought it was my shipmates at first, but even in the dark I could see them looking around just as I was. Within seconds, there was a loud thump at the door followed by more screams.

"I nearly jumped to the ceiling. We all did. My brother was there, right next to me. He wanted to open the door."

"Did you?" Lieutenant Jackson asked.

Dinesh fumbled his thumbs for a moment before answering in a whisper. "Yes."

Silverstein returned with a pitcher of ice water and a tray full of coffee cups. He set them in the middle of the table and dropped in his seat without a word.

Dinesh grabbed the pitcher and filled his cup, again spilling water on the table. He drained it and poured another cup.

"What did you see?" Rodriguez asked.

"They were all dead," Dinesh said. "Every one of them. Torn to pieces. We stared for a minute, wondering what could have happened, but once we saw the bodies move, we pulled the door closed and dogged it shut. All around, I heard the voices getting louder. People started to disappear. At one point, I would have sworn something whispered in my ear. I felt its breath as it called my name."

"Is that what happened on the mess decks?" Lieutenant Jackson asked as he looked over at Cairne and Edwards.

Cairne shook his head. "No, Sir. I didn't hear anything. Four Names just disappeared."

"I didn't hear anything either," Dinesh added, "but I felt it. I think whatever attacked the Lahore has moved to the Alexandria."

"Bullshit," Lieutenant Silverstein said.

"No, I felt it too," Rodriguez said. As soon as he spoke, he felt his cheeks flush as everyone turned to look at him.

"Is that right?" Lieutenant Henry asked, already smiling.

"Care to share, Petty Officer Rodriguez?" the Captain asked. He glanced at Dinesh and they both turned to stare at Rodriguez.

Rodriguez coughed into his hand and looked at the floor. "It was in berthing. I went to my rack and the floor lights went out. Then I heard someone whisper my name. It was just like you said," he looked at Dinesh, "only I felt something reaching for me too. I--" he choked on his words and coughed again, trying to cover it up.

"What's the matter," Lieutenant Silverstein asked, "did it get you?"

"I'm not going to ask you again," the Captain said. "Keep your mouth shut."

"Warner opened the door looking for me," Rodriguez said. "Then it all went away, just like that."

"When was this?" the Captain asked.

"On the way here, Sir." Rodriguez looked up when he answered. "Just a few minutes ago. I thought I was crazy so I didn't say anything."

The Captain sat back in his chair, his cigar burned down to just about nothing. A chunk of ash that had been hanging off the end dropped onto his leg. He brushed it away. "I don't think I like this," he said as he pulled the cigar from his teeth. "I don't think I like this at all."

"Captain," Lieutenant Silverstein began with considerably less vigor than usual, "you're not really buying into this shit, are you?"

"I've got a ship that's crashed into us, causing extensive damage due to flooding that took out our propulsion and most of our electrical systems, not to mention the damn thing is full of bodies and sinking with no explanation other than what Dinesh here has told us. I've got a radio room that's lost contact with everyone and everything in every way possible. I've got a radar that no longer shows Ertria, Yemen, or any of the islands in between. *And* I've got two sailors missing, one of which was seen disappearing into thin air." He leaned forward and stared at Lieutenant Silverstein. "So you got any better ideas, Sherlock-fucking-Holmes?"

The Lieutenant didn't answer. He stared at the tray of cups as Dinesh poured himself more water.

"I didn't think so," the Captain said. "Does *anyone* have a suggestion?" He looked around the room.

Lieutenant Silverstein didn't look up.

Lieutenants Henry and Jackson looked around at the others without speaking.

Cairne and Edwards both stood in the doorway shaking their heads.

"Any ideas, Dinesh?" the Captain asked.

"Nothing we did could stop it. It destroyed our ship without us even slowing it down. The Lahore was ripped to pieces from the inside out. No one survived, not that I know of."

"Except you," Lieutenant Silverstein added.

"Except me."

"And why do you think that is?"

"I...I don't know."

"Excuse my disbelief," Lieutenant Silverstein said, "but this smells like shit to me."

"Fucking Silverstein," the Captain roared. "Get out!"

"Oh, come on, Captain--"

"Out!" The captain's neck was turning red. He stood and pointed to the door.

"But--"

"Go to the fucking engine room and clean up some fucking oil. I don't want to smell you around here any longer."

Lieutenant Silverstein stood too quick and his chair fell to the floor behind him. "Yes Sir," he said. Without picking up his chair, he marched to the door. "Move it, fucker," he said as he elbowed Edwards on the way out.

"Someone remind me to fire his ass when we get home," the Captain said. "Rodriguez, you tell us everything? No bullshit?"

"Yes, Sir."

"Well, *fuck*." The Captain tossed his dead cigar into a cup and poured water on it.

The phone on the wall rang. Lieutenant Jackson reached over and picked it up.

"Ward Room," he said. After a pause his eyes went wide. "No shit?" He looked at the Captain and muttered, "Roger that," before hanging up the phone.

"What?" the Captain asked.

"Umm, Sir? It seems we've, uh, found an island."

"That right?" the Captain asked. He stood up and Lieutenants Henry and Jackson stood with him. "Dinesh, would you mind following us to Control? I'd like you to have a look."

"Yes, of course," Dinesh replied as he stood to join the others.

"Cairne? Edwards?"

"Yes Sir?" they answered nearly in unison.

"Get the fuck out of here."

"Yes, Sir," they muttered as they turned and bolted out of the room.

"Rodriguez?"

"Yes, Sir?" he replied, expecting the same command.

"Sorry to ask this of you, but I need you to suit up. You might have to go in the water."

Rodriguez swallowed hard. The click could be heard throughout the room. "Yes, Sir," he said as he watched the others walk out of the room.

Dinesh gave him a shrug before following the Captain into the passageway.

Rodriguez looked at his coffee cup and considered returning it to his rack. He shook his head and thought, *Fuck that*. He grabbed the cup and headed for the lower level. *I'll just jam it in my dive locker. No way I'm going back into berthing.*

No fucking way.

7

Cartwright stood at the back of the Engine Room watching oil drip off of a reciprocal pump and land on Adams' face. Although Adams' body lay in a heap on the other side of the pump, Cartwright liked the way his head looked on its own. He felt like he could stare at it for hours without getting tired. The other guys who had stumbled across Cartwright's path lay scattered around the deck, their bodies torn open, blood dripping into the bilges below.

Cartwright knew where the sub was heading. He could feel it getting closer. He looked up at the wires he'd hung in the overhead. They led from one power panel to the next, connecting the engine room in a web of insulated copper wire. When the time was right, all he had to do was close the circuit.

Just like on the Lahore.

"But I've never been on the Lahore," Cartwright said to the decapitated head of Adams.

Yes you have.

He heard a noise behind him. Footsteps echoed on the metal ladder leading down from the upper level. He didn't need to turn around to know it was Lieutenant Silverstein.

"Jesus H. Christ, what's that fucking smell?" The Lieutenant's footsteps landed on the deck behind Cartwright and moved closer. "Cartwright? What the fuck is going on? Why is there no one roving back here? And where's the...*shit*." Lieutenant Silverstein stopped walking.

Cartwright could feel the hesitation and fear building in the Lieutenant.

"What the fuck?" Lieutenant Silverstein yelled. "Is that you Cartwright?" His voice cracked when he spoke and his breathing sped up.

Cartwright heard Lieutenant Silverstein's heart pounding in his chest and smiled. *Goddamn Jew and a fucking goody two shoes, that's what you are. Always busting my balls. Time for a little payback.*

"Good morning, Lieutenant," Cartwright said. He turned

around, slowly, savoring the moment. "You know I've always hated you, right?"

"What did you just say? And what the hell's going on?"

"I'm just so glad you could make it," Cartwright said, ignoring the Lieutenant's question. "I was just thinking how much I'd enjoy a visit from you, and now here you are." He turned fully around, showing off his blood-soaked coveralls and sticky red-coated skin. Adams' guts were strewn at Cartwright's feet. He stepped on a chunk of intestine and a gas bubble squeezed out.

"Are you hungry, Silverstein?" Cartwright bent down and picked up Adams' liver. "Would you like a snack? Oh, no worries. It's kosher."

"W-what?"

"Okay, you got me," Cartwright said. "I lied. It's not kosher."

Lieutenant Silverstein stumbled backwards, tripping over a stretch of wire that ran along the deck and landing in an oily bilge.

"Oh good," Cartwright said. "Looks like you'll be staying for breakfast. Guess it will be kosher after all."

Lieutenant Silverstein called out for help, but no one came.

Cartwright's mouth opened wide as he let out a deep, throaty snort. He pointed and laughed as Lieutenant Silverstein struggled to free his foot from where it had gotten caught under a floor bracket when he fell backwards.

Cartwright expelled all the air he had and sucked back in quick. It created a small tornado in the back of the Engine Room that pulled the Lieutenant up out of the bilge.

Lieutenant Silverstein's ankle cracked as his twisted body slid across the rough metal deck plates. The wind died down and he settled at Cartwright's feet. He looked up and whimpered something that went unheard.

Cartwright held out his hands and claws extended from his fingertips, bloody talons that stretched out at least six inches from each hand. *I can get used to this*, he thought.

Lieutenant Silverstein screamed, but Cartwright only laughed some more.

"Who are you calling for?" he asked. "Everyone else is dead."

Cartwright laughed as the Lieutenant screamed. He looked down at Lieutenant Silverstein's head and brought his claws forward. *I might put it next to Adams,* he thought. *There's plenty of room down there.* He laughed to himself as he pulled the lieutenant's head and spine from his body. *Hell, there's enough room down here for the entire crew.*

Rodriguez stood in the Control Room as the Captain and Dinesh took turns on the periscope. The ship still couldn't move on its own power, so everyone on watch sat around staring at Dinesh; that, and staring into the shadows, eyes nervously twitching at every sound and movement.

News travels fast on a submarine, so everyone had already heard about the disappearances. They all fidgeted in their seats, and barely anyone spoke.

"Nothing," the Captain said as he pulled his eye away from the periscope. "Not a damn thing except for the Lahore."

"Is that thing ever going to sink?" Lieutenant Norton asked.

"Shut up, Navigator," the Captain said as he turned towards the navigation plot. "Are you sure there's an island out there?"

"No, Sir," Lieutenant Norton replied. "There's nothing on our charts, but there is a fucking huge radar return that doesn't move. I don't know what to tell you."

"Right." The Captain looked over at Dinesh. "Any of this making sense to you?"

"I'm not sure it makes any more sense to me than it does to you," Dinesh said, "but I can tell you this is how things started with the Lahore." He stepped up to the periscope and brought his eye to the sight. He looked out across the water, trying to see through the thick fog that had descended over the Red Sea.

Nearby, Rodriguez stared at the periscope monitor, leaning on the back wall and trying to stay out of the way.

"Can't see shit out there," the Captain said. He shook his head and sat on a bench, propping his foot up on the navigation plot.

"Sir, please," Lieutenant Norton said, motioning to the Captain's foot.

The Captain's boot tore the corner of one of the charts as he shifted his foot. "What?" he said. "It's not like its doing us any good. Neither are you, for that matter." He reached over and grabbed the torn corner and pulled it entirely off, dropping it to the floor and looking back at Dinesh. "Anything?"

"No, Captain. Only fog."

"Navigator, how far away is this invisible island?"

"Radar has it out at 13,000 yards and closing."

"And how is that?" the Captain asked.

"How's what?" Lieutenant Norton asked.

"How is it that the island is closing us if we're not moving? Is the island moving?"

"What?"

The Captain leaned forward and stared at the Navigator. "How is it moving if it's a fucking *island*?"

"I...I don't know, Sir. Maybe the Lahore is pushing us?"

"Are you fucking kidding me? Have you even *seen* that ship?"

"Well, without our GPS--"

"Stick your GPS up your ass," the Captain yelled. "You're the Navigator, so be a fucking Navigator. Get up in the bridge and look at the fucking stars or something. Find out where we are."

Lieutenant Norton stared at the Captain for a moment before dropping his pencil. He grabbed a pair of binoculars off a hook on the back wall. "Yes, Sir," he whispered as he stepped past the periscope and walked to the bottom of the ladder. "Up ladder," he called as he climbed up into the bridge.

"He won't be able to see it," Dinesh said. "Not until we all see it."

The Captain kicked the navigation plot and turned around. He looked at Dinesh and said, "That's what I'm afraid of."

###

"What the fuck are you doing up here?" Lieutenant Norton asked as Rodriguez's head popped up to the top of the ladder.

Seaman Sulley sat along the side, staring out into the sea.

Lieutenant Dawson, the current Officer of the Deck, stood next to Lieutenant Norton.

"Just wanted some fresh air, Sir," Rodriguez replied.

"Sorry to bust your bubble Diver Dan, but it smells like shit up here," Lieutenant Dawson said. "Between that smoking wreck of a destroyer sinking next to us and whatever's in this fog, it isn't exactly fresh."

Sulley snickered and picked his nose.

"Quit with the nose, Sulley," Lieutenant Dawson said.

"Sorry, Sir." Sulley pulled his finger out of his nose and held it up to his face, inspecting the glob of snot clinging to the end.

"And don't fucking eat that."

"Aw, man," Sulley whined. He wiped his finger on his shirt and brought his binoculars up to his face.

Rodriguez could see the booger smeared across Sulley's chest. He opened his mouth to say something but changed his mind. *It wouldn't help.*

Lieutenant Dawson shook his head. "How the hell did I luck out and get you on my watch?" he asked.

"Could be worse," Lieutenant Norton said. "You could have fucking Butterball up here."

"I'm amazed that fat hunk of shit can even fit through the hatch," Lieutenant Dawson said. "What are you guys in Sonar land feeding him to make him so fucking fat?"

"Not me, Sir," Rodriguez said. "It's all him. He must have taken his name too seriously." *Poor guy*, he thought. *I can't imagine having to go through life with the name Butterball. That's a name that might just be worth changing.*

"Well Doc needs to put that guy on a diet," Norton said.

"Yeah," Sulley said. "And he stinks like shit, too, the dirty Sonar Tech."

"Fuck you, booger man," Rodriguez replied. "I wouldn't talk if I were you, especially not until I'd washed my disgusting shirt."

Sulley looked down at his mucus-stained chest and sighed.

He turned and looked out into the fog without speaking.

"Anyone know what we're supposed to be looking for up here?" Lieutenant Dawson asked. "I've been on watch for three hours and no one tells me shit."

"Rodriguez's buddy down there says it's an island," Lieutenant Norton said.

"Why does everyone keep calling him my buddy?" Rodriguez asked.

"Ain't shit out here," Lieutenant Dawson said. "If you ask me, that fucking guy's got a few screws loose."

"Maybe he's a retard," Sulley said.

"*You're* gonna be a retard if you keep eating your fucking boogers," Lieutenant Dawson said.

"Seriously?" Sulley asked. He scrunched his face and held his fingers up for inspection. "Does that make you retarded?"

"No, you idiot," Rodriguez said. "And he's not retarded. Neither are you, for all your stupidity."

"Oh. Cool."

"Seriously, what's that guy's deal?" Lieutenant Dawson asked. "Is he really the last motherfucker left alive?"

"That's what he says," Rodriguez said.

"Damn." Lieutenant Dawson looked out and squinted through the thick fog. "That's got to suck."

"So how do we know he's not some crazy serial killer or something?" Sulley asked.

"First off, if he killed every motherfucker on the Lahore he'd actually be a mass murderer," Lieutenant Norton replied.

"Oh. Right." Sulley's finger made its way back up to his nose.

"Second off, we don't, but the Captain's got a hard on for him, so we lick his ass and hope he doesn't have a bomb stashed somewhere."

"That's not funny," Rodriguez said.

"Wasn't supposed to be."

"Hey, shut the fuck up," Lieutenant Dawson said.

"Fuck you," Lieutenant Norton replied. He held his middle finger out for emphasis.

"No, seriously. Listen." All four of them stared into the fog, their ears cocked towards a sound that no one but Lieutenant Dawson could hear.

"I don't hear shit," Lieutenant Norton said.

"That's because you mother fuckers can't shut up," Lieutenant Dawson said.

"Well, all I can hear is Sulley digging for gold."

Sulley's face reddened and he pulled his finger out of his nose.

"What am I supposed to be listening to?" Lieutenant Norton asked. The bridge fell silent again.

"Fuck it," Lieutenant Dawson said with a sigh. "I must be hearing shit."

###

"Are you ever going to get power back to my ship?" the Captain asked. He stood with hands on his hips, leaning in as he yelled at Lieutenant Jarvis.

Dinesh stood at the periscope, switching his view between the dense fog outside and the heated discussion between the Captain and his Engineering Officer.

"Come on, Cap, my guys are working as fast as they can," Lieutenant Jarvis replied.

"And why aren't you back there working right along with them?"

"Well sir, I...I--"

"That's what I thought," the Captain interrupted. "You don't want to hang around with your dirty nukes any more than the rest of us."

"Sir, Ensign Klein is well qualified to--"

"To what? Wipe his own ass?" the Captain asked. "I highly doubt that."

"What is that guy, like fucking twelve?" Lieutenant Henry asked from down the hall. He walked in the Control Room and slid past Jarvis to stand next to the Captain. "I can't believe the Navy was able to pry him off his mother's tit long enough to go to sea."

"What do you want, Henry?" Lieutenant Jarvis asked.

"A hand job. You buying?"

"You ass fuckers keep that shit to yourselves," the Captain said. "What's up, Henry?"

"Well, Sir, I just wanted to pass on that lower level is secured from flooding and general emergency."

"Oh yeah? No torpedoes got wet?"

"No Sir," Lieutenant Henry said with a smile. "Not a one."

"Well, that's good to know," the Captain said. "*Five fucking hours after our collision.*"

Dinesh drew back from the periscope and watched Lieutenant Henry deflate in front of the entire Control Room.

"Uh, yes Sir." He turned and sulked out of the room.

"Now," the Captain said as he turned his full attention back to Lieutenant Jarvis. "About my power."

"Sir, I can assure you--"

"I don't want to hear it, Engineer. All I want to hear from you is '*Yes, Captain, there's nothing to worry about, Captain, we've got our power back, Captain.*' If you can't make that happen for me then maybe I could arrange for a transfer for you and your entire fucking engine room. I bet the Lahore could use a new engineering team. How would you like that?"

"Not very much, Sir."

"Well, I should think not." The Captain sat on a stool and kicked at a small metal trashcan. It fell off its bracket and clattered to the floor, sending bits of torn paper and an empty Dr. Pepper bottle across the room. "*Shit.* Can someone clean that up?"

"Captain, Sir?" a voice from the loudspeaker called.

"What?" The Captain screamed loud enough that he could be heard in the bridge without a microphone.

Over the intercom, Lieutenant Dawson cleared his throat and continued. "Sir, it seems we've arrived."

PART II — THE FUCKING ISLAND

8

"That it?" the Captain asked.

Dinesh leaned back from the periscope and nodded his head. He swallowed hard and the click in his throat made Petty Officer Tito turn his head.

"Something you need to tell me, Quartermaster?" the Captain asked.

"Uh," Tito muttered, his compass twirling around between his fingers. "No Sir?"

"Well then mind your own fucking business."

"Yes Sir," Tito whispered. He dropped his compass, grabbed a pencil and a notebook, and began furiously scribbling on a blank page.

The Captain turned around, grabbed a microphone and keyed the handset. "Norton!"

"It's Dawson, Sir," Lieutenant Dawson responded from the bridge. "I'm the one on watch."

"Whatever. How far away are we?"

"Well, we're right about...uh..." After a moment of silence, Lieutenant Dawson replied, "Really fucking close, Sir. I'd suggest slowing, but it's not like we're not moving on our own."

"You think I don't fucking know that?" the Captain asked out loud. He didn't bother to key the mike. He stared at the floor for a moment before keying the mike to speak to the Lieutenant again. "So what exactly do you suggest?" The response was only silence. "Well is fucking Norton still up there? Can he take your cock out of his mouth long enough to give me a suggestion? What kind of Navigator is he, anyway?"

"Well, Sir," Lieutenant Norton replied from the bridge, "since I can't find this island on any of my charts, I'd say I was a piss-poor excuse for a Navigator. Maybe you should ask someone else." A loud clicking sound reverberated over the loudspeaker. Everyone present knew what it was, even Dinesh. It was the intercom equivalent of slamming the phone down on the Captain.

Dinesh looked around the room and saw everyone was

staring at the floor. No one looked up, not even when the Captain stood and threw the microphone against the wall. The handle shattered, sending chunks of black plastic flying around the room. The metal part that remained intact bounced around on a length of coiled wire.

"I fucking hate that guy," the Captain said before walking out of the Control Room. Three seconds later, the door to his stateroom slammed shut.

Lieutenant Jarvis walked through the mess decks on his way to the Engine Room. As he walked past, the men sitting around him stopped talking and stared, heads straight but eyes following him to the back of the room. On the tables in front of them lay cards, dominoes, popcorn, half-empty drinks and a cribbage board. No one spoke.

What's their fucking problem? he wondered. As soon as he passed through the aft door, the mess decks returned to life. The sounds of laughter and slamming of dominoes echoed into the hall. *Fuck 'em. They're a pack of idiots anyway.* He stopped and stared at the Engine Room door. *I've got bigger problems to deal with.*

He spun the handle just enough to break the seal but stopped when no air escaped. *What the hell?* He lowered his head to the hatch and waited. The first thing he noticed was the sound, specifically the absence of sound. It was quiet; the engine room was *never* quiet, not even when everything was shut down. He smelled something that made his eyes water.

"What the fuck?" he asked out loud. He cracked it open a bit more so he could see down the long hall. The passage was much darker than it should have been, but other than that nothing appeared out of place. He stood up straight and spun the handle until the hatch fully opened. He threw his leg through the door and pulled his body in after. When he brought himself upright, he could feel the cold air sitting in the passage. He wiped moisture from his eyes.

The Engine Room's never cold, he thought. *What the fuck is going on here?* Lieutenant Jarvis took a couple steps down the passage, leaving the Engine Room door behind him wide open. He got about halfway to the first intersection when he heard what sounded like a laugh. "Klein?" he called. "Vasquez? Porter?" He walked a little faster and noticed the lights ahead of him dimming as well. "Adams?"

"Well, well, well," a voice called from above him. "The mighty Engineer decided to show his face in the dirty Engine Room. You must have finally gotten over your filth phobia. That, or the Captain forced you to do your fucking job for once. Either way, I'm so flattered I could just *shit*."

"Who is that?" the Lieutenant asked. "Gregory? Where are you?"

"Clueless as ever, no surprise there. Maybe it's time you met your crew?"

"Cartwright? Fucking Cartwright, is that you?" Lieutenant Jarvis spun around in the narrow passage, looking through the piping that ran overhead. "You fucking putz. I've had just about enough of you. If you don't get your balls out here I'm gonna start a paper trail."

"Oh no, not the paper trail," Cartwright said in a falsetto voice. "Always with the threats, you're so predictable," Cartwright let out a soft chuckle. "As if anyone's scared of a piece of paper. Or you, for that matter."

"Where the fuck are you?"

"I'm right up here," Cartwright said. "Just past the first junction box."

Lieutenant Jarvis headed down the passageway. He felt the heat rising from his neck to his face. He knew it was turning red but couldn't stop it. His fists were clenched so tight he could barely feel them. *Fucking Cartwright*, he thought. *I'm going to enjoy misdirecting my frustration toward your sorry ass. I'm going to enjoy it a lot.*

"Did you get lost?" Cartwright asked. "Maybe you should have spent more time back here when you had the chance."

"By the time I get done with you, you're gonna be cleaning my Engine Room bilges with a toothbrush for the rest of--"

Lieutenant Jarvis rounded the corner and stopped speaking.

Cartwright was there, but so was the rest of the Engine Room crew. Each of them looked like they'd been pulled to pieces and then put back together by a child with a glue stick. They all stood behind Cartwright, each one staring at the Lieutenant with dead eyes.

"Oh no, Engineer," Cartwright said. "This is now *my* Engine Room. But thanks to you, soon the whole ship will be mine."

"What--what do you mean?"

"What, did you really think we were waiting just for you?" Cartwright asked with exaggerated surprise. "You're not that important. You just happen to be standing between us and the door."

Lieutenant Jarvis spun his head around and saw the Engine Room door standing wide open, the soft glow from the mess decks illuminating the passageway beyond. He could even hear a scream of joy as someone on the mess decks won a game of something.

"Fuck this," he said as he sprinted for the door, his boots echoing down the dark passageway. In his heart he knew he'd never make it, but at least he could die knowing he tried.

When the hand clamped on his shoulder he was jerked backwards so fast he crumpled to the deck. Before he could even scream they were on him.

Lieutenant Jarvis stared at his body as it was torn to pieces by the Engine Room crew. He felt no pain; he felt nothing at all, not even when they pulled his arms from his shoulders and his fingers from his hands. He could hear Cartwright laughing from somewhere behind him, but once his head rolled to the side he could no longer move. All he could see was the bilge, a sheen of oil floating atop a spreading pool of red foam.

Cartwright laughed even harder, but soon the Lieutenant's hearing began to fade. That, and everything else.

Rodriguez watched through the fog as the rock drew closer. That's what it really looked: a giant rock in the middle of the Red Sea that apparently no one but the Lahore had ever found.

69

He looked over the side at the deep blue water below. *Maybe there were others*, he thought, *but from the sounds of it, probably none that lived*.

"What d'ya think is in there?" Sulley asked.

"Where?" Lieutenant Norton turned to follow Sulley's gaze.

"In there," Sulley replied, pointing to an opening cut into the side of the rock. As they continued north, the fog began to lift and a cave was just coming into view.

"Fuck if I know," Lieutenant Norton said. "Maybe Bigfoot?" He let out a nervous laugh, but no one joined in.

"Come on Lieutenant," Rodriguez said. "Everyone knows Bigfoot lives in New Jersey."

"My cousin Terrance saw Bigfoot," Sulley said.

"What? Shut up Sulley," Lieutenant Dawson said. "Besides, whatever it is, I think we're gonna find out. Whether we want to or not."

They all stared at the cave as the submarine moved closer to the island.

He's right, Rodriguez thought. *We're gonna find out all right, we're headed straight towards that fucker*. He looked over at the Lieutenant. "Did Dinesh say anything about a cave?" he asked.

"I don't know, he's your boy," Sulley said.

"Yeah, why not give him a ring?" Lieutenant Norton added. He picked up the handset and held it out to Rodriguez with a stupid smile on his face.

In the corner Sulley snorted with laughter. "Yeah," he said, "see if he wants to go on a date."

"Screw you guys," Rodriguez said. He turned back towards the cave and grabbed a pair of binoculars hanging off the bridge box. He brought them up for a closer look at the island.

The fog looked to be surrounding the island, but it thinned out as they moved closer. Rodriguez could just make out the dynamic landscape of the rocky island, but only from the side. He had a feeling it was a lot bigger.

He moved the binoculars slightly to the right and tried to see into the mouth of the cave. Even though they were nearly within throwing distance, it was still too dark to see inside. He dropped the binoculars and grabbed the microphone.

"Decide to call your girlfriend after all?" Lieutenant Norton asked.

Rodriguez just looked at him and keyed the mike. "Control, bridge, Dinesh, pick up." He picked up the handset and held it to his ear.

"Do you really think that fucktard knows how to use that thing?" Lieutenant Norton asked. They waited for a moment in silence; the line remained dead. "I mean, seriously. Does he even understand English?"

"Yes, I understand English," Dinesh said from the ladder. "I've been speaking it my whole life." His head popped up into the bridge and he looked around.

Rodriguez dropped the handset and held out his hand to help Dinesh into the bridge.

"Oh," Lieutenant Norton said. "Sorry. I just figured you spoke...I don't know, Indian or something."

"That's not even a language," Dinesh replied.

From the corner, Sulley began to snicker once again.

"Something funny back there, booger man?" Lieutenant Norton asked.

Without a word, Sulley grabbed another pair of binoculars and turned towards the island.

"Hey Dinesh, what do you know about that cave?" Rodriguez asked.

"What cave?"

"That cave," Lieutenant Dawson said, pointing to the approaching entrance. "Did you guys go in there?" He held out a pair of binoculars for Dinesh, who took them and looked towards the opening.

"We went in no cave. We barely touched rock and then we were gone."

"No idea what's in there?" Lieutenant Norton asked.

"No," Dinesh said. "No idea." His eyes dropped to the barely-floating mess that had once been the Lahore. It somehow stayed ahead of the submarine, leading the way toward the approaching cave. At a glance, it didn't' even look like a ship much less a naval destroyer.

Dinesh let out a sigh and turned back toward the ladder. "I'm going back to Control."

"Great," Lieutenant Dawson said. "Just great."

The Captain sat at his desk, staring at the Engineer's report. *That guy's a fucking idiot.* According to the document, the Alexandria would not regain power for at least three days, and even that would only be a return of auxiliary power. *And where'd you get* that *timeline,* the Captain wondered. *The guy's been in the Engine Room all of ten minutes this whole deployment.*

Getting the reactor back online would require returning to port, which probably meant dry dock.

"Fuck," he said to his empty stateroom. "Fuck, fuck fuck, fuck, *fuck.*" If he ever wanted to get promoted he'd have to keep the sub at sea. Every day spent in port was a missed opportunity. *I'll never be an Admiral at this rate.* He dropped the papers and pushed them aside.

He leaned back in his chair and stared up at the ceiling. He was about to close his eyes when something crashed nearby. He held his breath and listened.

There was a noise coming from below him, somewhere in the middle level passageway. Outside his stateroom, someone ran by on their way to the Control Room. Whoever it was started talking so fast that the Captain couldn't understand a word of it.

From the middle level passageway he heard a scream, followed by more voices and the sound of boots marching on deck plates. He stood up and threw open his door. The passageway was no longer empty; the passageway was alive.

9

Rodriguez stared at the cave as the submarine drew close to its gaping dark mouth. The sides were too far away to touch and the distant roof remained shrouded in darkness. He had no idea how big this thing was, but it easily dwarfed the submarine.

The wreck of the Lahore disappeared into the cave first, one second there and then next completely gone.

"Here we go," Lieutenant Norton said as the bow of the sub followed the Lahore into the cave.

"Hey, you know," Lieutenant Dawson began, "this cave kinda reminds me of something." He stood with his head back, eyes staring at the rock ceiling above.

"What?" Sulley asked. He was once again picking his nose.

"I don't know, I can't quite place it. Huge and stinky, deep and dark, can't even touch the walls..." Lieutenant Dawson's voice trailed off. After a pause, his eyes lit up and he snapped his fingers with a smile. "Oh yeah, that's right. It's Sulley's mom!"

"Aw, that's messed up, sir."

"Cut that shit Dawson," Lieutenant Norton said. "You're giving the cave a complex."

The group laughed. Even Rodriguez joined in, but it felt hollow and the humor quickly died. Within seconds the cave had swallowed the entire bow of the sub and the bridge began to pass into the shadowy interior. The sound of splashing echoed all around them and the smell of sea air and algae became overwhelmingly strong.

"Fuck, man," Lieutenant Dawson said with a cough. "Someone hire a maid."

Rodriguez watched him wave a hand in front of his face and then all light was gone. The darkness of the cave had swallowed them completely.

No one spoke. They barely breathed.

The group rode in silence, blind in the darkness, all traces of humor gone. With nothing else to do, they simply waited.

###

Dinesh stared at the panicked sailors as they came up the

passageway, running straight towards the Control Room.

Warner and Cairne ran straight past the Captain's stateroom and headed into the Control Room. They nearly collapsed next to the periscope. They pointed down the hall and struggled to regain their breath.

"What the fuck?" Commander Barnes asked from the back of the room.

Cairne coughed into his hand and spit a glob of bloody phlegm onto the floor."It's the nukes, Sir," he said. "I don't know, some shit's fucked up or something." He glanced behind him and wrung his hands at his sides.

Commander Barnes walked up to the periscopes and stared at Cairne and Warner like they were diseased. "Are you two both fucking idiots? Would one of you please speak so I can understand you?" he asked.

Warner took a deep breath and pointed back down the passageway. "It's the nukes, Sir," he said.

"Something seriously fucked up is going on back there," Cairne added, still wringing his hands.

"So we've established," Commander Barnes said. "A little more detail perhaps?"

"They're on their way," Warner said. "Just listen." They all turned to look down the passageway.

Dinesh thought he could hear something in the distance, but it was too faint to discern. They all stood in silence, waiting, until the first person screamed. Then it became too loud to hear anything at all.

Two more sailors ran up the passageway towards the Control Room while a ferocious howl followed them up the ladder from the middle level. It echoed off the walls and roared into the Control Room, blocking out almost all other sound.

Dinesh covered his ears and stared into the storm as it crawled through the passageway. The tiles were being ripped up from the metal deck plates. Charts and pictures that had been hanging on the walls were torn away, whipped into a cyclone. The upper level passageway was torn to pieces.

The Captain threw his door open and it was pulled right out of his hand. It smashed against the side wall and splintered into thousands of pieces. The Captain stood looking at his hand; he still had the shiny brass knob gripped between his fingers.

"Captain," Commander Barnes shouted over the noise. "Get back."

The Captain looked into the Control Room and back down the other way. A pulsing light was creeping up the stairway and spilling around the corner.

Another sailor ran into view, one that Dinesh had seen before. It was Edwards, the kid who was on the mess decks when Four Names had disappeared. He took two steps towards the Control Room before stopping. He had his hand glued to his face and stood straight up, looking at the hatch in the ceiling. It was closed against the sea, but he stared anyway.

The Captain called out to him but he didn't seem to hear.

"Edwards, get over here," Commander Barnes added. "Get over here *right fucking now*."

Edwards looked over at the others and pulled his hand away from his face.

Dinesh could see right through his cheek. The flesh and bone had been torn away so he could see the glowing wall beyond.

Edwards staggered once and turned half way around. The back of his head was gone. Pieces of his brain slid out of his cracked skull, landing on the deck next to his boots before being caught up in the wind and circling through the air.

The Captain jumped out of his stateroom and ran into the Control Room, slamming the door shut behind him. "What the fuck is going on?" he asked.

No one answered.

Dinesh stood nearby, mute.

The rest of the crew either ran around screaming and crashing into each other or scrambling on top of each other to get to the rear exit.

Dinesh looked at the Captain and they made eye contact. Both of them looked at the ladder heading up into the bridge. Without speaking a word, they grabbed the metal rungs and started to climb.

###

As the submarine cruised blind through the pitch black cavern, Rodriguez tried to sort out the noises they heard coming from below. It sounded like a mixture of a hurricane and an overexcited episode of Animal Planet.

Lieutenant Dawson was on the radio trying to make contact with someone - *anyone* - in the Control Room.

Lieutenant Norton stood nearby asking, "Did you get anyone?" every ten seconds.

Sulley was somewhere nearby. Rodriguez couldn't see him, but he could hear the unmistakable scratching sound that meant he was digging in his nostril for a nugget of fortune.

"Shit, someone's coming," Lieutenant Norton said as the sound of boots on metal echoed up the ladder and through the hatch.

"Up ladder," the Captain screamed.

Rodriguez felt someone bump into him as the Captain barked, "Get the fuck out of the way, will you?"

"What's going on down there, Cap?" Lieutenant Norton asked.

Someone stepped on Rodriguez's foot and elbowed him in the ribs. "Shit!"

"What? Who's that, Rodriguez?" Lieutenant Norton asked. "Fucking move, will you? The Captain's up here."

"Make room for Dinesh," the Captain added.

"I think I'm gonna fall over the edge," Sulley said.

"Big fucking deal," Lieutenant Dawson said. "We've got plenty of new guys lying around. We'll just get a new one."

"That's – that's not funny, Sir."

"It wasn't meant to be."

"Will you two ass clowns shut the fuck up and fill me in?" the Captain interrupted. "I've got a nightmare down there and it's black as the inside of Dawson's mom's asshole up here. What the fuck is going on?"

"We've got no clue, Captain," Rodriguez said. "Is Dinesh up here?"

"Yes, I'm here."

"Any thoughts?" Rodriguez asked.

"Not good ones."

"Great," Lieutenant Norton said. "That's a big fucking help."

From below, the sounds of howling increased. Everyone on the bridge went quiet.

"What's down there, Captain?" Lieutenant Dawson whispered.

"I don't think I want to find out," Lieutenant Norton said. "Not from the sound of that shit."

"Fucking Norton," the Captain said. "You're one great big piece of shit, but for once I agree with you."

Cartwright rounded the corner at the top of the ladder and found the body of Edwards lying before him in the upper level passageway. He raised his boot and stomped on Edwards' crotch. "Prick," he whispered as he passed the lifeless body, giving it one more kick for good measure.

He continued on toward the Control Room, watching with intense pleasure as his creation shambled past the Captain's Stateroom and into the panicked Control Room. Cartwright had taken the best parts of Adams and Silverstein and fused them together into one massive Adams beast. It was an abomination of a man, and one perfectly suited to do all the work while Cartwright hung back and enjoyed the show.

Parker ran around the corner from the Sonar Room and slid to a stop in front of Adams.

Harrison crashed into Parker from behind, knocking them both to the floor at Adams' feet.

Adams grabbed hold of Parker and threw him against the bulkhead. His body smacked against the metal wall and slid down to the deck with a wet thump. He left a trail of clear liquid outlined in red that dripped down around his body.

Harrison scrambled to his feet and ran down the hall, nearly crashing into Santalino.

Santalino stood staring wide-eyed at Adams as if frozen to

the spot.

Harrison stopped next to him and yanked on his sleeve. "Fucking *go*, man," he said. "Parker's dead."

Cartwright snickered and pointed at him. "Let's clear out all these dirty Sonar Techs," he said.

Adams turned towards Santalino and shambled forward, his arms reaching farther than humanly possible.

Because he's no longer human, Cartwright thought with a smile.

"Fuck this," Santalino said before turning to run through the passageway. He slipped on a puddle of Parker's blood and fell on his face.

Harrison helped him to his feet before Adams could reach him and they both disappeared around the corner into the Electronics Space.

"You can run, but can't hide," Cartwright said as he followed Adams towards the group of sailors hiding in the Control Room. *Who knew how much fun I could have up here?* he thought. *This shit's like Christmas.* My *kind of Christmas. Too bad it's all got to end. But first, I'm gonna get you fuckers.*

"No sir," he laughed. "You fuckers can't hide from me."

The screaming echoed through the submarine, the voices melting together into a mind-numbing wail of agony. It droned on and on, echoing through the passageways and traveling through the bridge. Rodriguez couldn't see anything in the passage below; it had gone just as dark as the tunnel surrounding them. He looked around but could only guess the general direction they were heading based on the gentle rocking of the waves and the salty breeze flowing aft.

The darkness was complete in all directions. Besides those coming from below, the only sounds they heard were the slap of water on the hull and the occasional scraping sound as they rubbed against rock or coral.

Everyone in the bridge stood still, barely even daring to breathe. They waited that way until a horrible sound rode from below masking everything else. It shook the sail and rattled the bridge, so strong that it nearly knocked Rodriguez over the side. When the noise stopped, so did all the screaming from below.

The sound of metal against metal echoed up the ladder, causing everyone in the bridge to jump. Elbows jammed ribs and toes were stomped; someone fell to the deck, arms flailing for something to grab hold of.

Rodriguez kicked whoever it was that fell; he was pretty sure it was Sulley, but he wasn't about to open his mouth to ask. He was far more concerned with what might be heading up to the bridge.

Another pang of metal and the sound of breathing made them all press back away from the hatch.

Rodriguez stepped on someone's hand; he was now sure it was Sulley from the whimper that escaped as Rodriguez's boot ground his fingers into the metal mesh deck.

"Who's that?" a voice whispered from the ladder.

Rodriguez knew the voice, but wasn't ready to open his mouth and respond.

The movement came faster up the ladder, the occasional ping of metal now obvious to Rodriguez. *Santalino is married*, he remembered. *That's his ring.*

"Santalino?" Rodriguez whispered through the wall of bodies that pressed back against him. He felt like at any moment he might crash through the railing that surrounded the bridge. "That you, man?"

"Shit yeah," Santalino said. "That you, Rodriguez?" Although still a whisper, his voice became clearer as his head popped up into the bridge.

"What the fuck, man," Lieutenant Dawson said. "There's no fucking room up here."

"Yeah, well there's no fucking way I'm going back down there."

"Me either," Harrison said from further down the ladder.

"Harrison too?" Lieutenant Norton said. "What the fuck is this place, a lounge?"

"What's going on down there?" the Captain asked.

"Uh, Captain?" Santalino asked.

"No, it's Howdy Fucking Doody," Lieutenant Dawson said. "*Yes*, it's the fucking Captain, now how about giving us an answer?"

"Shit, Sir," Santalino said, "They're all dead. I mean, for real dead."

"How?" the Captain asked.

"Cartwright, I don't know what the deal is, but he's crazy or something. He's got this thing with him, I--" his words cut off with a choking sound. He stopped and cleared his throat before continuing. "He's got something. I don't know what it is, but it's no longer human."

"Is he still down there?" the Captain asked.

"It killed Parker," Santalino said.

"Yeah, it just smashed him into the bulkhead," Harrison said, his voice shaking. He popped open like a--"

"Shut up, Harrison," Santalino said. "I think it got Edwards too."

"Is he still down there?"

"Yeah," Santalino said. He cleared his throat again and took a deep breath. "Yeah, it's still there. Somewhere."

"Well, get up here before he sees you," the Captain said.

"Can someone get off my hand?" Sulley asked, his voice strained and weak.

"Sorry," Rodriguez said. He had forgotten all about Sulley. He shifted his foot to the side and felt Sulley's hand scrape along the metal deck as it was pulled out from under his boot. *That's gotta hurt.*

"Mother *fucker*," Sulley mumbled. It sounded like his mouth was stuffed full of his snot-coated hand.

"So what do we do now?" Santalino asked.

There was silence all around, only broken by the occasional scrape of hull on rock and the ever-more infrequent shuffle of movement from below. After the collision, all the fans and most of the machinery had been shut down. Now that the screaming had stopped, it sounded like a ghost ship.

"I don't know," Rodriguez said, "but I've never heard it so quiet."

As if in response, the ship lurched to the side. The sound of metal twisting and rock grinding shuddered through the entire hull. The bridge shook like it might crack off from the submarine, plunging into the water and carrying them to unknown depths. Bodies crushed each other once again as they struggled to hold on to the safety railing.

Rodriguez felt like the air was being choked out of him. He pushed out against the pile of flesh that threatened to bury him but could not make anyone budge. He felt the sub begin spinning as he was pressed against the inside of the bridge. Someone was crushing his leg against a pair of binoculars. He heard a crack and felt shards of plastic pierce his skin.

From the surrounding darkness came sounds they had not heard before. It could have been whispering or movement along the cavern walls, Rodriguez could not be sure. He heard splashing from all around; he couldn't tell if it was waves slapping against the hull or something else entirely.

To his left, someone started to scream. From the whiny, nasal quality he was pretty sure it was Sulley.

"If we get out of this, I'm fucking throwing your ass overboard," Lieutenant Norton said as he slapped the scream out of Sulley.

Rodriguez still couldn't see a thing. His head was full of noise, and he could barely think. All he could feel was the crushing weight and the spinning. Somehow, the blind sense of vertigo was worse than if he'd been able to see. His head felt like it'd been pumped full of helium, and his guts churned like spoiled yogurt. He burped and felt the burn of acid at the back of his throat.

"Puke," he whispered.

"Fucking what?" Lieutenant Dawson answered from right in front of him.

At least I know who's crushing me, Rodriguez thought. He burped again. "Puke. I'm gonna puke."

Sulley began screaming once again.

"Oh, no you're not," the Lieutenant said, his voice rising to be heard over Sulley. "Not on *me* you're not."

Rodriguez could feel Lieutenant Dawson trying to grab his shoulders and turn his body, but the inertia kept them pressed in place.

Rodriguez felt his guts boiling and tasted the burn of bile as it climbed to the back of his throat. Just as he thought he was ready to pop, the sub stopped spinning. He swallowed back his lunch and fell to the deck in a heap of bodies.

He tried to open his eyes but they refused to open; the unexpected glare felt like shards of glass scraping across his cornea. It was like someone had turned on the lights full blast. Even with his eyes closed, Rodriguez could see shapes moving around in front of him as the collected group of sailors struggled to stand. He had to use his fingers to pry his eyes apart.

Sulley continued to scream. He sat huddled in the corner with his eyes clamped shut and his hands over his ears to block out his own noise.

"Somebody shut that guy up," the Captain said. He was leaning over the railing, looking every bit as shitty as Rodriguez felt.

Lieutenant Norton reached over and slapped Sulley hard enough to knock his head to the side.

Sulley shut his mouth and blinked his eyes open, but he slammed them shut almost immediately. He kept his mouth clamped shut as well.

"Thanks," the Captain said. "Dinesh?"

"Yes?"

"Any ideas?"

"No, Captain," Dinesh said. "No ideas."

"Great." The Captain took a deep breath and exhaled. "Does anyone have any idea where the fuck we are?" He looked around at the sad collection of sailors huddled on the bridge. "Anyone? Navigator?"

"No Sir," Lieutenant Norton said. "Not a clue."

Rodriguez's eyes started to adjust as he turned around to look at their surroundings.

They had exited the tunnel and ended up in a small lagoon, blanketed in sunshine and surrounded by an odd mix of jungle and bare rock. The surrounding hills were so tall that he could not see anything past them. The water was dark and murky; not at all like the Red Sea. It moved like something churned just below the surface. There was a current that flowed from the tunnel and around the submarine, keeping it moving towards land.

They were heading for a small clearing in the jungle. It looked almost like a beach. Behind them, the darkness of the cave was so complete it stood in stark contrast to the bright sunshine in the lagoon. To Rodriguez, it looked fake, like it had been painted on the rock wall.

"What do we do now?" Lieutenant Dawson asked. All heads turned towards him as he asked the question that was likely on everyone's minds.

Even Sulley opened his eyes to look up.

Like a flock of birds changing direction, all heads turned in unison without anyone speaking a word. All eyes came to rest on the Captain.

He stood up straight and looked at the assembled group. He turned his head towards Dinesh and had just opened his mouth to speak when he clamped his mouth shut and looked back towards the beach. His shoulders dropped and his eyes dropped to his feet. "Shit guys," he whispered with a voice not at all like their leader. "I'm at a loss."

Rodriguez looked back over his shoulder at the approaching land. They were maybe twenty feet from shore. He thought they only had one real option, and he opened his mouth to share it.

"Uh, Captain?"

"What?"

"What if we just--" was as far as Rodriguez got before an inhuman scream echoed up the ladder.

Something was coming from the Control Room. Whatever was down there had found them.

10

Cartwright heard the voices from above, echoing through the upper level passageway. He had decided to leave them alone until he finished cleaning up below. He knew where the sub was heading. He knew the small group huddled in the bridge had nowhere else to go. *Why rush a good thing?* He thought with a smile. *I'm in no hurry.*

Adams rooted through the Control Room, sniffing the air and rummaging through the mess. It lurked through the room, searching for anything that moved. At one point, it picked up the barely twitching body of some new guy Cartwright didn't even know. Adams broke the sailor across its knee and leaned in for a bite.

"Okay, fuck it," Cartwright said to the monster.

Adams looked up at Cartwright with the chewed remains of an ear gripped between its teeth.

"Let's go," Cartwright said. He was pretty sure there were others left alive in the lower lever, but he didn't want to waste time searching for them. The sub had stopped spinning and he could see sunlight blanketing the upper level passageway. That meant they were home.

Rodriguez stared down the ladder at the passageway below. It was now illuminated by daylight, and he could see the once blue tile had been stained red. The walls dripped with blood and the drainage grate at the bottom of the ladder was clogged with something that looked like a mixture of intestine and hair. Footprints led back and forth between the Control Room and the forward end of the passageway.

From the Control Room, something was moving toward the ladder. Rodriguez felt his balls shrivel when the first foot appeared in the hall. He sucked in a breath and held it as his hand clamped on the top of the ladder for support.

Another foot came into view, but it was facing the wrong way. It slid in the blood, pushing more guts into the clogged drainage grate. The thing at the bottom of the ladder moved closer to the beam of sunlight, and it was all Rodriguez could do to not turn away.

The Captain moved closer to stand next to Rodriguez. "What the hell is it?" he asked.

A low moaning "*Uh*," was all Rodriguez could manage. He kept his eyes on the thing below as it fully entered his view.

It wore the same Navy coveralls that they all wore, but the body beneath was all wrong. Its chest appeared disjointed, lumps and muscles rippling under the too-tight coveralls in areas where they shouldn't be. Two arms hung from its sides, but they were not from the same man. One was large, tan, and muscular while the other hung limp and pale.

The weak arm jerked to the side as the thing stepped to the bottom of the ladder; it appeared to be useless. The larger arm flexed constantly, the meaty hand gripping the air repeatedly as the thing leaned back and looked up the ladder. Where there should have been a head was something completely different.

Rodriguez bolted upright and took a step back. His breath escaped in a hoarse cough that sounded like a gag. His knees went weak as he looked into the two sets of eyes staring back at him. The sides of two heads had been sheared off; the exposed cheek and bone were somehow fused together into a solid unit. Two mouths opened in unison, their jaws locked together as it let out an inhuman scream of anger.

Above its left breast pocket, a bloody name tape declared the thing to be Adams, but it was not the Adams that Rodriguez had known for years. It reached its strong arm up and grabbed the ladder, the hand clenching so hard Rodriguez could hear the metal bend. As it put a foot on the ladder, one more scream made its way up to the bridge. Rodriguez finally looked away.

Sulley was there, standing next to the Captain and staring down at what Adams had become. He was already shaking his head back and forth, a line of drool swinging to the side and clinging to his cheek. He backed up, stepping on Rodriguez's foot and bumping into Lieutenant Dawson.

85

"Fuck that shit," Sulley said. "Fuck that *shit*." He spun around, throwing an elbow into Lieutenant Norton and grabbing at the railing. "Fuck *that*, fuck *that*, fuck *that*," he repeated as he pulled himself up on the railing and threw his foot over the top.

"Sulley, *no*," Santalino screamed. He pushed his way to the edge and grabbed for Sulley's other leg, but was kicked back.

Sulley swung himself up and over the safety railing and hung above the churning water below.

"Fuck, man. Someone grab him," the Captain said.

Multiple arms reached for Sulley just as another scream echoed up from the submarine. The sound of bending metal grew in volume and intensity. Everyone in the bridge stopped what they were doing and looked towards the ladder.

"Yeah, fuck *that*," Sulley said for the last time. He propped his feet up against the side of the submarine's sail and bent his knees. Before anyone could even move, he jumped.

"Shit!" Lieutenant Dawson said, leaning out over the edge and staring at the water below.

Rodriguez pushed his way past Lieutenant Norton to have a look.

Sulley lay in a pool of blood, his broken body hanging half in the murky water and half stuck on the rough non-skid deck that covered the top of the submarine.

Rodriguez hadn't realized how low the boat was sitting in the water. There was hardly any of the topside visible at all.

Beneath the waves, something continued to churn the water. As the submarine floated sideways, it left an uneven wake that swirled around the boat as it moved forward. At the aft end, something created a current around the ship's rudder. The water flowed smoothly aft and back up the other side. Rodriguez followed the path until his eyes locked on land.

"Hold on," he screamed. "We're gonna crash." He grabbed the railing and held on tight.

"Shit, hold on," Lieutenant Dawson repeated right before the submarine ran aground. It hit so hard the round hull rolled sideways, tilting the sail towards the clearing and throwing Lieutenant Norton, Dinesh, Harrison, and the Captain out onto the sand.

###

Rodriguez shook his head and wiped the blood from his eyes. All he could see was the black metal of the bridge. His face had come to rest in the salty corner by the lookout pooka. He could hear someone screaming, but it sounded so far away. Everything sounded far away. He felt like he was being crushed by the submarine. It took him a minute to figure out there was someone on top of him.

Lieutenant Dawson pushed himself up and off Rodriguez. His face had been spared the impact of the metal bridge by slamming into Rodriguez's much softer ass.

It may have saved the Lieutenant a bit of pain, but it didn't feel so great for Rodriguez. He thought that if it had been anything smaller than the Lieutenant's huge melon head, there just might have been penetration.

"Damn, Rodriguez," Lieutenant Dawson said, "you've got a surprisingly soft yet firm ass."

"Thanks, Sir," Rodriguez said. "When you're finished groping me, maybe you could help me up?"

Lieutenant Dawson grabbed the railing and braced his feet. He stuck out his other hand.

Rodriguez twisted his body around and grabbed the Lieutenant's hand, and together they pulled Rodriguez to his feet. He stood up next to the Lieutenant and looked out at the scene in front of them.

The boat sat halfway up on the shore, angled approximately forty-five degrees to starboard. Down on the beach, the Captain, Lieutenant Norton, Harrison, and Dinesh lay sprawled in the sand. As far as Rodriguez could see, only Dinesh moved; the other three lay like driftwood baking under the burning sun.

Down on the non-skid deck, Sulley's body lay mostly in the water. Only his face and left arm were visible. The sleeve of his coveralls was caught in the non-skid; it appeared to be the only thing keeping him from sinking into the water.

Rodriguez heard a splash from the aft end of the submarine. He turned just as the sub lurched forward, sending it further up on the shore. A spray of sand and water flew into the air and rained down on the sailors on shore.

The water around the sub boiled with activity. Churning water moved forward, splashing across the hull and landing on the beach. The current was so strong that it pushed the boat even farther onto land. Rodriguez had to hold on to the railing to keep from falling overboard. He watched the water flow as something moved fast along the starboard side of the ship. It was heading straight for Sulley.

Rodriguez tried yelling for him, but Sulley didn't respond. He screamed for him anyway, watching as the thing moved ever closer. Rodriguez tried to climb over the railing, but the sub shook so violently that he slipped and nearly fell overboard. He pulled himself back into the bridge and looked back at Sulley.

Sulley's body was ripped into the water so fast that Rodriguez didn't even see it move. It was there one second, and gone the next. All that remained was a few scraps of his coveralls, a chunk of jawbone that had been caught on the nonskid, and a pool of blood that had almost completely washed away.

"Aw, fuck," Lieutenant Dawson said. He was staring at the water where Sulley had been. "I never really liked the prick, but damn."

Rodriguez looked back at the shore and saw that all three of the crew were moving now, although just barely. He breathed a sigh of relief until he remembered who else was in the bridge. "Where's Santalino?"

Rodriguez and Lieutenant Dawson both turned around to look for their friend when a scream erupted from the ladder that led to the upper level. A geyser of red shot out of the hole and sprayed into the air. Rodriguez and the Lieutenant were both coated in blood.

Rodriguez reached up and wiped his eyes as Santalino's head dropped to the deck in front of them. A massive hand reached out from the hatch and grabbed the top of the ladder.

"Fuckin' shit, man, *go*," Lieutenant Dawson screamed. He climbed up over the railing and was gone before Rodriguez had even moved.

There was a thump from below as Adams' head came up into view. Four bloodshot eyes focused on Rodriguez. The twin mouths chewed the air as Adams grumbled something Rodriguez couldn't understand.

Rather than try, Rodriguez got moving. He grabbed the rail and leaped over the edge without looking. The thirteen foot trip down was mercifully quick, and he landed on his ass right on top of Lieutenant Dawson. His leg twisted to one side and he screamed out in pain, but he didn't feel anything break.

Lieutenant Dawson let out all his air in a mighty breath. He clearly struggled for air. His face was changing color and his eyes rolled back in his head.

Rodriguez rolled off of him and tried to help him up. He didn't see the Lieutenant land, so he couldn't tell if he was hurt.

From the bridge above, the stump of an arm flew down. It landed in the water with a splash, sending inky black spray into the surrounding air. Adams screamed as it tore apart the bridge.

"Fuck, Sir, you need to get up," Rodriguez said against the backdrop of inhuman screams. Whatever was going on up there, Rodriguez wanted no part of it. He grabbed Lieutenant Dawson under the arm and started to drag him towards the shore. As he pulled, the Lieutenant's legs caught on the nonskid deck. It tore through his clothes and ripped the flesh underneath to shreds.

"Rodriguez, watch his legs," Lieutenant Norton called from the shore. He was trying to climb up onto the submarine.

The Captain and Dinesh stood watching the water. Neither of them looked like they could be any help.

Harrison stood nearby, nervously glancing between the submarine and the woods behind him.

"Hang on, I'm coming," Lieutenant Norton said.

"Fuck that, his legs'll heal," Rodriguez said.

The thing in the bridge had started throwing parts of Santalino at them. A leg landed next to Rodriguez. He could feel wet chunks of tissue splattering his back as he ran. He closed his eyes and pulled Lieutenant Dawson harder.

The Lieutenant made a great sucking sound and finally pulled air into his lungs. They had almost made it to the edge of the submarine where Lieutenant Norton was still trying to scramble up the side.

Once he made it to the edge, Rodriguez stopped and grabbed his chest. He hadn't worked that hard in years; he could barely breathe.

"Fuck me," Lieutenant Dawson squeaked through gasps of air. "My legs."

Rodriguez looked down and wondered if the Lieutenant would ever walk like a normal person again. His calves had been torn open, exposed muscle shredded into strips that fell to the side, revealing pure white bone beneath.

"Fucking help me," Lieutenant Dawson said as he tried to roll onto his side. "I can't get up."

"Grab my arm," Rodriguez said. He reached down to help the Lieutenant up when Dinesh called from the shore.

"Behind you!"

Rodriguez turned and saw Adams standing on the bent railing of the bridge. Both halves of the monster practically glowed in the bright sunshine. He thought he recognized the other face but a name escaped him. At that point he no longer cared. The monster held more of Santalino in its one muscular arm, as the other hung limp by its side.

Behind Adams stood one of the most hated members of the Alexandria crew. Cartwright sneered down at Rodriguez with a look that was somehow worse than Adams.

Cartwright's face looked different. It had changed from the familiar look of nasty ignorance to something much more vicious. He looked more than his usual pissed, he looked beyond furious. He barely looked human.

As Rodriguez watched, something moved under Cartwright's skin. His face swelled on one side, a dark shape passing along his cheek and subsiding near his ear. His eyes bulged and turned briefly red before settling down and going dark. He opened his mouth and let out a low guttural sound that Adams repeated.

"Fuck, man," Lieutenant Dawson said. "Get me the fuck away from that thing." He looked up at Rodriguez. "I can't get up." He flailed his arms around, unable to bring himself to an upright position. "Come on, man, that thing's gonna fucking eat

90

me."

"Fuck that shit," Rodriguez said. He put his heel to Lieutenant Dawson's back and kicked him off the side of the submarine. He jumped right after him, his arms out in front of like a shield. As he hit the ground, he rolled past the Lieutenant and came to rest at the Captain's feet.

"Come on," the Captain said, "get up."

"We've got to go," Dinesh added. With his help, Rodriguez stood.

Behind them, Lieutenant Norton grabbed Lieutenant Dawson around the waist and drug him away from both the submarine and the ferocious water surrounding it.

"Shit," Rodriguez said as he ran to give Lieutenant Norton a hand. Lieutenant Dawson's shredded legs left a trail of red in the sand. The water moved directly towards it, wiping away the blood and bringing it back to the sea. "Harrison, give us a hand, man."

Harrison shook his head back and forth and backed away.

Rodriguez grabbed one of Lieutenant Dawson's arms and Lieutenant Norton grabbed the other.

"On three," Lieutenant Norton said. "One, two--"

They both lifted and headed away from the boat. They had only gotten three steps when the water beyond them exploded, spraying the beach and blocking out the sky above.

Something darted out from under the waves, grabbing Lieutenant Dawson by the legs and yanking him back to the water. Like Sulley before him, Lieutenant Dawson was gone before Rodriguez could even react.

Lieutenant Norton and Rodriguez both dropped backwards on the shore, their feet kicking sand as they backpedaled away from the living sea.

Harrison screamed and ran for the woods. Before anyone could say anything, he disappeared into the thicket.

"Move," the Captain shouted, "Fucking *now*." He grabbed Lieutenant Norton by the arm and pulled him up.

Dinesh grabbed Rodriguez and did the same.

The water moved towards them like a living wave, grabbing at the beach with liquid claws. It came close to touching

Rodriguez's foot but he managed to pick up speed and run away from the beach.

Rodriguez stumbled once, but Dinesh caught him and they continued all the way to the edge of the jungle. There they stopped and finally turned around.

The water receded. The surrounding waves had calmed down and returned to the appearance of a normal lagoon.

Rodriguez dropped to the dirt and tried to catch his breath, but the Captain spoke up.

"There's no time for that," he said. "I'm sure that thing on the bridge will be down here any moment."

Rodriguez looked up to the submarine. He saw that, although Cartwright was still hovering in the tilted bridge, the creature that had once been Adams was no longer standing on the railing.

"Right. Sorry, Sir." Rodriguez stood and turned to look at the wall of trees and shrubs.

"There's a trail over here," Dinesh said. He pointed to a small overgrown path that snaked away between two shrubs.

"I'm not sure we want to know what made that trail," Lieutenant Norton said.

"I agree," the Captain said, "but I'm not sure we have much choice." He walked over to the trail, looked back once at his submarine, and started through the trees.

Dinesh and Rodriguez followed.

Lieutenant Norton trailed behind. "I don't like this shit." He looked back over his shoulder as he walked. "I don't like this shit at all."

Rodriguez kept his eyes down, watching out for the roots and rocks that littered the path. Things moved through the trees but Rodriguez tried not to pay attention. He tried not to think about the oppressing heat and humidity of the jungle. He tried not to wonder why there were no bugs. He tried not to think about anything, but he couldn't stop thinking about everything. The more he thought about it, the less he wanted to know.

Ahead, the Captain marched on without slowing.

Behind, Lieutenant Norton tripped and landed on his face. He picked himself up with a quick, "I'm okay."

Next to Rodriguez, Dinesh walked in silence, staring at their surroundings and scratching at his stubbly chin.

"What's up?" Rodriguez asked.

"What's up with what?"

"I don't know," Rodriguez said. He scratched his chin, an unconscious mimicking of Dinesh. "You look like, I don't know."

"It's this place," Dinesh said. "I think there is something very wrong here." He peered through the jungle ahead and kept his eyes away from Rodriguez.

"No shit," Rodriguez said. "Anything in particular?"

"I just don't know."

Cartwright watched them pass into the trees. He looked up towards the hills surrounding the lagoon and wondered how long it would be before they reached the cliff. That would cut their journey shorter than they expected.

Where you gonna go, bitches? he wondered with a smile that spread impossibly far across his face. If he stared long enough, he was sure he could see branches moving as they made their way to the end.

"I love it when a plan comes together," he said. "Time to go." He stood and climbed on the railing while Adams watched from below. It had already dropped to the forward deck but was waiting for Cartwright to give the command.

In front of Cartwright, a cone of water rose up from the lagoon, snaking its way to where he stood. The top of the water column flattened out like a platform for Cartwright to step on. He stepped off the submarine and floated on the surface. The water slowly lowered his body to the ground, moving out past the submarine and towards the sandy shore.

Adams followed, dropping off the side of the ship and walking up to where Cartwright landed on the beach.

They both walked silently towards the entrance to the trail that the others had taken. Cartwright stopped before passing through, and Adams stopped behind him.

"Here we wait," Cartwright said. He dropped his ass to the ground and leaned back against a nearby tree.

Adams stood nearby, staring down the trail as if waiting for something to do. He didn't have to wait long.

The Captain stopped walking and held his hand up above his left shoulder, hand clenched in a fist.

Dinesh and Rodriguez both stopped walking and stared at the Captain, waiting.

Lieutenant Norton didn't. He'd kept his head down the whole way and walked straight into Rodriguez. He stepped on the back of Rodriguez's boot and slammed his head into his back.

"Ow, Sir," Rodriguez said, pulling his foot free and rubbing the back of his neck. "That shit hurts."

"Shh," the Captain whispered from ahead. The party held their breath and watched the Captain stand perfectly still.

Beyond him, Rodriguez could only see more trees. *There's nothing there*, he thought, *or is there? Maybe the Captain's lost it*. He edged closer to Dinesh to see if he could get a better view.

"What is it?" Dinesh whispered. He looked around them, eyes darting from the trees to the Captain to Rodriguez. "Why have we stopped?"

"I don't know." Rodriguez moved closer to the Captain and slid to his side so he could see what lay beyond.

The narrow path led through the trees before giving way to a small clearing. The face of a rock wall shot straight up from the dirt floor of the jungle. Carved into this wall were various inscriptions, strange artwork surrounded by characters of a sort he'd never seen.

There was a carving of something that resembled a bear with wings. Wavy lines like rays of the sun shot out from the bear in all directions. Near that was a moth-like creature with unusually detailed facial expressions; piercing eyes above vicious fangs so meticulous they seemed to drip right off the rock.

In the center was something that could only be described as

a dragon. The coiled serpent snaked around a rough opening chiseled into the rock. This opening led to a length of tunnel shrouded in darkness that the dim light of the jungle could not penetrate.

The Captain stared into this tunnel, as if waiting for something to walk out.

Nothing did. The shadows inside remained silent and motionless.

Rodriguez glanced around the area, but besides the newly-found rock wall, the area they'd stopped in was no different from the surrounding jungle. There were still things moving in the trees, just out of sight, but after their uneventful hike he'd figured it was no concern. He stepped closer to the Captain.

"Uh, Captain?"

"*Shh.*"

"Captain, there's nothing here," Rodriguez said.

The Captain ignored Rodriguez for a moment before tilting his head to the side. "Did you hear it?" he asked.

"Hear what?"

"You didn't," he replied, his voice dropping to barely a whisper. "You didn't hear it." He turned towards the group. "None of you heard it."

"Uh, no, Sir. Sorry. Dinesh?" Rodriguez said, hoping for a little help. He didn't get the response he'd expected.

"I heard it," Dinesh said.

"You did?" the Captain and Rodriguez asked nearly in unison.

"I did," Dinesh said. "I heard it." He stepped up to the front and past the Captain. He too had his head cocked to the side, his ear angled towards the tunnel.

Rodriguez held his breath to see if he could hear something. All he heard was his heart pounding in his chest begging for oxygen. He let out his breath and sucked air in, the burn quickly fading from his lungs.

Dinesh looked back at him with his finger to his lips before focusing once again on the tunnel.

The Captain took a tentative step towards the entrance. He reached around to the back of his belt and grabbed his flashlight.

As soon as he twisted the handle, the LED beam illuminated the darkness.

It looked like the tunnel had been cut straight into the rock for about ten feet before turning sharply left. The walls were not rough cut like the entrance. It had a smooth, polished finish that shined in the glow from the Captain's flashlight. Torches were mounted on both sides of the walls, ends long since burnt down to little more than charred stumps.

Rodriguez took a step forward to stand next to Dinesh.

The Captain stayed where he was, shining his flashlight all around inside the tunnel.

Lieutenant Norton stayed behind, maintaining a safe distance while staring into space, fixed on a spot along the rock wall. He kept quiet, but for Rodriguez the eyes gave it away. The Lieutenant was terrified.

Dinesh grabbed Rodriguez's shoulder. His eyes grew large and his mouth dropped open. "There it is again," he said. "Did you hear it?"

Rodriguez thought he might have heard something, although he wasn't sure what it was. He cocked his head and turned his ear towards the tunnel, just as the Captain and Dinesh had done previously.

The three of them stood at the mouth of the tunnel, all lined up with their heads to the side, waiting for something to happen.

When the sound came again, Rodriguez not only heard it, but he heard it loud and clear. He knew what it was. It was a voice.

"Help me," a female voice called. "Help me, please."

Rodriguez stared at the tunnel, glancing from the Captain to Dinesh, waiting to see what they would do. *Did they hear it too?* Someone touched his shoulder. Rodriguez turned and saw that Lieutenant Norton had broken his trance and moved in for a better look.

"What is that?" he whispered.

"Shh." Rodriguez found himself hushing the Lieutenant just as the Captain had done to him moments before. *He heard it too,* he thought. *We all did. What the hell is going on?*

Next to him, Dinesh twitched like he was getting ready to

move. His foot shot out and hovered in mid-air before being pulled back. He did it again, and he leaned forward as if to build up momentum.

Better him than me, Rodriguez thought. *I'm not gonna be the first to step in there. Not for a million bucks.*

From behind and without a word, Lieutenant Norton pushed his way through the group. He moved past them, walking around the Captain and crossing in front of the beam of his flashlight.

Rodriguez's muscles tightened but then froze to the spot. He looked from the Lieutenant to the tunnel but couldn't bring himself to move. Something about the entrance kept him from following. The jungle, the rock, the darkness of the tunnel, and the voice. *This is all wrong.*

"There's a chick in there," Lieutenant Norton said. He paused at the entrance and looked back towards the group, catching each of their eyes. When he got to Rodriguez, they stared at each other for a silent moment before the Lieutenant spoke again. "Rodriguez, seriously?"

"Fuck that, Sir," Rodriguez said. "I'm not going in there."

"There's someone in there asking for our help. She also happens to be a chick. We've been all around the world, and I've never seen you leave the ladies hanging. Are you gonna wuss out on me now?"

"Fuck that. I don't care if she can suck a ball bearing through a thousand feet of hydraulic pipe. She can keep her creepy tunnel."

"I think we should go in anyway," Dinesh blurted out.

"What?" Rodriguez said.

"Huh?" Lieutenant Norton said.

"Look," Dinesh said. He pointed back towards the path they had just followed. The woods were closing in, the trees and shrubs taking on a life of their own. The path was being swallowed by the surrounding vegetation. The little bit that remained disappeared as they all stood watching, and the moving field of green began growing closer to the rock wall.

Rodriguez took a silent step backwards as vines crept along the ground toward his feet.

"Fuck," the Captain said. "I don't wanna go in there either, but at this point I don't think we have much choice." He stepped to the side and pointed at the tunnel. "Move it," he barked as he pushed Lieutenant Norton towards the entrance.

Dinesh's body jerked as he jumped into motion, headed for the entrance. He followed the Lieutenant and soon the two were swallowed by the darkness of the tunnel.

Rodriguez stared at the moving trees and the shrubs that spread their branches across the path, coming close enough to scrape at the leather of his boots. He jumped back as a branch tried to wrap around his foot. A large tear ran across the otherwise perfectly shined toe of his boot. He backed up until he bumped into the Captain.

They both watched in silence as the branches crawled closer. Once they got to within a couple feet, the Captain grabbed Rodriguez and shoved him towards the tunnel. He stepped behind Rodriguez and put his hand on his shoulder.

"Let's go, Rodriguez," the Captain said. "It's time to move." He shoved Rodriguez through the entrance and followed close behind. As soon as they had entered, Rodriguez glanced back over his shoulder. Branches crisscrossed in front of the entrance, climbing up the rock wall, cutting off the outside light, and sealing off their only exit.

The Captain shined his flashlight deeper into the tunnel.

Lieutenant Norton and Dinesh stood nearby, not far from the entrance.

"Looks like we go this way," Dinesh said.

"No shit," the Lieutenant said. He reached up and grabbed one of the burnt torches from the wall. "Wonder if we could light one of these bitches."

"You got a match?" Rodriguez asked.

"Yeah, I think I do," Lieutenant Norton said. "Hold this." He handed the torch to Rodriguez and fished around in his pockets, pulling out a notebook, three pens, a rock, a wad of paper towels, and a Zippo lighter.

"You got enough shit in there, Navigator?" the Captain asked.

"Fuckin' A right," the Lieutenant said with a smile. He held the Zippo in one hand while shoving the rest of his things in his pants pocket.

"Here, let me see that," the Captain said. He reached out and grabbed the lighter without waiting for a reply. He handed his flashlight over to Dinesh. "Hold this, will you?"

Dinesh took the flashlight and shined it on the torch.

Rodriguez turned the burnt torch nub over in his hand. "You don't think this thing will actually light," he asked. "Do you?"

"You got a better idea?" Lieutenant Norton asked.

Rodriguez stared at the charcoal nub and remained silent.

"Yeah," the Lieutenant said. "Me neither."

The Captain flipped open the top of the Zippo and spun the wheel. Sparks flew from the flint but it did not light. He shook the lighter and tried again, his thumb flicking over and over without success. "When's the last time you filled this thing?" he asked.

"Shit, I don't know. Can't be that long." Lieutenant Norton reached out towards the lighter. "Let me give it a try."

The Captain closed his fist around the Zippo and stared at the Lieutenant.

"Sorry," the Lieutenant said. "May I give it a try, Sir?"

"Better." He handed over the lighter and reached for his flashlight.

Dinesh turned it over to the Captain without a word.

"Fuck that lighter," the Captain said. "I'm going this way." He turned on his heel and stepped further into the tunnel, his flashlight igniting the curve at the far end.

As he walked away, the rest of the group was left in darkness.

Lieutenant Norton struck his Zippo repeatedly without success. "C'mon, you fucker," he mumbled.

"Sorry, Lieutenant," Rodriguez said, "but I'm sticking with the light." He turned and followed the Captain.

"Good idea," Dinesh agreed, following Rodriguez.

Lieutenant Norton flicked his lighter a few more times. He stood by himself and cursed under his breath.

Before turning the corner, Rodriguez paused to look back at the Lieutenant. "Sir?"

Lieutenant Norton let out an exaggerated sigh. "Fucking lighter," he whispered. He jammed the wheel one last time and the wick sparked into life. "Hey," he said. "Hey, guys, it works!"

"Hooray," Rodriguez said with little excitement in his voice. He stepped back toward the Lieutenant and held out the torch. "I guess we can try this thing."

Lieutenant Norton grabbed the torch and held up the lighter as he called to the Captain. "Hey Captain, it works," he said, but the Captain and Dinesh had already disappeared around the corner. The flame sputtered and died in his outstretched hand, leaving Rodriguez and Norton in darkness.

"Uh, Lieutenant?" Rodriguez said. He felt along the wall and tried to find his way.

"Where the fuck are you?" Lieutenant Norton asked. To Rodriguez, he sounded very far away.

"Just walk forward," Rodriguez said. He heard two footsteps and a bump. "What was that?"

"That was my fucking head," the Lieutenant said. "Someone put a wall here when I wasn't looking. God *damn*, that hurts."

A soft glow illuminated the tunnel. The Captain came around the corner and shined his flashlight at them. "You two idiots want to drop your cocks and join us?" he asked.

"Fuck," Lieutenant Norton said as he tried to light the Zippo one last time. It didn't catch.

"Yes Sir," Rodriguez said as he ran to the corner with the Captain.

The light faded from the tunnel, shrouding the Lieutenant in darkness. "Hey, wait for me," he said. He pocketed his Zippo and followed the group deeper into the rock.

11

The tunnel turned left at just over a ninety degree angle. It led few dozen steps deeper into the rock before turning to the right. Rodriguez followed the Captain around the bend and stopped to stare at the scene before him.

The tunnel opened to what looked like a huge outdoor amphitheater, a large rock quarry dominating the center. The bottom was full of water and the sides were piled with massive boulders larger than anything he had ever seen. The rock around the quarry spread out in all directions as far as Rodriguez could see. Aside from the wall they'd just passed through, the rock sloped away from the quarry at an angle that could easily be walked on.

There were no trees, shrubs, or vegetation of any kind. There was also no water, with the exception of what sat at the bottom of the center pit. There was no sign of the beach or lagoon they'd just left, and there was no trace of jungle.

Rodriguez looked to the sky above. It had taken on the surreal quality of dusk, but like much of the island, something about it looked wrong.

Dinesh stood nearby, staring at the field of rock surrounding them. He didn't speak, but his eyes showed a level of discomfort that Rodriguez could understand.

The Captain had continued on, staring down into the quarry as he skirted the edge. His eyes remained fixed on the water below, yet he made his way around the perimeter with no problem.

Lieutenant Norton stepped out of the tunnel and bumped into Rodriguez. "Watch where I'm going, fucker." His words trailed off as he looked at the clearing ahead of them. He stepped to the side, dropped the unlit torch he'd been carrying, and sat down on the sloping rock wall nearby.

"You okay?" Rodriguez asked.

The Lieutenant laughed but said nothing. He dropped his head in his hands and remained that way, not moving or speaking.

Rodriguez looked over at Dinesh. He had taken a step forward and was staring wide-eyed into the quarry.

"Hey Dinesh, what's up?" Rodriguez asked.

Dinesh made no move to acknowledge Rodriguez. He kept staring at the stagnant water below. His mouth hung open slightly and a glisten of drool appeared at the corner of his mouth.

"Dinesh? Hey man, you okay?" Rodriguez waved his hand in front of Dinesh's face until he finally blinked.

"Yes?"

"Dude, you were kinda zoning out there for a minute," Rodriguez said.

"This has all happened before," Dinesh said.

"Come again?"

"We're all going to die down here."

"What?" Rodriguez opened his mouth to say more but Lieutenant Norton interrupted.

"What are you fags talking about?" he asked from his seat along the outside wall.

"Nothing, never mind, fucker," Dinesh replied. He walked away, stepping towards the edge of the chasm and staring into the murky depths below. He slowly walked away from Rodriguez toward the opposite end.

That was weird, Rodriguez thought. *Never heard Dinesh swear like that*. He looked around at the others.

The Captain was on the far side of the quarry and heading back around the opposite side.

Lieutenant Norton was still sitting by the tunnel entrance. He didn't say anything else, and he didn't look like he was moving from his spot.

"Wait up," Rodriguez said as he jogged over to where Dinesh stood. He slowed as he got closer to the drop off, eyes unconsciously moving down the steep slope to the water below. He stopped a couple feet from the edge, staring at the loose rock that clung to the edge.

Dinesh stood at this loose border, the toes of his boots hanging over the lip toward nothingness.

On the opposite side, the Captain walked just as close, his

eyes locked on the depths of the quarry.

Rodriguez took a tentative step forward but felt his stomach churn at the depth of the drop off. *Fuck that*, Rodriguez thought. *I'm not playing* that *game*.

"Take a look down there," Dinesh said, pointing into the pit.

"What is it?" Rodriguez asked.

"Have a look."

Without moving his feet, Rodriguez leaned forward to see over the edge. He felt his balls tighten and he took a step back. "Fuck that," he said. "No way."

"There's something I think you should see," Dinesh said. "I think your Captain sees it too."

Rodriguez looked over at the Captain and saw that he had stopped walking. He stood at the edge, staring down at something in the water, just as Dinesh was doing.

"Look at it," Lieutenant Norton said from behind.

Rodriguez jumped and spun around.

The Lieutenant was only a couple feet away. He had left his seat by the tunnel and was walking slowly towards the edge. He stepped past Rodriguez and stopped next to Dinesh. They both stared down into the pit.

"Have a look," the Captain called, his voice echoing across the field of stone. He wasn't moving, but he seemed somehow closer to the group.

Rodriguez looked back and forth between the Captain, Dinesh, and Lieutenant Norton. They all stood at the edge, staring unmoving into the pit at what appeared to be the same spot.

"It's just down there," the Captain said.

"You wouldn't believe it," Dinesh added.

None of them looked up at Rodriguez as they spoke, and none of them displayed any emotion.

Rodriguez took a step back and shook his head from side to side. "No way," he said, his feet treading carefully backwards towards the tunnel entrance. "Not happening." He backed up while the others remained at the edge without moving. Soon his foot came to rest at the rock wall. He turned around and headed for the tunnel entrance; it was just a few feet away. When he reached the opening, he paused. Sounds echoed from the darkness inside.

"Hello?" he asked. From around the corner, the unmistakable sound of a lighter echoed out, accompanied by the soft glow of an open flame bouncing off the shiny rock walls.

A voice whispered from the tunnel. *"Rodriguez."*

Shit, Rodriguez thought. Shadows danced off the walls as something yet unseen moved through the tunnel, approaching the opening. Rodriguez heard slow, lumbering footsteps crashing along the floor, as if something huge was making its way through the darkness.

"Rodriguez, come back," Dinesh called from behind him.

Rodriguez turned and saw that Dinesh and Lieutenant Norton were both looking at him.

The Captain was also staring at him. He had moved so close, he was now only a few feet away from Dinesh and Norton. "Stay away from the light," he said.

"Come back," the Lieutenant said.

"Watch out for the light," The Captain said.

"We need you," Dinesh continued. "Come back."

"Rodriguez," the voice from the tunnel repeated.

Rodriguez felt the hair stand up on the back of his neck as the sound of movement increased. Something had nearly made its way to the bend, and light spilled out of the tunnel at Rodriguez's feet.

A shape slithered from around the corner, a long, syrupy appendage that stretched out along the rock. It held a torch at the end, even though there were no fingers or even a hand to grasp it with.

Rodriguez stepped back from the opening. *Oh, what the fuck is this?*

"Hurry, Rodriguez, *hurry*," Dinesh said from the edge of the pit.

Rodriguez turned away from the tunnel and looked at the group by the pit. The Captain, Dinesh, and Lieutenant Norton stood side by side, once again staring at the water below.

Rodriguez heard what sounded like a growl from the tunnel behind him, and he broke into a run towards the group.

"Come with us," Lieutenant Norton said without moving.

"It's the only way," Dinesh added.

Rodriguez slowed as the three men each held one foot out over the edge.

"No!" Rodriguez yelled, but the group did not respond. They all stepped over the edge and disappeared from view. The noises from the tunnel grew to an almost deafening roar. Rodriguez ran towards the quarry but stopped before he reached the edge. He dropped to his hands and knees and crawled closer.

The water came into view, and his eyes scanned the pit for any sign of the three sailors. No one clung to the rocky slope, nor was the water below disturbed in any way. Rodriguez crept closer and stretched his neck out to see where they'd gone.

As his head moved over the edge, he tried to ignore the sounds pouring from the tunnel. There was no other way out, so he had no real choice. Once he had a clear view of the water he paused, looking in all directions. There was no one there.

"*Rodriguez!*" someone shouted from behind him.

He turned to look back towards the tunnel as a massive hand came up over the quarry's edge, grabbing Rodriguez's shoulder. He tried to pull back but it had a firm grip on him. "Get the fuck off me," he screamed as he dug into the leathery flesh of its fingers, trying to get free. He could not even move them, much less pry them off.

There were more noises coming from behind him, and they were getting closer. He tried to turn, but the arm was dragging him closer to the edge. Soon he would be in the pit, and he knew if he went in he wasn't coming back out.

"Quick, grab him," a familiar voice called.

Rodriguez felt arms wrapping around his waist and legs. To his right, Lieutenant Norton stepped into view with one of the torches from the tunnel burning in his hand.

"Burn it," the Captain shouted.

Lieutenant Norton jammed the torch into the thing's forearm. An inhuman scream echoed up from the quarry, the sound reverberating through the tons of surrounding rock. The ground shook like an earthquake as the hand let go of Rodriguez's shoulder.

Rodriguez flew back from the edge and landed in a pile of bodies.

"What the fuck just happened?" Rodriguez asked.

"I might ask you the same thing," the Captain said. "You fucking disappeared on us, you prick."

"Yeah," Lieutenant Norton said. "You were standing there when I lit my torch, then you just up and walked away--"

"You never lit your torch," Rodriguez interrupted.

"Fucking-a right I did."

"As much as I hate to agree with Norton, he's right," the Captain said. "Good thing, too, because my flashlight died. It took us like an hour to find you. You know what it's like wandering around in that maze for an hour?"

"What the fuck are you talking about?" Rodriguez asked. "I followed *you* out of that tunnel. You were marching along like a fucking Nazi or something."

"Bullshit," Lieutenant Norton said.

"I don't think arguing about this is helping," Dinesh said.

"Who the fuck asked you?" the Lieutenant blurted out. "It's because of your ship that we're in this mess."

"Goddamn it, Norton," the Captain began, "cut the bullshit and leave him alone."

"No, Captain," Dinesh said, "it's all right. I can understand his frustration."

"Well I can't understand his rudeness."

"And *I* can't understand what the fuck is going on," Lieutenant Norton said.

"I second that," Rodriguez added. "I mean, seriously. What the fuck?"

"I think I might have an idea," Dinesh said.

"You see?" Norton said. "I *fucking* knew it."

"Cut the shit," the Captain said.

Lieutenant Norton closed his mouth and mumbled something through closed lips. He looked at the ground and kicked at a bit of rock but said nothing more.

The Captain turned back to Dinesh. "Go ahead."

"Well, I'm not sure, but I think this has happened before."

"Aw, shit," Rodriguez said, "not again." He started to scramble backwards, sliding his ass on the rocky surface as he moved away from the group.

"Rodriguez," the Captain shouted, "you want to end up in that pit?"

Rodriguez stopped and turned his head around. He had stopped mere inches from the drop off. His head began to spin and his stomach dropped. He slid away from the edge and stopped next to Lieutenant Norton.

"Sorry, it's just that I heard Dinesh say something like that before, only it wasn't Dinesh...at least I don't think it was." Rodriguez dropped his head into his hands and exhaled. "I don't really know."

"What did I say?" Dinesh asked. "Or, well, what did the other me say?"

"I don't remember," Rodriguez lied. "I'm sure it doesn't matter."

"Can one of you tell us what you're talking about?" the Captain asked.

Dinesh stared at Rodriguez in silence.

Rodriguez shifted his legs and scooted further away from the pit, his eyes not leaving Dinesh. *Exactly what is going on with you?* he wondered.

They stared at each other until Dinesh broke eye contact. He looked towards the Captain and said, "I can tell you what I know."

"We found it while out fishing," Dinesh said. "Singh and I, we used to own our own shipping company. It was a small operation, but profitable. Most of the runs were just the two of us." He stopped and looked up at the sky. "When we found it, it was kind of like this, only under water."

"You mean like a seamount?" Norton asked.

"Yes, like--no," he shook his head, "not like a seamount. It was like an island. Like this. With air and everything."

"An island?" the Captain asked.

"No, not an island. That's why this is so strange." Dinesh closed his eyes and rubbed his temples. "I don't know, maybe

I'm just tired from everything that's happened."

"But underwater?" the Captain asked.

"I know what this sounds like," Dinesh said. "It sounds ridiculous. Our boat was going down. We dove underwater to avoid the flames, and Singh saw the tunnel."

"Who's Singh?" Rodriguez asked.

"He's--" Dinesh cleared his throat. "He was my brother."

"Oh."

"He swam for the tunnel, and I followed. I guess I don't know what we were hoping for, but I know we didn't expect the tunnel to lead to a place like this." Dinesh stared up at the sky, watching the stars. "All this, where we are. It's not real." He pointed at the darkening sky. "You see those stars up there?"

"Yeah?"

"They do not move. Nothing up there moves."

Rodriguez stared at the stars in silence.

The whole group watched for what seemed an eternity. Nothing moved.

"So?" the Captain said. "They're so far away we wouldn't see them move, would we?"

"Maybe." Dinesh continued staring at the same spot, as if waiting for something to happen. "Maybe not. I don't know."

"Bullshit," Lieutenant Norton said.

"No, no bullshit. Just like what Singh and I found, nothing is real."

The Lieutenant kicked a small rock into the quarry. The sound of it falling echoed across the rock as it made its way down to a final splash. "That seemed pretty real to me," he said.

"Yes, the rock is real, but nothing that happens here is. At least I don't think so."

"I'm sorry, exactly where are we then?" Lieutenant Norton asked. "Is this the Twilight Zone?"

"Norton--" the Captain began.

"No, seriously, Cap. Where did this fucker even come from?"

"I've told you to keep your shit in line."

"Or else what?" the Lieutenant said. "You threatening to bust me out here in the middle of fucking nowhere? Last I checked, you don't really have a submarine anymore, so that makes you the Captain of jack and shit."

The Captain looked like he was getting ready to explode. His eyes bulged; a deep reddening grew from his neck and spread to his throbbing temples. The only thing missing was a cartoonish rush of steam pouring from his ears.

He counted through gritted teeth and waited until he reached ten. "Right," he said, followed by the longest exhale Dinesh had ever heard. It seemed that the Captain shrunk with every second that breath left his body. The red faded back behind his ears and his veins retreated beneath his skin. By the end, he looked almost normal.

"Okay, Norton," the Captain said, "I'll play your silly little game. For now." He turned to Dinesh and looked at his hands before speaking. They shook, but only slightly. "Dinesh, where exactly are we?"

"I don't know, but I think it's possible we might be underwater."

Before Dinesh could even close his mouth, Norton was speaking right up. "Bull--"

"Shut...*up!*" the Captain interrupted. "I'm sick of your shit. If you don't like this conversation, you know where we left the boat."

"Yeah," Rodriguez said. "I'm sure Cartwright will be waiting with his little buddy."

"Fuck you."

"That's what your mother said."

"Shut the fuck up, both of you," the Captain said. "So what does all this mean?"

"I think it means we need to leave," Dinesh replied.

"First fucking smart thing I've heard him say," Lieutenant Norton muttered.

"So how did you and Singh get out?" Rodriguez asked.

"We swam." He looked down into the pit and stared at the stagnant water below.

"Not in that shit, I hope," the Captain said.

"Not exactly," Dinesh said. "Something chased us, so we ran. We ran as fast as we could without really paying attention.

We eventually got through the tunnel to the lagoon beyond. Nothing was there to stop us, so we swam out."

"Well that sounds easy," Lieutenant Norton said. "Why don't we just do that?"

"We don't know where it is," Rodriguez said.

"I don't think it will be so easy," Dinesh said. "Singh, he tried to find the island afterwards. Many times. We never did. I think we were lucky to escape. It might not let us out this time."

"That's stupid," Lieutenant Norton said. "We should be able to go back the way we came, right?" He pointed towards the tunnel. "Hell, the boat's still back there. We could just sail it on out of here. There's enough of us. I'll navigate. Rodriguez, you can sleep in Sonar. Captain, you lead us out of here. You can point, just like Charlie Brown." He looked at Dinesh. "I don't suppose you can run a nuclear reactor?"

"Fuck that," Rodriguez said. "You see that crazy shit Cartwright had going on?"

"Fuck him," Lieutenant Norton said. "I'll kick his little faggot   ass."

"He's not so little," the Captain said. "And I'm not sure if he's gay or what that has to do with anything, but with his buddy Adams hanging around, I'd like to see you try."

"Yeah," Rodriguez added. "And don't forget about his pack of asshole nuke friends."

"Fuck you guys," Lieutenant Norton said as he turned and headed for the tunnel. "I'm heading back before things get any weirder. You all enjoy your stay in the Twilight Zone, okay?"

"I think we should stay together," Dinesh said. "It may not be safe."

"And fuck you too," the Lieutenant said over his shoulder. "I'm way past sick of hearing your shit. Anyway, I don't even like curry."

"What?" Dinesh asked with a glance over at Rodriguez, who only shrugged. "But the last time I was here--"

"Not interested," Lieutenant Dawson interrupted.

"But--"

"*Not. Interested.*" The Lieutenant held up his torch with one

110

hand and flipped his middle finger back at the group with the other before disappearing into the darkness of the tunnel.

Dinesh looked over at the Captain who also shrugged in response.

"So we're kinda screwed?" Rodriguez asked. "That's what you're trying to tell us?"

"Yes," Dinesh answered. "I mean, no?" It came out more as a question than a statement, which did nothing for Rodriguez's peace of mind.

"Fuck," Rodriguez muttered under his breath. He turned and headed after Lieutenant Dawson.

12

"Why am I not surprised at this?" Rodriguez asked.

"At what?" the Captain asked. "That it's so dark you can't even find your own dick?"

"That's no surprise," Rodriguez said. "I'm used to having...*shit*, there's no one here to rank on."

"Bummer for you," the Captain said.

"This is not the same tunnel," Dinesh said.

"Yeah," Rodriguez said. "That's what I was going to say."

"It's too wet, and I don't remember as many turns."

"Well we haven't run into Norton yet, so it's got to go somewhere," the Captain said. "Does anyone's flashlight work?"

"Sorry," Dinesh said. "I have none."

"Nope," Rodriguez said. "Mine is dead too. I forgot to bring batteries this deployment."

"Used them all in your vibrator, did you?" the Captain asked.

"Real nice. Anyone have matches?"

"Even if I had them, they'd be wet," Dinesh said.

"At least nothing's chasing us, right?" Rodriguez asked. "Well, at least I don't think so. I mean, it *is* pretty dark. Are we all together?" When no one answered him he let out a nervous laugh. "You guys are still here, right?"

"Still here, numbnuts," the Captain said. "Do you need me to hold your hand?"

"Gee, would you Cap?" Rodriguez asked. "That'd be great."

"Since when do you get to call me Cap?"

"Well, I figure if something's going to eat us we might as well be buds."

"Not a chance, ass head. Now shut your trap before I shove my cock in it."

"Roger that," Rodriguez said. He reached out to touch the wall but ended up punching Dinesh instead.

"*Ouch.*"

"Sorry," Rodriguez said.

"I'd love it if one of you could tell me where the fuck we

are," the Captain said from further ahead. "If you're finished playing happy slappers, that is."

Rodriguez stepped closer to the Captain's voice and reached his arms out so he didn't walk into him. He touched something warm and wet dripping from the rough cut walls.

"Uh, Cap?"

"Didn't I tell you not to call me that?"

"Not exactly," Rodriguez said. "Where are you?"

"If I was deep in your ass, you'd know," he said from what sounded like very far away.

Rodriguez felt along the walls and tried to trace his way out. It felt like he was moving in circles. "Dinesh?" he asked.

"Yes?" Dinesh answered from close enough to make him jump.

"Shit, man," Rodriguez said. "Don't scare me like that?"

"Like what?" Dinesh's voice was no longer close.

Rodriguez stopped moving. "Where are *you*?"

"If I was deep in your ass, you'd know," Dinesh said. He, too, sounded like he was much farther ahead.

"What? Dinesh?" Rodriguez asked. *Not again.* "Cap? Anyone?" The only response was his own increasing heartbeat. *Fuck.* The walls dripped warm thick fluid and the floors were slick with moisture, so much so that even his boots slipped on the syrupy rock. "Okay, this isn't funny anymore."

"Who ever said it was?" a voice whispered in his ear.

"Cartwright?" Rodriguez asked right before something hit him in the back of the head. He fell forward, crashing into the wall and sprawling out on the wet floor. He flipped over and kicked his legs out but the only thing he hit was the other wall.

"Hey, douchebag," the Captain called from farther down the passage. "You coming or not?"

"Fuck this shit," Rodriguez said as he jumped to his feet. He threw his arms out and moved along the wall as fast as he could. "Where you at, Cap?" he called.

"Call me that again and I'll shit on your face, rub your face in my shitty ass, and then leave you in this stinking maze."

The Captain's voice wasn't very close, but it was enough to get a direction, enough for Rodriguez to move towards the others. He picked up the pace, his arms flailing in front of him to find the twists and turns. His feet splashed in the pooling water and twice he nearly fell, each time because he turned his head to look behind. There was no need; he couldn't see anything, but he felt better by *not* seeing anything behind him.

"I hear you, *Captain*," he said. "You don't have to tell me twice."

"Don't bank on it." The Captain's voice was close now, and up ahead Rodriguez could see a glimmer of light. The floor became gravelly and the groundwater thinned out. He sped up so he was nearly running by the time the Captain's hand jammed into his shoulder. It nearly knocked him back on his ass.

"Whoa there, Chauncey," he said. "Might want to slow down before you jizz all over yourself."

"Sorry Cap. *Tain*," Rodriguez said, "Cap*tain* is what I said."

"Uh-huh, right." The Captain grabbed Rodriguez's shoulder and shoved him forward. "Go on," he said, "you've got the point."

"What? Isn't that an Army thing?"

"Are you going all Nancy on me?"

"Where's Dinesh?" Rodriguez asked.

"I'm here," Dinesh said. "At the exit. Well, *an* exit. Or an entrance, I'm not sure which."

Rodriguez squinted towards the shimmer of light and saw a slight form waving back and forth. "I see you," he said.

"A little less seeing and a little more walking, please," The Captain said as he shoved him again.

Rodriguez stepped toward the dancing sliver of light. As he got closer, things started to come into view. Dark glistening walls of rough cut rock towered high above. He could barely see a ceiling. "Is it just me or is this a different cave?" he asked.

"Different from what?" the Captain asked.

"It *is* different," Dinesh said. He was around the corner inspecting the dripping walls. His once khaki uniform looked to be soaked with oil.

"You're both crazy," the Captain said. "This is the only way in or out."

"Are you sure?" Rodriguez asked. He reached out and

touched the wall. His hand came back dripping with a warm red substance. He quickly wiped his hand on his pants; it didn't wipe off, it smeared.

"Did you see another gaping hole in the rock somewhere?" the Captain asked. "I admit, I might have missed it."

"We *were* in the dark for a while back there," Dinesh said.

"Thank you," Rodriguez said.

"You two ass hats can suck each other off later," the Captain said. "Right now I've got a hankering for some fresh air. Which one of you disgusting bastards shit your pants?"

"Not me," Rodriguez said.

Dinesh made a sound that could have been a laugh or a dismissal.

Rodriguez stepped closer and got a good whiff of what the Captain was talking about. "Oh man," he said as he waved his hand in front of his face. "That's ripe. Dinesh?"

"Oh please," Dinesh said. He had backed up slightly from the entrance and Rodriguez walked over to him.

"What *is* that?" Rodriguez asked.

"I don't know, man, but it's grossing me out," Lieutenant Norton said from the entrance to the cavern. Rodriguez could hardly even see him.

"Where the hell have you been?" the Captain asked.

"I've been here waiting for you jack holes," the Lieutenant said. "I wasn't going out there by myself."

"Scared, huh?" Rodriguez asked.

"Fuck you, shitheel" Norton said. His voice dropped to barely a whisper. "But there *is* someone out there."

"Who?" Rodriguez asked.

"How the fuck should I know? I can't see through rock." He rapped his knuckles on the wall. They came away wet, but he hardly seemed to notice. "Can you see through rock?"

"Well you're the one by the entrance," Rodriguez said.

"Oh fuck this," the Captain said. "Norton, quit hiding like a cock head and go see who's out there. Rodriguez, stick to his ass. Dinesh, you hang with me."

"Fuck you," Norton said, "I don't work for you anymore."

"Oh, is that right?" the Captain asked. "Rodriguez?"

"Sir?"

"Remind me to kick Norton's ass after this."

"Yes Sir."

"Hello? I'm standing right here," Lieutenant Norton said.

"I know, but you should be moving," the Captain said.

"Whatever." The Lieutenant stood, straightened his shirt, and stepped out of the mouth of the cavern.

As soon as he disappeared from view, Rodriguez stepped closer and tried to peek around the corner.

"Don't be such a pussy," the Captain said. "Get your ass out there and hold Norton's hand, would you? He gets lonely."

"I can't see him," Rodriguez said. He couldn't. All he could see were trees, a landscape of brown and green blocking everything else from view.

"No shit," the Captain said. "That's why you need to get out there."

"Maybe we should wait and see--" Dinesh began.

"Not a chance," the Captain said. "I'm not hanging around this stink fest any longer than I have to."

"But the smell is coming from out there," Dinesh said with a nod towards the trees.

"Then we should move past it," the Captain said. He gave Rodriguez another shove and added, "Move a little faster and there may be a medal in it for you."

"A medal?" Rodriguez asked. "Are you fucking kidding me?" He shook his head and stepped out of the cave. He looked around but saw no trace of Lieutenant Norton. The wall of trees crowded the clearing so he couldn't even see the sky above.

"Lieutenant?" he whispered. Rodriguez took one more step away from the cave and everything changed. The trees faded away only to be replaced by more rock walls, this time illuminated just enough for him to see the chunks of flesh and splattered blood dripping from the walls.

Lieutenant Norton was there, hanging upside down from a knot of rope tied around his ankle. "Rodriguez," he whispered, "cut me the fuck down."

"What happened?"

"Don't ask stupid questions," the Lieutenant said. "Where's

your knife?"

"Hang on." Rodriguez reached back and pulled a knife from his belt while his eyes scanned the cave.

"Hurry up, you prick."

"Fuck you," Rodriguez said as he brought his knife up and sliced into the rope. It was thick, not like any rope he'd ever seen. His knife was sharp, but he could barely scratch the surface. He turned the blade around and used the serrated edge. The teeth bit into the rope and managed to slice in about an eighth of an inch. Something dripped from where he cut, a watery, foul smelling liquid that seeped out and ran down Lieutenant Norton's leg. Rodriguez stepped back as the Lieutenant gagged.

"What the *fuck*?" he asked. "Did you shit your pants?"

"It's not me," Rodriguez said. The ceiling above them shook and the Lieutenant began to swing back and forth. The rope that held his leg started retreating towards the ceiling, carrying the Lieutenant with it.

"Hey man, cut the rope," Lieutenant Norton screamed as he moved closer to the high ceiling and further away from Rodriguez's reach. "Cut the rope, cut the rope, cut the *rope*!"

Rodriguez stepped forward and hacked away at the rope, but all he managed to do was let out more of the stinking liquid. "I don't think it's a rope," he said. Within seconds it was out of reach, too high for Rodriguez to cut anything but the Lieutenant.

Rodriguez grabbed him by his legs and tried to hold on. "Hey," he called over his shoulder. "Hey guys. Captain? Dinesh? Need some help in here, quick!"

"Pull," Dinesh said. He was already grabbing at Lieutenant Norton's outstretched arms before Rodriguez even knew he was there.

"What the hell did you guys do in here?" the Captain asked from behind them. "It smells like butt sex gone wrong."

"Someone get this thing off me," Lieutenant Norton yelled. He was now almost six feet off the floor and Rodriguez had to stand on his tiptoes to keep hanging on.

"Oh, for fuck's sake," the Captain said. "Give me that knife." He grabbed the blade from Rodriguez's hand and jammed his foot into Dinesh's hip. Before Rodriguez knew what was happening, the Captain climbed above them, one muddy boot on each of their shoulders. He began sawing away at the rope as it pulled the Lieutenant towards the ceiling.

"Hurry up," the Lieutenant begged. "It burns."

"Shut up," the Captain said, "I know." He had made it about halfway through, and the liquid flowed freely from the cut. It thickened and took on a more toxic smell.

Rodriguez felt some splash on his shoulder. As it started to burn, he looked up at the Lieutenant's legs and the Captain's hands. They were coated with the stuff, and Rodriguez could see the skin around the Captain's fingers start to bubble. As he watched, he felt his toes leave the ground. They were all hanging now, the group clinging together and spinning in a circle.

"Hang on," the Captain yelled.

"Hang on to what--" Rodriguez began, but before he could finish they had all crashed to the ground amidst a puddle of reeking filth. Above them, the rope swung wildly, slithering toward the ceiling as it sprayed its burning rain all over the cave. Everything hurt. Everything burned.

"Get him up," the Captain said.

"What?" Rodriguez asked.

"He's not moving," Dinesh added.

"He's not?" Rodriguez pulled at Lieutenant Norton's arm and watched his head flop to the side at an impossible angle. Rodriguez let go and stepped back. *"Oh Shit."*

"Now's not the time to get squeamish on me, Rodriguez." The Captain grabbed the Lieutenant by both feet and pulled so that his head straightened out. "Unless you want to be next, I'd suggest you grab his shoulders."

"Yes Sir."

"Dinesh, can you hold his head?" the Captain asked.

"Of course." Dinesh held each side of Lieutenant Norton's face as Rodriguez slid his arms under his armpits.

"On three," Rodriguez said.

"Fucking three," the Captain said with a tug on the Lieutenant's feet. "Let's get out of here, this shit burns."

Rodriguez pulled the Lieutenant as Dinesh supported his

lolling head. He glanced up at the ceiling but saw no trace of the rope.

"Where to?" Dinesh asked.

"Not back that way," the Captain said with a nod towards the passage they had come through. He was already walking towards the opposite end, where the soft glow of light seemed to be strongest. "I figure this way will either be really good or really bad, and there's only one way to find out."

"It may be a way out," Dinesh said.

"I'm not sure if that's a good thing," Rodriguez said. He was looking over his shoulder and nearly slipped on the wet floor.

"You want to hang in here forever, be my guest," the Captain said. "I'm all for getting the hell out of here."

"We don't know what's out there," Rodriguez said. "There might not even *be* a way out of here."

"Yes, but we know what's in here," Dinesh said with a glance towards the ceiling.

They walked in silence for a while, the Captain charging ahead through the twists and turns of an ever-brightening path.

Dinesh stared ahead as he walked, his hands somehow keeping Dawson's head perfectly still even as they navigated the slick and uneven tunnel.

Rodriguez kept glancing above. He couldn't see anything move, but was more concerned with what he didn't see.

"Hang on," the Captain said. He stopped, dropped Dawson's legs, and spun side to side to crack his back. Without a word, he stepped forward and walked around a corner in the tunnel.

Rodriguez and Dinesh stood in silence, both staring at the spot ahead where the Captain had disappeared. Half of Rodriguez waited for the Captain to return. The other half waited for him to start screaming. He wouldn't have placed a bet either way.

When the Captain came back around the bend, Rodriguez let out the breath he didn't even realize he'd been holding. The shadows from the tunnel made his smile look like it had split his face in two, the bottom half ready to fall off if handled without care.

"Let's go," he said as he grabbed Lieutenant Norton's feet.

"This is a way out."

It didn't make Rodriguez feel any better.

Tall trees, green grass, and blue skies; everything looked exactly the way Rodriguez should have expected it. However, as he stared into the woods, a sinking feeling grew that he just couldn't explain.

The Captain and Dinesh were on the ground checking out Lieutenant Norton. Neither of them really looked like they knew what they were doing, but they were both pointing and saying smart-sounding things.

I guess that's better than doing nothing, Rodriguez thought. *But not much.* He was less concerned with checking on the body. Not because the Lieutenant was an asshole, which he was, but because Rodriguez didn't trust the peaceful-looking woods. He also didn't much care for their situation.

From what he remembered, the submarine was in no position to be operational. There also wasn't exactly a yacht club anywhere nearby. Lieutenant Norton was either dead or on his way, and neither option was helping them get the hell out of there. They also had no clue where the rest of the crew could be, assuming there even *was* a rest of crew. He looked over at the Lieutenant and sighed.

"How is he?" he asked. *Like I don't already know.* The Lieutenant was still a person, a dude, a part of the crew. He didn't want to seem like a dick, and he didn't wish him any harm.

"Not so good, I think," Dinesh said. "I think his neck is broke."

"Yeah," the Captain added. "Definitely broke." He pushed the Lieutenant's neck and it flopped to the side with no resistance.

"So...we should go then?" Rodriguez asked. He watched a bird fly overhead until it passed from view. It didn't look like any bird he had ever seen. It didn't even appear to have feathers. It was more leathery, like a bat. "Yeah, we should go." He turned towards the others and saw then staring at him with wide eyes and open mouths. "What?"

"Really?" the Captain asked.

"Really what? Do you want to drag him around this place?" Rodriguez asked. "I know I don't."

"That's bullshit and you know it." The Captain stood and fixed his hands on his hips. "We're not leaving anyone behind."

"Spare me the war hero crap. This isn't like in the movies."

"In the movies, doesn't the punk kid get his ass kicked by the crusty old man?"

"Let's focus on the old part of that, yeah?" Rodriguez asked. "What are you, like eighty?"

"Can you two be quiet for a moment?" Dinesh asked.

"*What?*" The Captain and Rodriguez simultaneously turned to face Dinesh, each sharing an equally unpleasant scowl.

"Someone's coming."

They all stopped speaking. Rodriguez looked around at the woods and back at the rocky entrance to the cave but couldn't hear anything, couldn't see anything.

The Captain crouched down and looked through the trees while Dinesh held his head cocked to the side as if it would make listening easier.

"What if it's not some*one*," Rodriguez asked, his voice barely a whisper. "What if it's a some*thing*."

"Ssh!" The Captain held his hand out towards Rodriguez as something close by stomped through what sounded like a pile of leaves and branches.

"Yeah, fuck this," Rodriguez said. He stood and turned to head back into the cave when Poole burst out from between the trees, seemingly out of breath.

"Shit," he breathed, "Fucking shit on toast. I thought I was the only one that made it out of there."

"Poole?" The Captain stood up and stepped back.

Rodriguez turned back and stared at Poole. "You're dead," he said.

"What?" Poole asked. "Who's dead?"

"You," Rodriguez repeated. "You died. I heard about it."

"Uh, are you sure?" Poole asked.

"Don't fuck with me," Rodriguez said.

"Now wait a minute," the Captain said. "Maybe it was someone else--"

"Disemboweled in an Engine Room bilge?" Rodriguez interrupted. "Not likely. I know some crazy shit went down back there, but this happened way before Cartwright's band of nukes went batshit insane."

Poole looked down at his stomach and poked a finger at his shirt. "Feels pretty solid to me," he said.

"This is bullshit," Rodriguez said.

"Am I dead too?" Lieutenant Jarvis asked as he strode out from between two trees. "I've always wondered what that felt like."

"Where the fuck were you?" the Captain asked.

"Just hanging out, waiting for someone to come along so I didn't feel so lonely." He looked down at Lieutenant Norton. "What's up with the Navigator?"

"His neck is broken," the Captain said.

"What?" Lieutenant Jarvis asked. "No it's not." He stepped over to Lieutenant Norton and reached down to shake his shoulder. "Get up, man."

"Don't do that," Dinesh said, his voice rising with a hint of panic. He reached out to grab the sides of Lieutenant Norton's head but it was too late.

Lieutenant Jarvis grabbed the Navigator with both hands. He repeated, "Wake up, wake up, wake up," as he shook him back and forth.

Lieutenant Norton's head flopped to one side and then to the other before his eyes popped open. He stared as everyone gathered around. "What the fuck are you pricks doing?" he asked.

The Captain and Dinesh each jumped in opposite directions, both nearly falling backwards.

Lieutenant Jarvis reached down and grabbed the Navigator's hand to help him sit up. "Welcome back buddy," he said with a face-splitting smile. "Thought I was gonna have to feed you to the bears."

"What does that even mean?" Lieutenant Norton asked.

"There aren't any fucking bears around here."

"Wait, there are bears?" Poole asked. His eyes grew large as he craned his neck from side to side, scanning the trees.

"What are you looking for, the wily and elusive oceanic grizzly bear?" Lieutenant Norton asked.

"Are...are there really bears out here?"

"No, you idiot," Rodriguez yelled. "There's no fucking bears out here."

"I'm not really sure what *here* is," Dinesh said.

"Do you know more than you're telling us?" the Captain asked.

"No."

"No, you don't know," Rodriguez asked, "or no, you're not telling us?"

"No," Dinesh repeated. "I don't know. I only know that we should be leaving as soon as we can."

"Well," Lieutenant Norton said as he jumped to his feet. "Best listen to the man and head out. I mean, he *is* the expert, right?"

"You're feeling much better," the Captain said, one eye narrowing as he stared at the Navigator.

"I'm no expert," Dinesh said.

"Well let's go then," Poole said. "Time's wasting."

"Yeah, does it get dark out here?" Lieutenant Jarvis asked. "I mean, do they turn out the lights?"

"Who's *they?*" Rodriguez asked.

"Hopefully not bears," a voice muttered from a nearby shrub.

Rodriguez stepped over and moved a few branches to the side.

Harrison was hiding inside the shrub, his face a mess of scratches and blood. He was clinging to the trunk and looking up at Rodriguez with red-rimmed eyes. "Are you real?" he asked.

"Dude, Harrison, where the hell have you been?" Rodriguez asked.

"I took off when the water ate Lieutenant Dawson," he said. I've been hiding here ever since." He looked around the woods and leaned forward to whisper. "I've seen things moving around out here," he said. "Things that kind of creep me out."

"Well get your ass out here," Rodriguez said as he reached in to grab Harrison's arm. "We're leaving." He pulled Harrison to his feet while everyone else stared in silence.

"Am I the only person here who doesn't have a clue what the fuck is going on?" the Captain yelled. Everyone turned to stare at him. "I'm kind of the boss here, you know? The boss? Fucking guy in charge?" He looked from one person to the next. "That ringing any bells?"

"What the fuck are you talking about?" Lieutenant Jarvis asked. "Out here you're in charge of Jack and shit."

"Yeah," Lieutenant Norton added, "that's what *I* said."

The Captain's face slowly reddened. The muscles on his neck stood out against his collar and his veins pulsed in his temples. He looked ready to explode. "Why you little prick," he said in a voice much calmer than he looked. "Exactly what is stopping me from stomping the shit out of you right here and now?"

Lieutenant Norton only laughed. "Yeah," he said with a spin of the heel and a step away from the group. "Good luck with that."

Poole and Lieutenant Jarvis joined in laughing, and the three of them began walking away. They headed in the direction of the submarine.

Harrison stared at the Captain but took a tentative step towards the departing group.

"Well, come on Indian dude," Lieutenant Norton said once he was out of sight, hidden beyond the wall of foliage.

"Yeah, you said we should leave," Poole said.

"So come on," Lieutenant Jarvis added. The sound of their heels crunching on downed leaves and branches carried on well past the point when they could no longer be seen.

Rodriguez looked over at the Captain and took a step back.

The Captain still looked furious, and Rodriguez didn't want to be the one to feel the brunt of his misdirected anger.

"Shouldn't we follow them?" Harrison asked. He was taking little side steps around the Captain as he headed towards the path.

Dinesh stayed close to the Captain, either oblivious to the impending fit of rage or choosing to ignore it.

"Dinesh?" Rodriguez asked. "Thoughts?"

"I think I'm all out of them," he said.

"Well standing here isn't doing us any good," Rodriguez said.

"Yeah, what he said." Harrison had reached the point where the group had disappeared into the woods. When both Rodriguez and Dinesh looked over at him, he stopped walking and glanced down at the ground. He opened his mouth but slammed it shut before saying a word. He turned on his heel, slipped on the leaves, and fell to the ground. He scrambled to his feet and without another look took off after the others.

"Is he always like that?" Dinesh asked.

"Sadly, yes," Rodriguez said. "He's not going to be much good to anyone out here."

"Maybe we *should* go," Dinesh said.

"Cap?" Rodriguez asked, but as soon as he looked over he realized he'd made a mistake.

The Captain's body started shaking as he glared at Rodriguez. "You," he hissed. His finger shot out and pointed at Rodriguez. He shook so much Rodriguez thought he could feel the ground moving under their feet. It took a moment for him to realize that it actually was.

"I think it's time to go," Dinesh said. He was already moving towards the woods as the rocky cavern behind them began to crumble.

Chunks of rock flew in all directions as Rodriguez backed away. "Captain, come on," he said.

"You," the Captain repeated. He made no move; he didn't even seem to notice what was happening around him.

Rodriguez glanced over his shoulder and just caught a glimpse of Dinesh as he disappeared into the woods. Somewhere deep inside the cavern, a sound like a deep growl grew out of the crumbling rock.

"Sorry, Cap," Rodriguez whispered. He turned and followed Dinesh into the woods as chunks of stone pelted the ground at his feet. They continued to fall around him as he burst through the cover of trees and ran straight into the back of Dinesh. Both of them crashed to the ground in a tumble of arms and legs.

Harrison helped them to their feet as Rodriguez looked around the clearing.

In the distance, he could see the silhouette of the Alexandria moored at a pier. Aside from the bizarre surroundings, the ship looked perfectly normal. It floated on a sea of inky blackness that rolled like thick oil. The tide moved in and out towards a distant cavern cut into the rocky wall, far beyond where the boat was moored.

The wall stretched in both directions just as Rodriguez remembered it, although a jagged rocky ceiling had replaced the previous simulated sunny sky. He could not tell where the light was coming from except that it was all around them, making everything stand out in perfect clarity. There was a group assembled at the pier, like a welcoming party that had been anticipating their return.

It was an unexpected collection: Lieutenants Dawson, Norton and Jarvis were there. Nearby stood Cairne, Adams, Tito, and Porter. Poole, Four Names, and Butterball stood off to one side near Edwards, Parker, and Vasquez. Ensign Klein was on his knees, along with Brett and Bone. Their hands were tied behind their backs, and they were looking up at Rodriguez's group with a mixture of fear and hope.

Lieutenant Dawson stepped forward and nodded at them with a huge smile. "Hiya, folks," he said. "Been a while."

"Not long enough," Rodriguez said. "How'd your swim go?"

"Oh, you know," the Lieutenant said with a laugh. "A doggie-paddle here, a side-stroke there. It's like riding a bike, only there's no bike. Because it's in the water. And that would be weird. Unless of course it was a water bike. Do they make them?"

"I don't think so," Lieutenant Dawson said. I think that'd be weird."

"Yeah, too fucking weird."

"I bet." Rodriguez shifted his feet and looked over at Dinesh.

Dinesh stood without speaking, his eyes locked on a point behind Rodriguez.

"Dinesh?" Rodriguez saw the look in Dinesh's eyes and didn't want to turn around. Within seconds, he didn't have to; the voice said it all.

"Hello, shit heel," Cartwright said in his ear. "Welcome back."

13

Dinesh stared at Brett, unsure what to say or if he should speak at all. He felt like he should do *some*thing, but instinct told him to keep his mouth shut.

Brett was hanging upside down from a heavy nylon net that had been draped over the side of the submarine. His hands were tied behind his back and his head was only about two feet from the waterline. His deeply tanned skin had turned nearly purple around his face from all his effort struggling to get free. Now he barely moved.

To Dinesh, he looked like all the fight had drained out of him. When Cartwright had ordered them tied up, Dinesh didn't fight. Maybe it was because there were so many of them; maybe it was because of what Cartwright had become. Dinesh had always considered himself more of a thinker. Even so, he was having a hard time thinking of how the hell to get out of there.

Since Dinesh didn't fight, they at least left him vertical. He was tied with his back to the flag staff, bound in something that felt like piano wire digging into his wrists and ankles. The waves of the vile sea rocked so hard he felt like he was going to tumble forward. The only thing keeping him upright was the same painful wire that kept him a prisoner.

Cartwright stood on the bridge, far enough away that Dinesh couldn't hear what he was saying but close enough that he could clearly be seen. He stood up there with Poole and Lieutenant Dawson. Rodriguez hung suspended from one of the masts. It looked like he was tied the same as Dinesh. All the others had either gone below or had headed out into the woods for reasons that Dinesh couldn't guess.

The waves splashed against the hull as the boat rocked back and forth. Dinesh closed his eyes and tried to think. He clutched his hands and flexed his legs, bouncing from side to side as much as he could move. He tried to picture the Lahore, before the attack, before the fire, before the death. He felt the sea rock him back and forth but couldn't keep the screaming out of his head; that and the smell of smoke. They were constant. He shook his head and opened his eyes.

"Brett," he whispered, careful not to let his voice carry as far as the bridge. No answer. "*Brett.*" There was only the slightest twitch of his head, but it was enough to keep Dinesh going. "Can you move at all?"

Brett glanced over at Dinesh but remained silent.

"I can't move my hands," Dinesh said. "They're tied with some kind of wire." He glanced up at Cartwright; he appeared to be deep in conversation with Poole.

Good, stay that way. Dinesh looked back at Brett. "Can you move your hands?"

Brett looked back towards the water and closed his eyes.

There's no help coming from him.

A strong wave rolled the ship and he tipped forward enough to see how close Brett had gotten to the water. He looked to be less than a foot away. Dinesh stared at the waterline and saw that with each wave it was slowly creeping closer to Brett.

Past the rudder, the water splashed in the air as something below the surface moved around the back of the boat. A wave followed, sending thick black water splashing at Dinesh's feet.

"Did you see that?" he asked as the water surrounding them began to churn. "Brett?"

"No." Brett's eyes popped open and he looked up at Dinesh. "You didn't?"

"I can't move them."

Dinesh looked at Brett's hands as he tilted slightly to one side. They were clearly bound with the same kind of wire that held Dinesh.

"I can't get free," Brett said.

"We have to get out of here."

"Did you hear me?" Brett asked. "I can't move."

"Yes, I heard you," Dinesh said. "But if you lay there much longer you're going to find yourself swimming, and I don't think whatever's in there is friendly."

Brett looked at the water just as something broke the surface no more than twenty feet away.

Dinesh caught a glimpse of scales and a flash of red before it disappeared. "No, not friendly at all."

"What the fuck was that?" Brett asked. His eyes grew large and he somehow found the energy to struggle against his bonds with renewed vigor. "What the fuck was *that*?"

"Brett, quiet down," Dinesh said as he glanced up at the bridge.

Lieutenant Dawson was looking back towards them.

Rodriguez's head was swinging side to side as he tried to see what was happening below.

Brett was getting louder. He repeated a series of *oh fuck*s and *what was that*'s in a voice that barely sounded human.

On the bridge, Cartwright, Lieutenant Dawson, and Poole all disappeared from view.

Rodriguez began struggling to get free.

Dinesh looked all around the sail. Except for Rodriguez, he could not see anyone.

Brett continued to squirm in his net and had dropped any attempt at words in favor of incoherent screaming.

The thing under the waves moved in closer, churning the water around the submarine. Waves lapped the side of the submarine, noxious blackness flowing across Dinesh's feet as it rolled to the opposite side.

Dinesh twisted his hands but only managed to bring more pain. The wire bit deep into his wrists without giving even a little. He kicked at the deck but the flag staff was not going to budge. He tried twisting around backwards and slowly made his way to the other side. All he could see was the rocky walls in the distance. He looked up at Rodriguez.

Rodriguez had stopped struggling. He was staring down at the water, mouth open and eyes wide.

Behind Dinesh, Brett stopped screaming. The silence was somehow much worse than his screams.

The boat lurched so far to the side that Dinesh found himself face to face with the water. He was close enough to smell it; it reminded him of burning tires. It made his eyes and nose burn but thankfully he was soon flying backwards. The rocky ceiling above blurred past as his back slammed into the water.

His body twisted to the side and his mouth opened to scream. Instead, it filled up with the noxious sea. He had no chance to catch a breath as his lungs began to burn. Something around him was moving. He felt the current swirling around him like a whirlpool. The water pulled at him, and for the first time he was glad he was bound to the flagpole. At least until it broke.

Dinesh felt the sharp crack of metal as the heavy threads gave way. He struggled to be free, kicking and thrashing around blindly as he fought for the surface. He was still bound to the pole, and the weight of it pulled him down. He sank ever deeper into darkness, his mind racing as his lungs screamed for air.

He barely registered when the pole broke free. It slipped through his bindings and plummeted into the depths. He feebly kicked towards a surface he could no longer see, but he was losing strength. His brain began to shut down. Before long, all he could do was float.

So he floated.

Rodriguez felt like he was flying. In a way, he was. As the boat rolled over on its side he found himself hanging in midair by his bound wrists, the wire tearing through his flesh with ease. He looked down and saw the violent surface of the water for only a moment before the rolling submarine changed direction, sending him rocketing away from the sea.

His arms twisted around as his body swung to the opposite side of the mast. The ship finally stopped rolling and his body jerked around so hard he thought both his wrists were broken. They felt warm and sticky; he could feel blood rolling down his arm as he dangled once again above the inky black sea. He looked around for a sign of the thing that had gotten Brett, but thankfully it was nowhere to be seen.

He closed his eyes and tried to purge the image from his mind. *So huge...and the teeth*, he thought as his stomach turned, threatening to force up the little bit of bile that remained. *I'll never forget the teeth. They tore through Brett like he was a scrap of paper.*

The boat shuddered and he threw his eyes open, half expecting the thing to be back for more. It wasn't.

He looked around for Dinesh but the back of the boat was mostly under water. He couldn't even see the flag staff any more. *How are we still floating?* he wondered as the boat rolled once again. A wall of spray erupted around him as the ballast tanks flooded, purging the air and sinking the boat to where Rodriguez was almost touching the water. *I had to ask.*

As the submarine dropped lower in the water, Rodriguez saw it. A flash of red cut through the haze of water, coming in fast. Rodriguez was dangling off the mast like a worm on a hook, just begging to be snatched up in the thing's jaws. He'd seen the way it got Brett, and he didn't want any part of it. He pulled as hard as he could, pain racing through his arms as fresh blood poured from his wrists.

As it moved closer, Rodriguez felt himself beginning to lose control. He began kicking madly, trying to swing himself up and hook a leg around the mast. With his arms twisted behind him, he could not find the leverage to swing. He bounced around but he could not pull himself away from the water. Nothing worked, he was stuck.

The thing was nearly on him. It drew so close Rodriguez could smell it, a putrid combination of fish and what smelled like rotting meat. It broke the surface and came in like a shark, with just enough of its scaly flesh exposed that Rodriguez could see how big it really was.

I'm toast, he thought. He closed his eyes and relaxed. *I hope I taste like shit, you fucker.*

With a rumble of air, the boat shifted and he found himself under the water. Metal groaned all around him as the ship twisted, and soon he was flying through the air yet again. He opened his eyes just as the boat settled out in a somewhat upright position. In the water, a flash of red tail splashed under the waves and disappeared.

Rodriguez looked around. The boat was sitting so low he could not see the deck. Only the bridge remained above the water; even the rudder was completely submerged. *We're just high enough to save me from becoming lunch*, he thought. *That's good enough for me.* He leaned back to stretch his bruised limbs and nearly fell over.

The mast he had been tied to was mostly gone. Only a chunk of jagged metal remained, the break close enough for him to slip his hands free. Once he did that, the wire came off easily. It wasn't tied in any way, it was just wrapped around enough times that he couldn't pull free. The ends were twisted around each other but they quickly came undone.

Rodriguez looked around but saw no one on the shore. No one floated in the water, and aside from him the bridge was clear. He couldn't tell if the submarine was still moored to the small dock. There were lines tied to the pier but they hung limp in the water, the ends submerged and out of sight. He looked at the beach and thought, *I bet I could swim for it.*

That thought was almost immediately followed by, *Fuck that.* There was only one place to go, and although he would have wished for just about anywhere else, he moved over to the ladder and grabbed the rail. He listened at the hatch but only silence waited for him below decks. Silence and darkness.

When his boot landed on the first rung he paused, glancing back at the hostile water. Off in the distance, something that looked like a body broke the surface. *No thanks*, he thought. *I know what's out there, and I'm not messing with that.*

Rodriguez moved down the hatch, skipping the damaged ladder rungs and dropping most of the way to the bottom. As soon as he landed, he found himself in complete darkness.

Dinesh dreamed that he was in a vast ocean, peacefully floating without need for lungs or air. He could see clearly, strange shapes gathered around him, moving in unison as the investigated his intrusion into their world. He started to smile but lost all traces of humor as the darkness crept in from all around. He opened his mouth and felt like the darkness poured into his soul.

He woke to a burning sensation as he choked on a mix of air and vile water. He splashed at the surface and struggled to keep his head above water as his body shook with the convulsive coughing. He could feel himself spinning as the water swirled around him. He was floating on the water's surface; there was something in the water with him.

He cracked his eyes open and stared at the grey metal hull not more than five feet in front of him. He looked up towards the bow, knowing what would be there before he even had a chance for his eyes to adjust to the light. It read *INS LAHORE*.

A rope ladder hung down from the side railing, the end dipping into the water nearby. Dinesh stared at it and began treading water backwards. The ship looked like hell, but it sat straight in the water with no evidence of damage. It appeared solid, but somehow looked like it had been underwater for months.

Brown algae clung to the metal just about everywhere he looked. Not enough to cover the hull, but enough to make the ship appear dull and lifeless. When last he saw the ship, it was barely afloat. *This isn't the same ship,* he thought. *It can't be.* He turned around to look for the Alexandria. Although it was nowhere to be seen, something else was.

Dinesh saw the water moving, a wave crashing in the distance as something dove below the surface. It was large enough to change his mind. *I'm not messing with that thing,* he thought. *I'll take my chances on the Lahore.*

He swam for the rope ladder as fast as he could move. He could barely feel his legs but he didn't want to stay in the water any longer than he had to. With all he had left, he pushed forward and grabbed the ladder. With shaking arms, he pulled himself out of the water and climbed.

Half way up he heard the snap of metal. The ladder dropped about two feet and he clung to the one side of the rope ladder that somehow held. He looked at the water below. It spun in circles below his feet. Something dark passed beneath him and dove under the ship.

He climbed the rest of the way, taking care not to look down again. When he reached the top, there was a section of the metal railing that had broken from his weight. It had torn one end of the ladder, the frayed rope hanging far below. The other end was tied to a cleat. It was the only thing that kept him from falling. He took another glance below and pulled himself over the edge.

Dinesh stepped onto the deck as everything around him swirled as if under a breeze. The rust blew away like dust and the algae faded from the paint. Before long the ship looked as it had before they'd set sail: clear bow, immaculate paint, polished metal. It looked brand new, like it could have been sitting in dry dock waiting to be launched. Not a thing out of place, it was all shiny new and stowed for sea. There was only one thing as missing: the crew.

The ship was devoid of life, and for that Dinesh was grateful. He knew where he was and knew where the ship had been. *This is not the Lahore*, he reminded himself. *This is not the ship I know and love*. It was not even a ship; it was a floating abomination.

He stepped towards the bridge, staring up into the unblemished glass and the vast darkness beyond. As with the rest of the ship, it stood empty. All around him waited nothingness, a vast shell of metal that had not so long ago been his home. He had never felt uncomfortable on the deck of the ship. With many things, that had changed.

Below the bridge, a single watertight door stood open. All others were buttoned up tight. Hatches were closed, gear was stowed, the deck was clear. Only the one door stood out of place. It was the same door he had passed through when he fled the fire that had burned below.

Dinesh glanced back at the inky black sea and wondered if he may have been better off taking his chances in the water.

He turned back as the door slammed shut. Everything inside Dinesh made him want to turn and run, but instead he moved closer. As he moved closer, the door began vibrating on its hinges. He tried to stop walking but it was no use; something beyond the door was calling to him, and he was on his way.

As he reached the door, his hand automatically moved towards the hatch. He wanted to pull back, but his hand moved of its own will. He had no real control over himself. He could have been watching the whole thing from a distance.

His hand grasped the handle and turned. The door shook uncontrollably, the dissonance of metal on metal ringing through the superstructure. He ignored the sound, and as he pulled the hatch the vibration stopped. The pristine door creaked open on what sounded like rusted hinges.

Wait, clean doors don't creak. It was enough to break the hold the ship had on him. He blinked and shook his head as the flawless paint before him melted away, exposing the charred remains of the ship. The metal under his hand grew hot and he snatched it away. From below decks, he smelled smoke.

The door flew open, slamming into him and knocking him into a pile of bodies that was not there a moment ago. He scrambled away from the pile, his feet slipping on a mixture of dried blood and ash. He couldn't see through the darkness and smoke pouring from the hatch, but he could feel something in the distance moving towards him. Dinesh jumped to his feet and ran to the hatch, slamming it closed and reaching for the handle.

He threw the latch just as something crashed into the other side. It hit so hard it knocked Dinesh to the deck. He scrambled to his feet and leaped towards the door, reaching for the handle as it snapped open. He held on tight as the door shook, his body pressed against the frame, skin searing against the heated metal as he struggled to keep the hatch closed. The ship lurched to the side and he was lifted nearly off the deck.

All around the ship, water flew into the air, spraying across the deck and slamming Dinesh against the shaking bulkhead. He clung to the latch and squeezed his eyes and mouth shut as he was drenched in a barrage of liquid. His feet slid out from underneath him but the water kept him in place. From the hatch, something clawed at the other side as if trying to get out.

As quickly as it had begun, everything stopped. The ship settled out and floated on a deceivingly calm sea. The remaining water flowed over the side of the ship and Dinesh dropped to the deck in a heap of soggy flesh and pain. A fading squeal resonated from the other side of the hatch, but at least it stopped shaking.

Dinesh lay staring at the door, half waiting for something to come through and half knowing he wouldn't be able to do anything about it if it did. He tried to lift his head but it fell to the deck, limp.

He lay back and stared at the rock ceiling above him. *That's it*, he thought. *I'm done.* He closed his eyes and took a deep breath. *I don't care anymore. I'm going to take a rest. I need it.*

136

###

The Control Room looked like it had been on fire. Everything was coated in a thick layer of blackness; not a single piece of equipment was powered on. Rodriguez couldn't remember ever seeing it so dark.

He took a step forward and kicked something soft. *There's nothing soft in the Control Room*, he thought as he blocked the images that flooded his head. *Gross*. He reached around to the back of his belt and grabbed for his flashlight. He twisted it on but nothing happened. *Dead battery*, he remembered. *Fuck, I forgot about that*.

He stepped back and turned towards the Command Passageway. Since there was nothing but empty hallway below the bridge ladder, he had at least a bit of light shining down from above. It was still dark, but he made his way to the opposite end with ease. The door to the Sonar Room stood open. He stepped inside and squinted, waiting for his eyes to adjust to the darkness. It was even darker than the Control Room had been, so of course they never did.

Rodriguez took a deep breath and let it out. He needed to grab a flashlight before anything else, and he knew there was a huge triple D-cell Maglite in the locker above the laptop. *I can do this*, he thought. *I've worked this space for almost five years, I can find a damn flashlight*.

He slid behind the operator seats and ran his hand along the workbench until he touched the keyboard. He reached into the darkness above and found the locker. When he opened it, he was immediately struck with most of the locker's contents, including the flashlight he was just looking for.

"Mother *fuck*," he whispered as he rubbed his head. "That's gonna leave a mark." He felt along the floor, brushing aside the reams of paper and rolls of duct tape until he found the flashlight. He closed his eyes, crossed his fingers, and turned it on. Even with his eyes closed, the light hurt. He smiled and stood, turning the light towards the open door leading to the Control Room.

He cracked open his eyes and stopped. All along he'd thought he was alone in there. He was wrong.

###

Dinesh didn't want to get up, but something woke him. It was moving on the other side of the rusted door. He was sitting up, his back leaning against the hatch. He could feel the slight vibration of metal shifting as a wave rocked the beaten ship sideways. It resonated through his body and buzzed through his head, making everything hurt. Against his body's will, he stood.

He turned and placed his hands against the door. He felt a mild sensation, like electricity running up his arm and down to his feet. He placed his ear against the door. He could hear the muted sounds of movement, but nothing familiar. He kept silent, waiting to see who or what was there, but when he heard a voice mutter something too low to hear he felt a spark of hope.

He balled his hand into a fist and held it in front of the hatch, waiting. After a moment's hesitation and a stretch of silence from the other side, he gently knocked. The frame shifted and dropped to the deck, a plume of rust blowing in Dinesh's face. He stepped back, waving a hand in front of his face in a fit of coughing.

The door leaned forward, and Dinesh had just enough time to jump to the side as it crashed to the deck. He wiped at his eyes and squinted into the gloom but it was too dark to see. He could tell that something was moving, but he didn't know what. When the blinding light caught his eyes, he squeezed them shut and dropped to his knees. He brought his hands up to shield his face but let them fall to his sides; it hurt too much to hold them up.

Dinesh turned his head to the side and tried to hold his breath, expecting at any minute something would reach out and drag him into the demolished ship. He could feel his body shake but could do nothing to control it. The dust from the rusty door coated his nostrils and burned his throat; he felt it scratching beneath his eyelids as he tried to keep still.

When a hand clamped on his shoulder, he opened his mouth to scream. All that came out was a series of hacking coughs and a cloud of rust. He tried to drop back and scramble away but hands grabbed both his shoulders. The light went away. He wiped at his eyes tried to block his face.

"Dinesh?"

He knew the voice but it couldn't be real. He tried to open his eyes to see if Rodriguez was there. Bad idea; it felt like the inside of his eyelids had turned to sandpaper. They scraped across his cornea and blurred his vision until everything was covered in a pinkish haze. It was even worse when he slammed his eyes shut once again.

"I can't see," Dinesh said. "My eyes--"

"Relax, man," Rodriguez said. "There's an eyewash station at the back of the Control Room."

"I can't make it up there," Dinesh said. "I can't climb the ladder."

"What ladder?"

"The ladder to--" Dinesh began but stopped to ask a question of his own. "What Control Room?"

"The...one you're standing in?" Rodriguez said.

Dinesh tried to open his eyes again but the pain kept them clamped shut.

"What's going on, Dinesh. How did you even get down here?"

"I...don't know."

"I saw you go over the side," Rodriguez said. "You went in the water. I thought you were dead, what happened?"

"I...don't know." Dinesh leaned forward and dropped his hands to the deck. He felt the rough non-skid that coated the weather deck of the Lahore, just as he expected. He held his breath and listened to the oddly thick sound of wave slap so far below. He could still detect the smell of smoke and rust and the faint toxic scent of the water. The moisture of the sea air coated his skin. Even without sight, there was no denying it; he was still outside.

###

Dinesh crawled around the Control Room, sniffing the air

139

and feeling along the floor like he was looking for something.

Rodriguez stared at him for a moment but couldn't figure it out. He shined his flashlight around the Control Room, but except for the place being trashed everything was where it should be.

Whatever, he thought. *At this point, the day can't get much weirder.* He spotted the eyewash at the back of the room and reached for Dinesh.

"Can you stand?" Rodriguez asked. "I can take you to the eyewash."

"There is no eyewash," Dinesh said.

"I'm looking right at it. Let me help you."

"It can't be."

"Just trust me," Rodriguez said. He grabbed Dinesh by the arm and helped him to stand. "Just watch for the periscopes."

Rodriguez led Dinesh between the twin scopes to the back of the Control Room, all the while shining his light between the forward and rear doors. He saw nothing moving but didn't trust that it would stay that way.

Next to the eyewash station was the aft door. From the looks of it, there was really no door left to speak of. The hinges remained, but that was just about it. He glanced over towards the front doorway but it was also empty. It led to the equally empty Command Passageway beyond. As far as he could tell, they were alone.

When they reached the eyewash station, he stopped Dinesh. "Lean forward," he said.

"Where are we?" Dinesh asked.

"Eyewash station."

"I don't know what's happening," he said.

"Don't feel bad," Rodriguez said. "Neither do I."

14

Dinesh felt cool water flowing across his face. He had no idea what was happening, but he had never felt anything quite as comforting as clean water. He reached up and pried his eyelids open, holding back the screams that wanted desperately to escape as he washed away as much of the rust as he could stand. Everything looked like it was underwater, but soon he could see a glowing light beyond.

The water seemed to be coming from nowhere. It made no sense, but he went with it. It felt too good to complain. He splashed some on his face and rubbed away the slime from his earlier swim. He didn't exactly feel clean, but he felt better than he had in quite a while. More than anything, he really just wanted a shower.

He closed his eyes and wiped the water from his face before opening them back up and looking around. Everything looked fuzzy, but he could see clear enough to see Rodriguez standing next to him with the largest flashlight he'd ever seen in his life.

This isn't real, Dinesh thought. *It can't be*.

Although there was enough light to see, Rodriguez shined his light back and forth between the hatch he'd first come through and the ladder that hung over the side. It was the ladder Dinesh had used to climb out of the water. Rodriguez kept glancing down like there was something coming up, but Dinesh could see or hear no movement in the water below.

"What are you doing?" he asked.

"What?" Rodriguez jumped as if he'd been caught doing something wrong.

"What are you looking for?"

"I don't know," Rodriguez said. He leaned forward and shined the light over the side.

Dinesh watched as Rodriguez put his hand on the metal railing that had broken earlier. "Watch out," he said as he grabbed Rodriguez's arm.

"What?" Rodriguez leaned back and stopped in midair, supported by absolutely nothing as far as Dinesh could see. He looked at Dinesh like he was crazy, but Dinesh just shook his head.

"What's happening?" Dinesh asked.

"I have no idea," Rodriguez said, "but I keep hearing noises from below."

"From the water?"

"The water? What water?" Rodriguez asked. "I'm talking about the noises from middle level." He peered below and dropped his voice to barely a whisper. "I think it may be coming from the galley."

"I don't hear anything," Dinesh said. "Except for the waves, at least."

"*Shh*, listen." Rodriguez held his finger to his lips and tilted his head.

Dinesh did the same but couldn't hear anything. He was about to open his mouth when he finally heard something that didn't sound like wave slap. He closed his eyes and listened. If he held his breath and ignored the pounding of his heart, he could just make out the clink of metal on metal. It mixed with the familiar sound of water splashing against the bow of the ship, although even that sounded different.

"What is that?" he asked.

"I don't know," Rodriguez said, "but...do you hear water?"

"I hear more than that." Dinesh moved closer to the edge, his brain screaming to back away but his body unable to stop itself.

Rodriguez leaned back with his flashlight clutched in his hands. He aimed the light towards the open hatch but kept glancing over his shoulder towards the ladder.

There was another sound of metal from below. Something was definitely moving down there. Where it had once been calm, Dinesh could hear the water splashing all along the side of the ship.

"Do you see anything?" Rodriguez asked.

"No." Dinesh edged closer.

"Watch out, man," Rodriguez said.

"Quiet."

"Take this." Rodriguez held out his flashlight but Dinesh

only stared at it.

"It's bright enough. I can see." He leaned just far enough that he could see the water swirling below. *Although I'm not so sure I want to see*, he thought. He crawled to the edge and placed his hand on the top of the ladder.

He heard Rodriguez shift behind him. He was waving his flashlight around but not making a sound.

Dinesh took a deep breath and leaned closer to the edge. A massive hand slapped down on the deck not three inches in front of his face.

Dinesh opened his mouth and let out a low moan as all the air escaped his lungs. He rolled backwards, the nonskid biting into his flesh as he scurried away, whimpering like a wounded animal. Another hand came up and grasped the guardrail as the thing pulled itself up onto the deck.

Rodriguez wasn't moving. He had the flashlight clutched in his hands as the light danced around the room. He looked unable to focus on anything as his eyes darted back and forth.

Dinesh tried to say something, tell him to run, say *anything*, but he couldn't do it. He felt hot breath from behind him as the ship listed under the thing's weight. It reached out to touch Dinesh and he finally found his voice, but only just enough to scream.

Dinesh jumped to his feet and ran for the open hatch. It was open wide, the rusty door shattered across the deck, the corridor beyond shrouded in darkness. Without thinking, he ran through, continuing long past the point where he could even see. He screamed the entire way.

Rodriguez watched in horror as Dinesh ran screaming into the darkness of the Sonar Room. He heard something moving up the ladder but couldn't bring himself to look. He tried to convince his legs to move but they would not obey. He kept the flashlight as still as he could, but no matter how hard he squeezed he couldn't keep the beam of light steady.

He looked at the hinges that hung empty along the aft

Control Room door. *Even if the door was still there, I don't think it would do any good.* The frame had been burnt so badly a door probably wouldn't even close, much less lock. He flashed his light over to the Sonar door but saw no sign of Dinesh. He could no longer hear him screaming.

Behind him, he heard the chain at the top of the ladder jingle, as someone removed the hook that secured it across the hatch. He brought his light over and saw a hand grasp the doorway. Something was pulling itself up the ladder. From the sound of heavy breathing, it was with no small amount of effort. The grunting and breathing froze Rodriguez where he stood. *Maybe coming back down here was a bad idea.*

"Hey Rod," a voice whispered up from the darkness. "Welcome back."

Yup, Rodriguez thought as he finally convinced his legs to move. *A* very *bad idea.* He glanced at the Sonar door. *And fuck that. Dinesh never came back, I'm not going to follow.* He ran past Sonar without another glance and headed straight down the Command Passageway. Behind him, the Control Room echoed with laughter.

He slid to a stop below the forward hatch. It was open wide, a light but steady flow of water pouring in from topside. The water dripped down on the floor and seeped through the cracks down to middle level. *I hope the power's out down there*, he thought. *On top of all this, we don't need a fire.*

He looked up and saw the weird rock ceiling high above, but the ladder to climb through the hatch was missing. He tried to pull himself up but couldn't grab hold of anything. His hands caught but slipped off the wet hatch ring. He landed on his back, his head cracking down on the metal deck. His flashlight rolled into the darkness, the beam of light extinguished.

"*Ow*." Rodriguez shook his head to clear the impending fog of dizziness before pulling himself to his feet. He felt the back of his head and his hand came away wet. *Water or blood?* he wondered. *Too dark to tell.* The passageway around him spun; he leaned back against the bulkhead to keep himself from falling. He scanned the floor for his flashlight but could not find it anywhere. *Shit.*

144

He looked back towards the Control Room and saw Cartwright standing between the periscopes, his arms spread out to the sides past the point that Rodriguez could see. He wore a ridiculous grin that stretched beyond what was humanly possible. He looked like a twisted and evil version of a sick child's puppet.

"Where you heading, Hot Rod?" Cartwright asked. "The only thing that way is *down*."

"I'll take my chances," Rodriguez said. He turned and jumped down the stairway, his hands gripping the dual handrails for support. Before he was halfway down he saw that the wall at the bottom of the stairs had been removed. It was the only thing separating the foot of the stairs and a hatch that led straight down to the lower level. It was too late to stop, he was going down.

"Told you," Cartwright said from the Command Passageway.

Rodriguez tried to slow himself but the railing was too wet. He couldn't get a grip. He continued to slide toward the hatch, but it was coming so fast. He stuck out his legs and tried to stop. His boot got caught between one of the steps and twisted back. He heard his ankle crack before he felt the pain. His leg stopped, but his body didn't. He flew face first towards the hatch.

Above, Cartwright laughed even harder.

Rodriguez threw his arms out just in time for them to slam into the metal hatch. His head crashed into his arms and bounced back so hard he felt like his neck was made of rubber. His leg felt like it was broken just about everywhere, but he managed to pull it out from where his foot had gotten stuck. His head spun and he felt like he might throw up, pass out, or both. With Cartwright's howling laughter just above, all he really wanted to do was scream.

Instead, he grabbed at the ladder and pulled himself towards the very hatch he almost fell through. He could pull his busted leg along, but was pretty sure he wasn't going to be able to stand much less climb down a ladder. He glanced down the middle level passageway. The lights burning on the mess decks looked so far away, but there was also an escape hatch just beyond.

That way also leads to nuke land, he thought. *Cartwright comes from nuke land. Bad things come from buke land.*

Rodriguez looked down the hatch to lower level but it was too dark to see. There were no lights down there at all.

"Looking for this?" Cartwright asked.

Rodriguez looked up as the beam of light from his flashlight caught him in the eyes. *Fucking shit.*

Cartwright's howling rang even louder from the upper level. It soon mixed with laughter from the mess decks. Down the middle level passageway, a horde of something moved around the corner, their shadows dancing along the far wall.

"Fuck this." Rodriguez pulled himself to the hatch and slid his bad leg over the edge.

"What--oh that's *good*," Cartwright said with another laugh.

"Yeah? Well fuck you too," Rodriguez said. He grabbed the ladder and let his body fall through the hatch. He tried to grab the hatch ring but underestimated how slippery everything was. He slid right through and down into the lower level. He was unable to grab anything as he dropped to the deck below.

Rodriguez fell into a pile of random shit that he could barely see. Some of it was soft; it felt like the mattresses piled up from the torpedo room bunks. Some of it was not so soft. His legs bent to the sides as each moved in opposite directions.

He screamed out, his voice echoing in the darkness. He reached down and grabbed his balls, now throbbing from both his impromptu split and whatever it was they'd landed on. He sat that way, barely able to move, waiting for the wave of nausea to pass and the haze of sparkling blackness to fade from his vision.

There were noises coming from above, drawing closer, but at that point he didn't care what they were. It could have been Cartwright and company, or it could have been something else entirely. He didn't want to move; at that moment he didn't even want to exist.

Once he knew he wasn't going to black out, he leaned to the side to start his body moving again. His shoulder scraped against something cold and wet, something with jagged edges that felt like they could cut right through him. He pulled his arm back and leaned to the other side. With a wave of vertigo he leaned too far, too late to realize there was nothing there.

Rodriguez fell to the deck into a puddle of fuel oil. It was slick and wet and made his skin burn. As his body slid sideways he smacked his head against a locker, sending his body spinning around in the oil, powerless to stop moving. His leg howled in pain as it twisted around uncontrollably. He opened his mouth to scream but shut his mouth when he heard someone moving in the small office space nearby.

"Hey, Rod," someone said. "Where you been?" The voice was somewhat recognizable but garbled to the point where it no longer sounded human.

Rodriguez struggled to pick himself up. He thought he could hear something moving in the nearby Torpedo Room but tried to ignore it. The Torpedo Room could wait; the voice behind him was much closer.

He grabbed for the ladder and his hand landed on an emergency lamp. *What are the odds?* he wondered with a fleeting smile. He yanked it off the wall and tried again for the ladder. This time he found it.

He pulled as hard as he could but lacked the strength to pull himself upright. He let go and clutched the lamp to his chest. His finger hovered over the switch as he wondered, *Do I even want to see?*

The voice called out from the office once again. "Where are you going?" it asked. "Back up there? But you were in such a hurry to leave." The voice was getting louder. "And you just got down here."

"Fuck you."

"That's not very nice, but given your situation I can forgive you."

"Thanks," Rodriguez muttered as he dropped the lamp to his feet and pulled himself up to try and stand. Pain shot through his leg and he leaned on his good side to keep from falling. His hand went out for balance and landed on something that rolled away from him. He hopped toward it and pulled it close, holding it for support. *A tool box*, he thought. *On wheels. Perfect.*

He leaned over the metal frame and reached back to pull up his busted leg. Someone in the darkness was moving things around, the sound getting closer every moment. *Time to go.*

He reached over and grabbed at the pipes among the wall.

He shifted his body and the lamp dropped to the deck, sliding along the oily floor. "Shit," he whispered. He reached down and felt around the floor, but couldn't find the lamp. He held tight to the pipe and leaned as far as he could. *If these wheels slip, I'm getting a face full of floor tile.*

Nearby something fell to the deck, metal clanking on metal as things scattered across the floor.

"Why do you want that lamp?" the voice asked. It was much closer than before. "I thought you didn't want to see me."

Rodriguez leaned to the point where he started to slip off the side. He tried to shift his leg, but it lay useless across the toolbox. He kicked with the other to try and move himself closer. His hand flailed around the oily deck until it finally connected with the flashlight. He grabbed and flicked it on.

Santalino stood before him, his face so close Rodriguez could smell the lavender body wash he used to mask the stink of the submarine. It made him smell nice in Sonar, adding an oddly pleasant feminine ambiance to offset the entirely male crew. Now it made Rodriguez feel sick, an overwhelming stench that made his nose run and his eyes well up with tears.

Santalino had a slight smile on his lips that partially masked his dazed expression. His face had lost its olive complexion; it had paled nearly to ash, his skin dry and cracking. Chunks fell off as something moved just below the surface. His smile was accented by shreds of torn skin hanging from the gaping hole of his exposed cheekbones. His back teeth were no longer molars; they had been shaped into jagged fangs that resembled a bear trap, clearly visible where the flesh had been torn away. His head sat atop his neck at an odd angle that Rodriguez almost wanted to reach out and fix. Almost.

The two stared at each other, neither speaking, neither moving.

This is no longer my friend, Rodriguez thought. He tried to pull himself away from the nightmare standing before him but he leaned too far on the top-heavy toolbox. Before he even realized he was falling, he crashed to the deck. The lamp went dead as he flailed around to try and get away from the thing that had once been Santalino.

His hand landed on something hard, a pile of tools that had spilled out of the toolbox. He grasped a long chunk of metal between his fingers. By the shape of the handle and the clatter of the teeth, he knew it was a pipe wrench. *Perfect.*

A hand reached out and clutched his shoulder.

Rodriguez spun around with the metal in his hand. He tightened his grip on the wrench and swung into the darkness. As soon as it connected, he met with a deafening roar that pierced his ears. If was followed by a nauseating stink that quickly filled the space, so strong he felt like he might vomit or black out.

His head swam and the room nearly shook around him. He shook his head, drew back his arm, and swung again. The wrench connected with a sickening crunch, the end of the wrench sticking in the mess that had once been Santalino. Before Rodriguez could yank the wrench free, it was ripped out of his hands.

He ran his hands along the floor and grabbed every wrench he could. Amidst the backdrop of Santalino thrashing about the room, Rodriguez found four wrenches and his flashlight. He clicked it on and shined the beam of light towards the horrible noise. What stood there no longer made any effort at appearing human.

Santalino's face had split nearly in two, the wrench sticking out from where his nose should be. The sides of his head ran like hot wax dripping nearly to the floor. His twisted body resembled nothing like a human. Skin ran down in gelatinous pockets of fat which sprouted far too many arms to be useful. They flailed in all directions like wicked tentacles spreading out in a tornado of discolored flesh.

Santalino screamed through a mouth that opened up in his chest. The gaping hole was lined with teeth that looked every bit like a rusty metal bear trap. Things moved around inside its mouth that Rodriguez no longer wanted to see. He shone the light on the floor, grabbed two more wrenches, and crawled to the nearest standing toolbox. He threw the wrenches on top and then hauled up his broken body. He rolled the toolbox into the Torpedo Room.

Santalino followed, his body spreading across the space

more than moving. Soon it blocked the starboard side torpedo racks, so Rodriguez grabbed a pipe in the overhead and pulled himself and the toolbox towards the port side aisle. One hand at a time, he pulled himself to the opposite side of the Torpedo Room.

The sound of bent wheels scraping against rusted casters echoed through the open space. It was nowhere near as loud as Santalino's screaming, but the grating reverberated through the metal deck plates and seemed to fill the room.

Soon Santalino grew quiet.

Rodriguez grabbed another pipe and pulled past the center console. He waited until he reached the port side aisle before shining the light behind him.

Santalino hadn't exactly followed Rodriguez, but he was still getting closer. His body had rooted to the spot. What were once legs wrapped around two torpedoes, squeezing with such force they looked to be breaking apart. His arms, now at least ten feet long, slid across the torpedo mounting brackets and spread towards Rodriguez. Small shoots grew out of the main tentacles and coiled around equipment wherever it could find purchase. His cleaved head had sprouted tentacles that were taking root in the overhead. It was becoming one with the room.

One of the tentacles reached for Rodriguez.

He grabbed a wrench and slammed it down, smashing it against the corner of the metal torpedo rack. The beast screamed out and the arm shrank away. Rodriguez smiled before turning the light towards the port corner.

Petty Officer Butterball stood no more than a foot away. Rodriguez nearly fell off the toolbox. The stink coming from Butterball's open mouth burned his eyes and singed the hairs in his nose. Without thinking, Rodriguez slammed his wrench into the side of Butterball's face and grabbed for another overhead pipe.

As Butterball struggled to pull the wrench from his shattered skull, Rodriguez pulled himself around the corner. The boat listed to port and the front end rose out of the water. The toolbox rolled right along with it.

Because of the angle, he didn't have to pull himself aft. He couldn't stop himself either. He turned his body around to look behind.

Butterball had pulled the wrench from his head and was running after him.

Rodriguez grabbed another wrench and threw it at Butterball's head, but it did no good.

Fuck. Rodriguez grabbed another wrench and looked around the room. The torpedoes on either side flew past faster than he would have liked. He didn't need to turn around and look; he knew he was going to slam into the back wall within seconds.

From the starboard side, Santalino's arms were spreading across the room. They followed the overhead, branching towards the port side but staying just out of Rodriguez's reach.

Butterball was closing the gap, running impossibly fast and nearly catching the toolbox.

Almost there, Rodriguez thought. He reached down and yanked off a length of nylon strapping, making a loop out of the end and tying it around the top of the toolbox. He closed his eyes and held on as best he could. He may as well not have even tried.

When the toolbox hit the back wall, he slammed into the row of lockers and dropped to the deck like a rag doll. The drawers of the toolbox flew open, spilling their contents across the space. Wrenches and screwdrivers flew past Rodriguez's head as he tumbled backwards away from the flying debris. He kept one end of the strap in his hand, the other still tied to the smashed toolbox. Ignoring the nearly overwhelming pain, he rolled through the open door at the back end of the Torpedo Room and slammed it shut.

Before Rodriguez could even catch his breath, Butterball was grabbing for the handle.

Rodriguez braced his shoulder against the wall and pulled on the strap as hard as he could. He heard a crash as the toolbox tipped forward and spilled its remaining metal guts across the aisle.

Butterball didn't scream; he didn't make a sound at all, but the handle on the aft Torpedo Room door *did* stop moving.

Rodriguez waited with his hand wrapped tightly around the strap until he could hold on no longer. His arms burned and everything else hurt. He dropped his head to the deck and allowed his eyes to close. He took a few slow, deep breaths, each one bringing sharp pain to his chest. One of his legs hurt like hell, the other he could no longer feel.

Thankfully, his arms both seemed to be in working order. Aside from a mounting tension headache, his head seemed to be in one piece. He reached up and grabbed an emergency flashlight from under the stairs and made a quick scan around the short hallway. He saw nothing moving. With a deep, painful breath, Rodriguez crawled towards the steps.

Dinesh stared down the hallway, his eyes and nostrils burning from the smoke that slowly filled the compartment. All he could see was the glow from the ladder ahead. It led down towards the engine room. That was where the fire had started. From there it spread until it overwhelmed nearly the entire ship and most of the crew, including Singh.

He took a step back and hit the metal handle of the hatch. Although he hadn't closed it, the hatch stood shut against the main deck outside. The metal was hot; not enough to burn him, but enough to be uncomfortable. He pulled at the handle but it would not budge. The glow down the hall grew stronger as something in the middle of the passageway came into view.

He tried to peel his eyes from the snakeskin boot. "Singh," he whispered. "No." The boot rested in a pile of melted flesh just past the ladder to the lower level.

Dinesh pulled at the handle again, but it still wouldn't move. There was no other place he could go except down the ladder to the fire below. That, or head down the passage to find his brother's remains.

This isn't real, he thought. *I know this isn't real*. It all felt real enough to be unnerving but not enough to be convincing. He didn't know what he would find if he went to his brother's remains, but he was pretty sure he knew what waited below.

"Better to deal with the devil you know," he said, his voice echoing through the otherwise empty corridor. He stepped forward slowly, his eyes not leaving the snakeskin boot. As he crept, he ran his fingers along the wall. As soon as they touched the warm metal ladder, he slid his boot onto the top step. Before he could convince himself otherwise, he closed his eyes and headed down toward the Engine Room.

The heat was almost unbearable. His skin ran slick with sweat. It felt like he was going to melt. Dinesh looked around and saw flames in every direction. All but one. There was a small break in the fire that lead to a cramped office in the back. Dinesh knew it very well. It had been his brother's.

I can't go back there, he thought. *I won't go back there.*

"Dinesh?" a voice called out.

"No," Dinesh said. "You're not real."

"You left me."

"This isn't happening."

"You left me to die."

"*You're not my brother*," Dinesh screamed. He felt the tears well up in his eyes but they evaporated before they could spill past his cheeks.

"No," Singh said. "Not anymore."

Dinesh heard the telltale click of a wooden heel on the metal deck. The dark shadow of a man came into view, just beyond the flames.

Dinesh could no longer hear the groaning of metal or the burning of the overhead. All he could hear was his dead brother's one remaining heel. He pictured the other one still waiting in the upper level but banished the thought as soon as it came.

"I didn't leave you," Dinesh said. "I tried to get to you."

"And then you left." The shadow passed through the wall of flame and took the very shape Dinesh didn't want to see. Singh's boot came into view first, followed by the rest of his body. Although his pants looked normal, his 70's-era polyester shirt had melted into his chest. If it hadn't been for the boots and the shirt, Dinesh might have lied to himself that it was someone else.

Singh's face was burned beyond recognition. The only things remaining were little bits of charred flesh clinging to his skull and a ring of burnt stubble on top of his head. Blackened teeth ground back and forth as bits of bone cracked away from his jaw.

His fists came together with a crack, bone slamming into bone as he slammed his fist into his palm. "You left me here to die," Singh said. "We were supposed to find the island together."

"This island is a lie," Dinesh said. "It was always a lie, we never should have found it."

"*You* never should have found it," Singh said. "It called us back, but you wanted nothing to do with it. I had to volunteer us for every bloody mission to the Red Sea just for a chance to come home. I finally made it back, but then you let me die. Now I'm stuck here. *Forever.*"

"This isn't real," Dinesh said.

"Time for you to join me," Singh said. "Time for you to join *us.*"

A choir of voices echoed in Dinesh' ears as the Lahore's dead simultaneously cried out in pain. Ghostly shapes flailing in the flames grew more solid as fallen sailors took shape, burning in the fire.

"Not real." Dinesh closed his eyes and hugged himself tight. *Not real, not real, not real.* He continued the mantra in his head, wishing it would all just go away. Singh's clicking heel grew louder and Dinesh started to speak out loud again. His voice rose as Singh drew closer.

"Not *real*," Dinesh screamed as a bony hand landed on his shoulder. He felt electricity travel through his body and down his leg, connecting with the metal deck under his feet. He opened his eyes and the feeling went away.

The flames around him burned out of control, the dead crew now dancing wildly about the room. Bodies singed as they spun through the flames, their dance growing more frantic as Dinesh watched.

Singh was no longer there.

Dinesh turned and climbed the ladder as fast as he could. Someone grabbed at his leg, a bony hand attached to an unrecognizable body. It burned like a hot poker, melting through his khaki and searing the flesh around his calf.

Dinesh kicked out and the hand lost its grip. He climbed

faster.

He reached the upper passage and turned towards the hatch, but something behind him let out a soft chuckle. Dinesh stopped and turned slowly around, his mind screaming for his body to just *run*. His body did not listen.

Singh stood where his boot had once lain. Dinesh looked down and watched him pick it up and pull it onto the bone and burnt muscle of his foot. Somehow seeing the abomination before him wearing his brother's boots was more difficult than anything else.

Dinesh stumbled backward, nearly spilling himself onto the deck as his legs gave out underneath him.

"Leaving so soon?" Singh asked. There was not enough flesh on his face to show emotion, but the charred sinew connecting his jaws stretched into what could only be a smile. When he started to laugh, something fell out from between his blackened teeth, something that moved across the deck even as its slimy body sizzled on the hot metal.

Dinesh found strength in his legs. He turned and ran towards the hatch. *It's not going to open*, he thought. *It'll be locked and I'll to be stuck in here with Singh*. He threw himself at the hatch anyway, his hand grabbing the handle right as the Engine Room exploded below. His body slammed against the metal frame as the ship shook out of control. The surrounding bulkheads bowed as if they might collapse at any moment. A cloud of rust flew into the air to mix with the waves of thick black smoke from below. The hatch fell outwards, crashing to the main deck in a spray of salt and rust.

The handle fell to the deck, tripping Dinesh as he tumbled through the jagged opening. He slid to a stop on the rough nonskid deck, his tattered uniform tearing back to expose newly-shredded skin. His back burned from the hot metal shards that flew through the air.

Without looking back, he crawled away from the hatch. The deck scraped at his hands and knees until they were torn and bloody. He could no longer feel his hands, but the end of the deck was fast approaching. He could smell the toxic fumes mixing with the salty sea air. He could hear the violent waves crash against the crumbling hull. He closed his eyes and kept crawling towards the drop off.

I'm not going to make it, he thought as he felt himself running out of both energy and will. His arms turned to jelly and he dropped to the deck.

He heard the screaming from below mix with a series of smaller explosions. He could feel the heat pouring from the depths of the ship as clouds of smoke rolled overhead. The ship listed to the side and the bow tilted down, dipping into the water on its way to an eternal grave at the bottom of the sea.

Dinesh slid, his face scraping into the nonskid before he tumbled over backwards and crashed through the safety lines. With nothing to grab hold of, he fell. An expanse of nothing surrounded him as he floated in a cloud of darkness. It felt wonderfully free.

Once Dinesh hit the water, everything went black.

Rodriguez stared at the crumpled body splayed out at the bottom of the stairs. "Dinesh?" he asked as he crawled forward for a closer look. He poked Dinesh in the ribs but received no response. He aimed his flashlight up the ladder towards the middle level but there was no one there. An orange glow flickered slightly in the distance, but he could detect no movement.

Rodriguez grabbed Dinesh's shoulder and shook but there was still no response. He lowered his head to look for the rise and fall of his chest. *At least he's breathing.* It wasn't much, but it was enough to know he was alive.

There was only a few ways out of the lower level, and Dinesh had just fallen from the easiest of them. The hatch in the Torpedo Room was out of the question. Even though the noises from the other side of the door had subsided, Rodriguez had enough of that room for a lifetime. There was another hatch in the Machinery Room, but it was so small he wasn't sure he could get them both out. Unless Rodriguez could wake him up, Dinesh was going to be dead weight.

I can barely drag myself, he thought. *I can't drag him too.* He shook Dinesh one more time and called his name. He thought he detected a slight flutter to his eyelids so he gently slapped his cheek. "Dinesh?"

Dinesh didn't open his eyes, but he did wince slightly.

Maybe I should slap him again, Rodriguez thought, *just for good measure. It always works in the movies.* He pulled his hand back and slapped one more time, but it made no difference. *Stupid movies. They're always lying to us.*

He felt along the deck until he found the outline of the hatch that led to the storage tank below. Dinesh was lying partially on top of it, so Rodriguez tried to push him to the side. It didn't work. He crawled to the other side and pulled. By grabbing a nearby door frame, he had just enough leverage to roll Dinesh onto his back.

Dinesh muttered something as his head flopped to the side. His eyes stayed closed and his body remained limp.

Rodriguez grabbed the handle and pulled up the hatch. Below waited a darkness even blacker than he'd remembered. He reached in and flicked the light on but nothing happened. He felt around until he found the safety line that was stored at the top of the ladder. He pulled most of the line out at once, but one end was caught on something below.

He grabbed his flashlight and aimed it down into the storage space. The reflection of two yellow eyes made Rodriguez jump back and drop his flashlight. "*Shit.*"

Rodriguez heard something crawling across the boxes below as it made its way out of the storage space. He pulled out as much of the line as he could before slamming the hatch shut. He rolled on top to force it closed as he dogged the handle. The line was caught in the hatch, and no matter how hard Rodriguez pulled it would not come free.

Whatever was in there made it to the top of the ladder. It started scratching and banging on the other side.

Rodriguez looked up and noticed the flickering orange glow from middle level was growing brighter. He could now see well enough without the flashlight. *As much as I appreciate the light*, he thought, *this can't be a good thing.*

He crawled forward and saw a Leatherman multi-tool that had fallen underneath the stairwell. It sat just within his reach.

Fucking-a. He grabbed the tool, flipped out the knife, and sliced through the rope. He put the blade away and stuffed the tool into his pocket. *Might come in handy.*

He unraveled the rope and made a loop. He tied it around Dinesh, weaving it through his belt loops and tying it tightly around his waist. The other end he tied to his belt loop before climbing up the stairs. The rope was long enough that he made it to the top before taking the slack out.

Even with no lights on, the middle level was much brighter than below. He could see everything clearly, even better than with normal submarine lighting. The passageway back towards the mess decks was well lit, while the corridor headed forward remained dark. *Light or dark?* he wondered as he looked towards his unconscious friend. *Maybe I'll just get Dinesh first.*

He untied the rope from his belt loop and wrapped it around the handrail. He crawled back towards the mess decks and took out the slack until the rope was tight. With one last glance around, he pulled. Dinesh didn't budge.

Fuck. He braced his shoulder against the wall and tried again. Still, Dinesh would not move. He jammed his only functioning foot between the railings and pushed back with all he had, but it didn't help.

Fucking fuck. He checked the rope for snags as he crawled back to the stairway. *I'll never get him up here like--*

Rodriguez dropped the rope, his thoughts dying off as his mind struggled to take in the scene in lower level. The storage tank hatch was open. Dinesh was gone, a pool of black slime covering the area where he once lay. At the bottom of the stairs, the thing from the storage compartment was climbing its way up to the middle level.

The creature did not even resemble a human. It had an impossibly long body that was covered in slimy fur. The mouth resembled a bear trap, its teeth offensively long and razor sharp. They were dwarfed only by the thing's eyes, huge yellow discs that like a prism reflected light from middle level. There were nearly a dozen of them wrapped around its skull so the thing could see in all directions. Every time it opened its jaws, the closest set of eyes blinked shut only to open again when the jaws snapped shut. Rodriguez tried not to stare at them; there was something moving behind the lenses that made him want to start screaming.

Tentacles along the side of its body slid up the railing and felt along the wall, as if tasting the wood and metal along the way. It climbed the stairs on all of its legs, of which there were more than could be counted. There appeared to be hundreds of them, short dark legs moving so fast Rodriguez couldn't keep track of them.

It slithered up the stairs and was already half way up before Rodriguez broke his trance. He didn't stop to think. He turned and crawled towards the light.

Dinesh limped through the darkness towards the back of the Machinery Room. He had no idea how he'd gotten back on the Alexandria, but whatever had come out of that hatch, Dinesh wanted nothing to do with.

He felt his way through the nest of machinery towards a square of light in the ceiling. It came from a hatch leading to middle level. It was just bright enough to light his way.

He only glanced back once, and only to follow the trail of rope that hung from his waist and drug on the floor behind him. The end was still near the ladder; it was oily and frayed where the thing had bitten through on its way up the steps. He breathed a sigh of relief that that it was headed up to middle level and away from him.

Good luck Rodriguez, he thought as he turned back towards the hatch. He heard movement in the passageway above him. *Hope that's you getting away, because if not, it's something headed to meet me.* Based on how far he'd walked, he guessed that the mess decks were above him. That meant the hatch at the aft end would lead him outside. *I don't fancy wandering through those woods again, but it beats being stuck down here...or back on the Lahore.*

He tripped over an uneven deck plate and fell down next to the massive diesel engine. He lay for a moment on the cool deck,

159

enjoying how it felt against his burned skin. He rolled over on his back and looked up. In the darkness of the Machinery Room, he could just barely discern the outline of a fire axe hanging nearby. It was close enough for him to grab. He pulled himself to his feet and unfastened the clasp holding the axe in place. *Nice.*

It was damn heavy, but not too heavy to carry. He wasn't a hundred percent convinced he could swing the thing, but as long as he remained on the sub it helped his sense of security. He continued on towards the glowing hatch until he was standing directly beneath it. The ladder heading up was incredibly short, so short that he didn't even need to climb it to reach the handle.

Dinesh opened the hatch and pushed it slightly up. It moved easy enough that he knew nothing was there. *At least not on top of it*, he thought. *But don't get too excited. I'm not in the clear just yet.* With the axe in one hand, he pulled himself up and pushed the hatch open completely. He popped his head up into the middle level and immediately dropped back down to where he could just peek out through the hatch.

There was light filling the mess decks, mostly coming from the adjoined galley. Flames shot out of the door and licked up the walls, although nothing was actually burning as far as he could tell. There was no heat and no smoke, no bitter smell of melted plastic and charred wood. There was only light.

At the forward end, Rodriguez was on the deck crawling onto the mess decks. He was looking around, eyes wide and full of pain, but he seemed to be ignorant of the fire dancing right next to him. One of his legs was helping him along but the other he dragged limp behind him. Rodriguez continually glanced over his shoulder as he crawled.

Dinesh climbed all the way through the Machinery Room hatch and looked up. The ladder leading topside was clear, the hatch open wide to a clear night sky above. *I know it's not real sky, but it's better than nothing.* He turned back towards the mess decks. "*Rodriguez.*"

Rodriguez didn't answer. Even when Dinesh repeated himself, he didn't react at all. He had stopped crawling and was staring at the empty space behind him. A shadow passed along the bulkhead and onto the mess decks. It was only for a moment, but it was there. Rodriguez rolled over and tried to drag himself under one of the tables. For no apparent reason, he began to scream.

Dinesh ran over to his friend as fast as he could.

Rodriguez held his hands up in a defensive posture, his eyes closed tight, body shaking. His screams had dropped to a whimper as the shadow from middle level moved toward him.

As the shadow passed by, Dinesh swung the axe through the air. He was equally surprised and thrilled when the blade buried itself in something. He was less thrilled when it let out an inhuman noise that filled the room and somehow made the fire behind him die out.

Thick brown blood sprayed in all directions, coating the walls and soaking Dinesh's uniform. He let go of the axe, reached down, and grabbed Rodriguez.

Blood coated his body and sprayed in his open mouth, but Rodriguez did not respond.

Dinesh dragged his friend from under the table and pulled him toward the escape hatch. He took the rope from around his waist and wrapped it under Rodriguez's arms. The rope was slick with blood so he had to triple-knot it to get it to stay. Once secure, Dinesh climbed the ladder.

Half way up, the rope went tight. Dinesh had the full weight of Rodriguez, and he wasn't going any higher. He braced his legs and struggled to climb, but Rodriguez had curled up in a ball and was not helping.

No way am I getting him up here like this, Dinesh thought. He looked around and saw a life ring hanging on the wall. *But maybe with this…*

He grabbed the ring and climbed down the ladder. He pulled Rodriguez out of his ball and slipped the ring around his waist. He tied it as best he could.

Rodriguez did not help, but he also did not resist.

Dinesh climbed up the ladder with the other end of the rope in his hand. It was long enough that he could climb all the way up without having to pull Rodriguez. Once Dinesh was topside, he looped the rope around the top of the ladder and tied the end around his waist. He leaned back and pulled. Far below,

Rodriguez started to rise.

"Rodriguez," Dinesh yelled. "You've got to help me."

At the bottom of the hatch, Rodriguez stirred. He swung to the side and hit the wall before bouncing off. He put his hand out to stop himself from hitting the opposite wall. He looked up at Dinesh as if he had no idea where he was.

"I need your help," Dinesh said.

"My leg," Rodriguez said. "I think it's broken."

"I know. Try and pull yourself up."

After a pause the rope shifted. Dinesh thought he was going to drop him, but then the load became much easier. He glanced below.

Rodriguez had grabbed the ladder and was pulling himself up hand over hand, rung by rung.

Dinesh continued to pull until he saw a hand reach out and grab the handle. He dropped the rope and reached out to grab his friend. He leaned back to pull Rodriguez out of the hatch and they both tumbled onto the deck.

Rodriguez rolled to the side and looked up at the sky. "What the fuck was that?"

"I don't know, but can we close this?" Dinesh asked. He pointed to the open hatch.

Rodriguez shook his head. "Not from up here. It's hydraulic. The valve's below."

"Great." Dinesh looked out across the water. He was not surprised to see that everything looked different. The night sky above stood out of place against the distant rocky silhouette of land. A glow came from somewhere beneath the dark brown rock along the shore.

Dinesh dropped to his knees, ignoring the fresh blood that flowed when his skin connected with the nonskid deck. "I'm so tired," he said. He barely registered that he'd said it out loud until Rodriguez spoke up.

"I don't think I have anything left."

"Me either. How will we get out of here?"

"I don't know," Rodriguez said. "Maybe we won't."

"No," Dinesh said. "We will. We have to."

"Cartwright has got to be around."

162

"I know."

"You know they'll be coming up for us."

"Yes," Dinesh said. "I know."

The two men stayed where they were, both staring up at the sky, Dinesh wondering if he'd ever see the real one again. It was a moment of silence that they both needed, but one that could not last. Soon, the scratching below roused them from their daze.

"It's coming," Rodriguez said.

"Can you stand?"

"No. One of my legs is definitely broken. Maybe both, I can't really tell. I can move this one but can't feel either." He wiggled his left leg and looked at Dinesh. "Can you carry me?"

"No." They looked at each other as Dinesh nodded his head towards the water. "We could always swim for it."

"I don't want to go in there," Rodriguez said. "Fuck that. We don't know what's down there."

"Unfortunately we do," Dinesh said.

"My legs won't get me far."

"They'll have to."

"We'll probably drown."

"It's not like we have much choice."

The scratching from below grew louder as the stench of rotting meat wafted through the hatch from the Mess Decks below.

Dinesh coughed and waved his hand in front of his face. "Or we could just wait it out," he said. "I guess we do have a choice."

As Rodriguez opened his mouth to respond, something reached up from under the water and grabbed his ankle. Black arms like tentacles rose from beneath the waves and led all the way to the back of the sub. Another one reached up and grabbed Dinesh. Neither man bothered to fight. They each sat there, waiting to see what would happen. They didn't have to wait long.

15

The aft end of the submarine exploded, jagged chunks of black steel flying in all directions. What once was a reactor room now resembled a fleshy pit of hell, toothy spikes of metal circling the edge. Two gigantic arms reached out and grabbed the sides of the submarine as Cartwright's massive form climbed out from the reactor pit. He had grown disgusting and huge, an oversized blob of putrid flesh and vicious anger that shook the boat and sent waves across the water.

"You two," Cartwright said in a voice that was no longer his own, a voice that buzzed like a wasp drowning in thick tar, shrill and dripping with spit. "Why aren't you two dead?"

"I should have known it'd be you," Rodriguez shouted over the sounds of collapsing metal. "Only a fat fuck like you could shake this boat."

"You piece of shit," Cartwright screamed. "I will squash you."

"I wish you would," Rodriguez said. "You stink like Butterball's boiled ass and I don't think I'm having fun anymore."

Cartwright's face twisted as he brought his arms up into the air. He beat his chest and raised his fists. "*I will smash you into paste.*"

Dinesh reached over and grabbed his friend's hand. "This can't be good."

"I'm sorry, man," Rodriguez said. "I know I just made it worse, but I fucking hate that guy."

"No need to be sorry," Dinesh said. "He is so unpleasant to be around, I think I would prefer being paste." He closed his eyes and waited for the world to go dark.

The tentacles around their ankles let go as something in the water rocked the broken ship nearly on its side. There was a scream so loud it shook the air around them. Waves of murky water spilled over the deck and poured into the exposed Engine Room.

Dinesh opened his eyes and stared at the thing rising from the water. He could barely recognize the face, but the eagles pinned to his collars gave the Captain away without question. Like Cartwright, he had grown offensively huge, his body a slithering nest of tentacles and muscle. He still had the stub of a long-ago burnt-out cigar clenched between his teeth.

"Cartwright, you little shit," the Captain growled. "This is *my* boat."

Cartwright turned and his eyes grew huge, spreading across his face like giant expanding discs of yellow nightmare. He dropped his hands to his sides and clenched his fists, his fingers wiggling like sweaty sausages.

On the sub, Dinesh was grabbed from behind and pulled away from the water. The thing from the mess decks had made its way to the top of the ladder. Its huge eyes peered up from the darkness as its tentacles tightened around Dinesh's waist, dragging him back towards the hatch.

With another tentacle, the thing from the hatch grabbed Rodriguez by the neck and tightened around his throat. His face grew red as he struggled to breathe. He reached in his pocket and pulled out the found multi-tool. He fumbled with the blade but couldn't get the thing open.

"Give it to me," Dinesh said. Rodriguez tossed him the tool and reached for the thing around his throat. He dug his fingers into the tentacle and tried to pull it away. It didn't give at all; he looked like he was on the verge of blacking out.

Dinesh caught the tool and flipped out the blade. He thrust it at the tentacle around his waist and it sliced through with ease. He winced as he cut through to his stomach, but not deep enough to worry about. He rolled toward Rodriguez and hacked at the tentacle around his throat, careful to cut away from his flesh.

The thing in the hatch screamed, the sound echoing through the hatch as it lost its grip and dropped to the bottom. It slammed into the Mess Decks with a disgusting sloppy sound. The screaming stopped.

Rodriguez pulled the limp tentacle from around his neck and threw it into the water. He sucked in a great breath of air before coughing it right back out and dropping his head to the deck. His breathing came across ragged and wet as he struggled to for air.

Dinesh stuffed the tool in his pocket, climbed to his feet, and grabbed Rodriguez beneath the arms. He pulled him away from the hatch and toward the front end of the boat. He stared up at Cartwright as he turned his massive bulk to face the Captain.

"This is *my* boat now," Cartwright said. "In my world, you're the Captain of Jack and shit."

"Everybody says that," Dinesh muttered as he dragged Rodriguez away. "What is it with the Jack and the shit?"

"Well I've got news for you, dickhead," the Captain said. "Jack just took over." He drew up his arm and swung a mighty fist towards Cartwright. He had grown so big that he moved like he was in a slow motion film.

Cartwright was just as slow, and even if he wasn't he was so big that he couldn't have moved out of the way. He tried to bring his arms up to block the punch but was too late.

The Captain's fist smashed into his face.

Cartwright's head flew back as thick black blood spewed from his mouth. It splashed down across the deck and flowed into the water where it floated away from the submarine. The surface exploded with activity as things swam up from the depths to devour Cartwright's blood. Huge scaly creatures broke the surface, taking in great mouthfuls of the vile fluid before diving back to the hidden sea floor.

Cartwright screamed and slammed his jaw shut so hard his teeth cracked and chipped away around the edges. He brought his hands up to his head and tilted it to the side, cracking his neck with a sound like cannons going off nearby. He smiled and balled his hands into fists as he took a swing at the Captain.

The Captain was already leaning out of the way.

Cartwright's fist flew past the Captain, the momentum drawing him in close to the Captain. The submarine tilted along with Cartwright, and the aft end dipped well below the waves. As soon as Cartwright had passed the point where he could do any damage, The Captain moved in.

The Captain's other fist came up and caught Cartwright under his jaw. Blood poured from the holes along the side of his face where his ear had been. He screamed out and brought his chin down, his mouth open wide to expose rows of pointed interlocking teeth. He clamped down on the Captain's hand and ground his jaw back and forth. His teeth tore through the Captain's flesh and exposed sections of bone. Chunks of meat fell into the water to be devoured by the nauseating feeding frenzy.

The Captain's face turned red; he bit down on his cigar, slicing the thing in two. The end dropped into the water, a single brown leaf from the wrapper still stuck between his teeth. He brought his other arm above his head, balled his fist, and slammed it down on top of Cartwright's head like he was hammering in a nail. "Let go of my *fucking hand*," he screamed.

Cartwright's mouth dropped open and a gush of blood flew out. It mixed with the thick, chunky fluid that seeped out from his nose, flowed around his mouth, and dripped off his chin. Blackness welled up at the corners of his yellow eyes, spreading across the blazing pupils like a twisted sunrise. He rocked back and nearly fell over before leaning forward and swinging both arms towards the Captain. His fists flew through the air, coming together in an eight-knuckle hammer.

The Captain dropped down into the water, his body disappearing beneath the surface before Cartwright's fists even came close. A series of bubbles and an expanding ripple of water were the only indications he had even been there.

Cartwright's mouth dropped open. He scanned the water, his eyes darting independently of the other as his head shifted back and forth. He opened his fingers and held them out like a shield. They followed the back and forth flow of his head as he searched for the Captain. Blood flowed freely from his mouth, nose, and both ears. He was covered in dark red and black chunks of living coagulated blood that crawled around in the mess pouring out of his head.

On the submarine, Dinesh pulled Rodriguez away from the war between Cartwright and the Captain. He headed for the forward end of the boat, holding a safety line as he slid Rodriguez down the narrow strip of non-skid by the submarine's sail. The ship rocked with every punch the two giants threw, but Dinesh managed to keep them both out of the water.

As Dinesh cleared the sail and headed towards the bow, a wave slammed into the side of the submarine, forcing them nearly sideways and carrying a noxious wave across the hull. Dinesh grabbed the nearest line and held on as Rodriguez slid across the deck, his legs dropping over the edge so far his boots dipped in the water. Dinesh pulled him out but could not haul him up to the deck. Rodriguez lay there, his boots a mere foot away from the surface, with only Dinesh's hand clamped onto his sleeve to keep him from taking a swim.

The Captain flew out with the wave, his massive body rocketing up with both fists held high. He rose well above Cartwright, who stared up at the Captain with a look that blended hatred and fear.

As he reached the crest, the Captain brought his fists together and swung them like a sledgehammer, forcing them down as his body dropped towards the water. He slammed them on the top of Cartwright, splitting his head in two and sending a wave of blood, bone, and rotting brain in all directions. His fists continued into Cartwright's neck, pushing him down and forcing his body back into the Reactor Room.

As the Captain splashed back into the water, he brought Cartwright and the submarine down with him. With a crack of breaking steel, the entire boat submerged.

Dinesh found himself choking on the vile water and swimming for the surface. He lost his grip on Rodriguez as he struggled for air. The water swirled around him like a torrent so dark that no light penetrated the surface. He was not even sure which direction was up. He kicked his feet and paddled as hard as he could. Soon his head broke the surface and he was able to breathe.

The aft end of the submarine was gone. The bow bobbed up out of the water, belched out a final gasp of air from the ballast tanks, and slid below the surface.

All that could be seen of Cartwright were his two hands reaching out of the water, his fingers clutching the air as they sunk below the waves. The water around rocked with such violence the waves rose and crashed over the Captain's head.

The Captain didn't budge. He smiled, his teeth still clenched as he stared down at the surface. His hands were below the water, shaking Cartwright back and forth beneath the waves.

Dinesh reached down and felt along his waist. The rope was still there. He pulled the slack out of the line and followed the direction. It led down into the water near where the submarine went down. He could feel something tugging on the end, and soon he found himself under the water once again. He let out the slack and broke the surface, swimming backwards and pulling on the rope. Dinesh looked back and saw land; he swam for shore.

He struggled, the rope pulling tight as the waves crashed against him like he was in the middle of a storm. He could still feel something moving on the other end of the rope. He couldn't tell if it was the movement of the waves or of something alive, but he hoped it was Rodriguez.

He looked back and saw the pier close by. It had been crushed the point where it could not support their weight, but he reached out and grabbed the closest post for support. It leaned to the side but held. Dinesh grabbed the rope and wrapped it around the post, pulling his body along with it. He took a deep breath and pulled as hard as he could. The post dipped down below the water, but popped right back up when the line went slack.

Dinesh scanned the rolling surface until he saw a flash of orange jump out of the water. Rodriguez was still inside the life ring, so Dinesh pulled him closer to the shore. With his other hand, he grabbed the shattered support beams above and pulled himself along the pier until he was within a few feet of land.

He dropped his foot, expecting to find a bottom to stand on. He slipped beneath the water and returned to the surface choking. He reached up, grabbed the support above, and pulled himself the rest of the way to the water's edge. He kicked his feet in front of him and found a rock wall where the beach began. There was no gradual slope; the drop off was a ninety-degree angle straight down.

He rolled to the side and pulled himself up onto the beach. He pulled the rope to bring Rodriguez towards shore, but the line had gone slack. Dinesh yanked on the line but there was no resistance. He looked out among the waves but didn't see the bright orange life ring floating anywhere. He looked back towards the rapidly sinking submarine and watched the creatures rise up from the deep to consume the remaining blood that floated on the surface. There was no sign of Cartwright or the Captain.

He pulled the line faster. It moved freely but Dinesh did not stop. *The rope is not that long*, he thought. *He should be here by-*

His thoughts were broken by a hand coming up out of the water just a few feet away. The fingers were curled around the motionless body of Rodriguez as he lay in the massive palm, curled up in a ball.

The Captain rose from the sea, a wicked smile on his face. He towered over Dinesh, looking down on him like he might have been a bug. In his other hand, he held the crushed head of Cartwright. One of his yellow eyes was missing and the lower half of his jaw had been ripped away, exposing a row of broken teeth that somehow looked sharper than when they were in one piece.

The Captain threw the head onto the beach with a mighty laugh. It landed so close to Dinesh he was nearly covered in the spray of foul seawater, blood, and sand as it slid to a stop. The smell was horrible; it overwhelmed even the stink from the water, making it hard to breathe.

"You," the Captain said. "You did this." He pointed at Dinesh, his index finger so close it nearly blotted out the sky. The one finger was bigger than Dinesh's entire body. "You brought me to this island, but you never said it would be like this."

"I didn't know it would be like this," Dinesh said. "I had no idea what Singh was doing, I never wanted to find this island again."

"You *lie*," the Captain screamed. "I invited you into my home and you lied to me, you killed my crew, you sank my boat."

"I didn't sink it," Dinesh said. He dropped his voice so low that the Captain couldn't possibly hear it. "You did."

"What's that?" the Captain asked. "You want this?" He grabbed Rodriguez with his thumb and forefinger and held him in the air, his limp body dangling over the water. "You want this piece of shit? Your little faggot friend?"

Dinesh stared up, taking shallow breaths, barely able to think, unable to respond. In the sea beyond the Captain, the feeding frenzy came to an end, the stragglers finally dipping below the surface in a swirling pool that faded as he watched. *I never should have come back here*, he thought. *Not even for Singh.*

Dinesh felt in his pocket and found the lump of metal he was hoping for. He pulled out the tool Rodriguez had given him and flipped open the blade. Above him, the Captain laughed.

"Weak," he said. "Pathetic. What will you do with that?"

"It's not for you," Dinesh said. "It's for me." Dinesh brought the blade up to his throat and closed his eyes. He tried to slide it over, tried to force his arm to move. He pressed down into the soft flesh beneath his jaw and felt the sting like a needle searching for a vein. He sucked in a breath and flexed his muscle.

Before Dinesh could pull the blade across, the Captain's fingers closed around his body. He squeezed Dinesh, pressing his arms to his sides and forcing the air from his lungs.

Dinesh couldn't breathe; the agony was overwhelming. He could feel his guts being pressed together, like they were being forced into places they shouldn't go. It felt like they could shoot out through his neck and spray through the air. All he could hear was the booming voice of the Captain.

Dinesh felt the Captain's laughter through the shaking of his fist. It created a sense of vertigo that made it hard to think. He tried to take in a breath, but when he opened his mouth blood shot out in a stream.

Dinesh tried to move his hand back and forth, slowly inching the blade into the Captain's hand. He pressed with what little strength remained and felt warmth begin to ooze all around him. The grip on his body loosened, and Dinesh could finally take a breath. He didn't wait to see what would happen. He gripped the handle tight and drove the blade into the Captain's hand.

With a scream, the Captain's fingers flew open. His palm

thrust out and Dinesh found himself dangling above the water, hanging on to the blade for his very life. Below, the water churned as blood poured from the Captain's hand. The blood flowed around Dinesh, and he felt his grip on the tool begin to slip.

He reached up and grabbed the Captain's finger. He pulled himself between the knuckles and dragged the knife with him. The blade twisted around, opening the wound even more. There was so much blood that it forced the blade out. Dinesh climbed around the back of the Captain's hand and stabbed at his knuckles.

The Captain continued to scream as Dinesh twisted the blade back and forth, jamming it against bone and peeling away flesh.

The Captain's fingers flexed open and closed but somehow Dinesh managed to hang on. The blood flowed out like a river; Dinesh was completely covered, his hand slipping as the viscous flow coated everything.

Dinesh lost his footing and nearly slipped; he jammed the blade between two knuckles, turning it sideways so that it would hold. Soon there was nothing that wasn't slick with blood, including the Leatherman's handle. He clung to it as best he could, but he was losing his grip.

When the tool slipped from his grasp, Dinesh felt like everything slowed down around him. He was falling towards the water, his arms and legs flailing on their own. He couldn't stop their movement; it was as if his subconscious was trying to convince his body that it could fly. He couldn't see where he was heading, but against the backdrop of night sky above he could clearly see Rodriguez falling nearby. The life ring was gone, but the rope still connected them together. However, the thing that dominated the sky was the Captain.

The Captain's face had turned red. His teeth were clenched tight and the cords of his neck stuck out, offensively erect. Blood sprayed from his hand in all directions. His other hand came around to grab at the wound; he brought his thumb and index finger to his knuckle and pulled out the blade. He dropped it and turned his eyes to Dinesh. They looked like they might erupt into flames at any minute.

The fall seemed to last forever, but just as the Captain started to reach for Dinesh he hit the water. He landed flat on his back and the impact took the air out of him. The pain was so complete he thought it had killed him. The water rushed in from all sides, tinted red with the Captain's blood but still so dark he could barely see. He tried to kick for the surface but his body wouldn't respond; he had nothing left.

He opened his mouth and let out what little air he had left. It wasn't enough to bring him up, and he wasn't coming up on his own. He was spent. He was done. Dinesh closed his eyes, still feeling the foul water that burned his throat and clawed at his eyes. He willed the darkness to return to finally take him away. Then he hit bottom.

Rodriguez woke to pain. He couldn't breathe, and by the burning sensation he instantly knew where he was. Water was everywhere, and there was no mistaking the sickening feeling it left on his skin. The last thing he remembered was being on the submarine. Everything after that was a blur of sound and color filtered through the lens of unconsciousness.

He tried to kick at the water but his legs did not work. He flailed his arms but they weren't doing much good. He felt himself sinking deeper into the sea, and there seemed to be nothing stopping him. Soon it was too dark too see. The familiar burning returned to his lungs, his peripheral vision turning white as he felt his tenuous grip on consciousness rapidly slipping away.

When he hit the bottom, he was surprised to find it smooth and rigid. He expected a bottom of sand and slime, but this felt like polished rock. He wanted to investigate but needed to breathe. It was enough to bring him back from the edge, made him want to stay awake. He threw out his arms and scanned the bottom for something to grab hold of. He found what had to be the water's edge; a ninety-degree angle that led straight up. It also felt like smooth rock but had ridges all along like handholds.

He grabbed and pulled as fast as he could. Consciousness was still threatening to slip away, but he knew he could hang on if he could just make it up and out of the water. He felt something tugging around his waist but barely registered it. He just climbed. His legs were no good, but the handholds were deep enough for him to keep his momentum going.

When his hand cleared the surface, he stopped. His head spun and his body shook. His hand flailed above the surface, looking for the next handhold but finding only air. He stayed that way until someone grabbed him and pulled him out onto the small beach.

He couldn't see, he could barely breathe. Rodriguez choked until he threw up seawater. The air returned in ragged breaths as he rolled onto his back and waited for his body to slow down. He heard voices around him and felt something tugging at his waist once again. He couldn't pay it any attention. He was somehow alive, and that was good enough for him.

He couldn't tell how long he'd been lying there, but he finally opened his eyes. There was a group of people standing around him, and another smaller group crouched a few feet away. He couldn't recognize them, but he knew from their coveralls that they were from the submarine. Everyone was fuzzy. Even their voices were fuzzy.

"What?" he asked. He wasn't sure who he was asking, but he needed to say something to make it real.

"Rodriguez," a voice said. "Just relax, man. We'll get you out of here."

"What?" Rodriguez tried to sit up but then everything *did* go black. He was out before his head hit the sand.

PART III - GET ME THE HELL OUT OF HERE

16

Rodriguez woke up and looked around. Although things were still dark and fuzzy around the edges, his vision had cleared enough to see. Harrison and Bone were standing not far off, talking quietly amongst themselves while Ensign Klein was crouched nearby, hovering over another person laying in the sand.

"Harrison?"

"Rodriguez, you're awake." Harrison came over with a smile spread across his face. "Thought we might have lost you."

"Is this real?" he asked.

"The real deal, my man."

"How are you feeling?" Lieutenant Jackson asked. He was talking with Lieutenant Henry by the edge of the woods. He stepped closer and stood over Rodriguez.

"Like shit."

"Well, hopefully you'll feel better. We're fixing to get the fuck out of this place."

"How the hell are we going to do that?" Rodriguez asked. He brought his elbow underneath himself and tried to sit up.

"Whoa buddy, let me help you with that." Harrison pushed Rodriguez to a sitting position and stepped back. "You okay?"

"Sure, man. Never--" was all he could get out before vomiting once again. He got his head turned just in time to miss his already-soiled coveralls.

"Eew." Bone scrunched his face and stepped back a couple steps. "Dude, that's nasty."

"Not as--*urp*---nasty as your mom," Rodriguez choked. Harrison and Bone looked at each other and started laughing.

Lieutenant Henry walked toward them. "How's this prick doing?"

"Better, if he could stop fucking puking," Lieutenant Jackson said.

"Yeah well, I'd take puking over the bottom of that cesspool any day," Lieutenant Henry said.

"How's Dinesh doing?" Lieutenant Jackson asked.

"I don't know. We'll see, I guess."

"Dinesh made it out?" Rodriguez asked.

"Sorta," Bone said. "The fucker was tied to your waist."

"Yeah, when we pulled your dumb ass out, he came out too," Harrison added. "It was like a bonus. A two-fer."

"Where were you guys?"

"In the woods," Lieutenant Jackson said. "The nukes had us tied up, but once Cartwright and the Captain started going at it, they all took off. Turns out none of them really knew how to tie a knot, so we bagged ass and here we are, fishing you two pricks out of the drink."

"Well thanks for that," Rodriguez said.

"Don't thank us yet," Lieutenant Henry said. "Thank us when we're finally out of here."

"And how's that supposed to happen?" Rodriguez asked.

"On that." The Lieutenant pointed towards the water, where the Alexandria sat moored to a small but fully functional pier. Rodriguez stared at the boat, floating straight and looking solid and normal.

"What the fuck is going on here?"

"I don't know," Lieutenant Henry said. "But as soon as we get her fired up, I'm pretty sure I won't care."

The mighty USS Alexandria fired right up as faithful as she ever had. There were not many left of her crew, but after searching the surrounding woods they found enough nukes to start the reactor and keep it from exploding. On any other day, Rodriguez wouldn't have felt a warm fuzzy from that thought. *Not exploding is good enough to get our sorry asses out of here*, he thought. *Not exploding works just fine for me.*

There were two Sonar technicians, Rodriguez and Harrison. Harrison sat at the Basic Sonar Operator's stack while Rodriguez sat in a chair at the door between Sonar and the Control Room. His legs hung beneath him, bandaged but not very well. They were starting to hurt like holy hell, which he figured may or may not be a good thing.

Only three officers remained: Ensign Klein, Lieutenant Jackson, and Lieutenant Henry. Lieutenant Jackson took watch over the nukes in the Engine Room, Ensign Klein took watch in the Control Room, and Lieutenant Henry, being the senior man remaining, took watch as Officer of the Deck in the Bridge.

"So Lieutenant," Rodriguez said over the phone circuit. "You think we're really getting out of here?"

"I fucking hope so," Lieutenant Henry said.

"We've got ten people doing like forty jobs."

"I know," the Lieutenant said, "But as long as we don't have to shoot anyone we should be fine."

"I wish I had your optimism."

"Well find some, because I need you to run Sonar and Control."

"Me? I can't even walk. What about Ensign Klein?"

"Seriously?" Lieutenant Henry said. "Klein? That fuck stick can barely tie his shoes. He's my last choice to do pretty much anything. I only stuck him on the periscope so he feels useful."

"I'm just not sure I'm the guy for the job."

"That's bullshit and you know it. You've got more leadership potential than half the officers on board, you just don't fucking see it."

"Uh, okay. If you say so."

"Grow a pair of nuts, Rodriguez. Now's not the time to wuss out on me. It's time to go." With that, Lieutenant Henry hung up the phone and keyed the bridge microphone.

Rodriguez felt his stomach tighten up when he heard the Lieutenant's order.

"Back full, left fifteen degrees rudder," Lieutenant Henry said from the bridge. The order echoed through the nearly empty submarine. Ensign Klein jumped up and looked around the Control Room before grabbing the periscope and having a look around.

Bone sat in the driver's seat. He reached over with an unsteady hand and rang the order to maneuvering. When they responded, he brought his hand back to the steering wheel, both hands gripping too tight as he turned it to the left.

Rodriguez stared at the periscope display as the Ensign swung the optics around wildly. The boat pulled back from the pier and turned slowly around to face the black hole that was the tunnel they'd first entered.

"Rudder amidships, ahead one-third," Lieutenant Henry said as soon as they'd straightened out. Soon they were moving towards the tunnel. As they approached the entrance, he ordered "All stop."

The propeller stopped churning the water and the boat slipped quietly into the tunnel. They maintained forward momentum as if caught in a current. No order came from the bridge, and the tunnel was black as night.

Rodriguez looked back and forth between the periscope display and the Sonar display, but there was nothing to see. No one spoke. They barely even breathed. The trip was dark but short and uneventful. Soon, there was light.

They were back in the open ocean. The salt air poured through the ship, smelling every bit as fresh as Rodriguez had remembered. *It feels like it's been forever,* he thought as he leaned back in his chair and watched the natural flow of the waves across the Red Sea. The periscope display followed Ensign Klein's constant spin to the left. It took a few times around before Rodriguez noticed something was missing.

"Hey, where's the island?" he asked.

"What?" the Ensign asked without stopping.

"The island. The one we were just on?"

"Ida know."

Rodriguez leaned into the Sonar Room and asked Harrison, "Anything out there?"

"What?" Harrison asked. He stared at the screen as if he wasn't even seeing it. "No, man. Ain't shit out there."

Rodriguez picked up the handset and called the bridge. "Hey Lieutenant, where's the island?"

"Fuck that island," Lieutenant Henry said. "Go check the GPS and see where we are."

"I don't know how to do that."

"It's just like in a car, idiot," the Lieutenant said. "Well, sort of like a car." There was a pause as he took a deep breath.

"Yeah, it's not really like a car at all. Don't touch it, you'll just fuck it up."

"I *know*."

"All right, send up Ensign Fuckstick. I'll be right down."

"Roger that." Rodriguez hung up the handset and turned towards Ensign Klein. "Lieutenant Henry needs you in the bridge."

"What?" the Ensign asked. "Why?"

"Fuck if I know," Rodriguez said. "Maybe he needs to take a piss."

"Fine." His shoulders slouched and he let out a huff. "Take the scope."

"Uh, hello?" Rodriguez said as he pointed to his bandaged legs.

"*Fine*." Ensign Klein huffed again and stomped towards the ladder. He grumbled something under his breath as he climbed up to the bridge.

Not only does he look twelve, he acts twelve, Rodriguez thought as the Ensign disappeared around the corner.

In Sonar, Harrison was busy falling asleep at the stack.

Rodriguez slapped him in the back of the head. "Wake up, prick."

"Ow, man," Harrison said as his eyes popped open. "That hurt."

"It'll hurt a lot more if we run into something, so wake yourself up."

"Relax, there's nothing out here," Harrison said. "Can you get me some coffee?"

"Not until the mess decks are wheelchair-accessible."

"You're not in a wheelchair."

"I know that, you dick." Rodriguez leaned back and looked at the periscope monitor. He took a deep breath. *Okay Rodriguez, relax. Maybe there really* is *nothing out here.* He slid his chair over to the bottom sounder and looked at the chart. Supposedly they were in 500 feet of water. He looked over at Seaman Bone. "Hey Bone?"

"Yeah?"

"You know how to work the radar?"

"I'm a mechanic," he said. "What do you think?"

"Sorry. Just thought I'd ask."

"Don't fuck with the radar," Lieutenant Henry said. "You'll just fuck *that* up too."

Rodriguez turned around to see the Lieutenant stepping off the ladder and heading into the Control Room.

"Who let you out of your hole, anyway?" he asked.

"*You.*"

""Oh. Well, get back to Sonar."

"You told me to hang in here."

"Whatever," the Lieutenant said. "Just get the fuck out of my way. I need to find out where we are." He leaned over Rodriguez and keyed a few buttons on the GPS before moving over to the chart table. "Hmm."

"Hmm?"

"Hmm."

"Hmm what?" Rodriguez asked.

"It seems I have no idea where the fuck we are."

"What the fuck does *that* mean?" Bone asked.

"Shut up and drive, prick," Lieutenant Henry said. "Let the big boys handle this."

"I'm almost three hundred pounds," Bone said. "I *am* a big boy."

"Whatever, Nancy," Lieutenant Henry said. "That weight's all in your tits."

Bone looked down at his chest and dropped his head.

"So what's the deal, Lieutenant?" Rodriguez asked.

Lieutenant Henry walked to the other side of the Control Room, grabbed a stool, and sat down. He looked at the compass, but it spun in circles without stopping. "I have no idea," he said. They sat in silence for a bit, with only the sound of Bone breathing and the gentle rocking of the boat to keep them company.

"Wait," Rodriguez said. "Where's Dinesh?"

The Lieutenant cocked his head and said, "Good question. I kind of assumed he was with you."

"I haven't seen him since we stepped on board."

"I saw him," Bone said.

"Where?" Lieutenant Henry asked.

"Topside," he said. "Right before we left."

"Did he come aboard?"

Bone shrugged. "Don't know. Maybe he took a swim."

"You're an idiot," Lieutenant Henry said.

"I know."

As if in response, the wheel jerked out of Bone's hands. It moved all the way to the left and the ship lurched to the side.

Rodriguez fell out of his chair and rolled to the side to avoid being crushed by a loose chart locker. It crashed to the deck and slammed into the bottom sounder.

Lieutenant Henry's stool tilted and fell over, but he managed to grab on to the nearest periscope for balance. "What the fuck, Bone?"

"Dude, it's not me."

"Don't fucking call me dude."

"Control, Bridge, we're taking on water," Ensign Klein screamed through the loudspeaker. A wave of sea water began pouring through the bridge hatch and into the Control Room. It flowed through the upper level, tapering off to a trickle as the boat settled out and floated straight once again.

"Hey, Supervisor," Harrison called from Sonar. "You might want to see this.

Rodriguez pulled himself to his feet, biting his cheek until he tasted blood. He grabbed a nearby cardboard chart tube and leaned on it like a cane. That and the splint around his broken leg were strong enough to hold him upright. It hurt like a bitch, but by hanging onto nearby lockers or piping in the overhead with his other hand, he could at least move around. He headed for Sonar.

"Okay Harrison," he called as he made his way through the Control Room. "What have you got?" He made it to the door and leaned in through the frame.

"Fuck if I know, but it's big."

"I know it is, but you don't have to keep telling me," Lieutenant Henry said. "It's getting weird."

Rodriguez and Harrison stared at him as he walked over to the Sonar door.

"You know, my cock?" he said. "Because it's big?" He

looked back at the two but received no response. He cleared his throat and leaned past Rodriguez to stare at the Sonar screen. "What have you got, Sonar?"

Rodriguez pointed at Harrison's stack where a giant glowing contact was blocking out everything else on the display. He had only seen that happen once before, and that was when they had a near collision.

"What the balls is that?" Lieutenant Henry asked.

The loudspeaker came alive with the sound of screaming. Ensign Klein was shouting into the microphone but his voice came across as static. After a few seconds, the speaker cut out.

"Fuck." Lieutenant Henry headed for the ladder. "Rodriguez, come with me." He looked over his shoulder and his eyes darted to Rodriguez's bandaged leg. "Never mind," he said. "Can you get to middle level, gimpy?"

"I think so," Rodriguez said. He started for the aft ladder on the other side of the Control Room.

"Then here," the Lieutenant said as he pulled the cord of keys from around his neck and tossed them to Rodriguez. "Get to the small arms locker. Grab what you can."

"Pistols?" Rodriguez asked. "You think they'll do any good?"

"No, but it might make me feel better."

"What about me, Lieutenant?" Bone asked.

"Drive the fucking boat," the Lieutenant said. "Just go straight. Hopefully no one will get in our way."

"What if we reach land?"

"Land? Seriously?" The Lieutenant paused long enough to give Bone a disgusted look. "If we reach land, fucking turn around." He disappeared up the ladder without another word.

"Harrison, come with me," Rodriguez said.

"But who's going to man Sonar?"

"Are you fucking kidding me? Get your ass over here." Rodriguez made it to the ladder and lowered himself one rung at a time. He closed his eyes and chewed on his bloody cheek as he made a slow but steady descent to middle level.

Harrison stood at the top of the ladder, staring down at Rodriguez. "You need any help, boss?"

"Shut up." Rodriguez made it to the bottom and took a deep breath. He looked at the small arms locker by his foot. *At least the damn thing's right here*. He knelt down and found the correct key. He opened the locker and three boxes of 9mm ammunition spilled out on the deck. *Fuck.*

He reached in back and pulled out four Berettas and four loaded magazines, lining them up on the deck next to him. *Whatever's out there, this isn't going to help*, he thought as he loaded each pistol. He looked up at Harrison and held up a pistol.

"You know how to use this?"

"Of course," he said. "I'm qualified Topside Sentry and--"

"Fuck that," Rodriguez interrupted. "Do you know how to *use* this?"

Harrison nodded his head and said, "My dad was a hunter. He taught me how to shoot when I was nine."

"Good," Rodriguez said as he handed it up. "Take these." He handed three of the pistols to Harrison and stuck the third in his belt before grabbing the ladder. "Now head up to the bridge. Give one to the Lieutenant and one to Klein."

"What about you?"

"I'll be up," Rodriguez said. "I might be a while climbing this fucking ladder."

"Roger that." Harrison disappeared around the corner and the hall went quiet.

Rodriguez looked down the passageway. He listened for the sound of someone moving but the submarine was quiet. The mess decks were basked in fluorescent light; no flames cast dancing shadows on the walls. Middle level seemed completely normal.

He closed his eyes and climbed the ladder, one rung at a time. It felt like an eternity before he pulled his broken leg up the final rung and stood in upper level once again. *This is* really *gonna hurt later*, he thought as he made his way through the Control Room to the bridge ladder. He looked up but didn't see anyone near the top of the ladder.

"Hey, Harrison," he yelled. "Lieutenant? Ensign Klein?" He stared at the clear blue sky above and counted the number of rungs that led to the bridge. He pulled the Beretta from his belt and checked to be sure he had chambered a round. He had.

He stuffed it back in his belt and looked up towards the sky. *I'm not gonna make it*, he thought as he grabbed the ladder and pulled his leg up to the first step.

"Up ladder."

###

Rodriguez reached the top of the ladder, his legs numb and his arms like jelly. He climbed into the empty bridge and looked around. "Lieutenant?" He leaned over and saw the emergency ladder draped around the side. Harrison was hanging off the end, his eyes closed and a pistol clutched in his hand.

"Harrison," Rodriguez called.

Harrison opened his eyes and pressed the trigger. A bullet bounced off the sail and shot into the water. "*What the fuck was that*?" he screamed.

"That was you almost shooting yourself, you fucking idiot." Rodriguez looked around the sail. "Where's the Lieutenant? And Ensign Klein?"

"I don't know man, I think it got them."

"*What* got them?" Rodriguez asked before looking towards the aft end of the submarine. The top of the rudder showed through the churning water, slicing the waves as the Red Sea rushed by. Sitting atop the rudder was Dinesh.

He had grown bigger, nowhere near as large as Cartwright or the Captain had been, but he easily dwarfed the rudder he was perched on. In one hand he had Ensign Klein and in the other he had Lieutenant Henry. Both were waving their arms and kicking their legs as they stared at the rushing water below.

"Rodriguez," Dinesh said. "Good to see you again."

"I doubt that," Rodriguez said. "What the fuck, Dinesh?"

"What the fuck? What the *fuck*? This was supposed to be *our* time. Me and Singh. We had the Lahore on her way and you assholes came by and messed it all up. Well, the pirates messed things up too, but still. It's easier to blame you."

"What are you talking about?"

"*Then*, We've got the Alexandria...there...*on the island*...and that asshole Cartwright tries to take what's rightfully ours. Then

185

your Captain gets all righteous and even fucks *that* up. And *then*...you pricks manage to just...sail *away*?" He stomped his foot and the rudder shook, rocking the boat back and forth. "What. The. *Fuck*?"

"Come on, man," Rodriguez said. "You had nothing to do with all this, you know it."

Dinesh growled and slammed the Lieutenant Henry and Ensign together. They both stopped moving. "No," he said. "Not at first. It was Singh's idea, but when he showed me the power, it all became clear."

"What are you talking about?"

"You wouldn't understand," he said. "It's all about the *power*."

"What power?"

"Watch," he said. He draped Lieutenant Henry over his shoulder and held Ensign Klein up in the air. Dinesh's jaw opened to the point where it became unhinged and he stuffed the Ensign in his mouth whole.

Ensign Klein screamed as Dinesh crunched down. Streams of blood ran out at the corners of Dinesh's mouth. His eyes rolled back in his head as he savored the meal. His body grew in size as he consumed the Ensign. Soon Dinesh was almost too big to stand on top of the rudder. He choked down the final bits of broken bone and smiled at Rodriguez.

"Now turn this thing around," he screamed as he grabbed the rudder and leaned to the side. The boat lurched to port and the bow dipped below the waves.

Rodriguez fell to the side, his makeshift cane falling to the deck and dropping down to the bottom of the ladder. He pulled himself up and looked over the side. The boat had submerged to the point where the water was only a few feet down. He grabbed the bridge box and keyed the microphone, but the unit let out a pop as smoke poured from the speaker.

Shit. He yelled down the ladder, "Bone, can you straighten this thing out?"

"Won't...budge," Bone said through a series of grunts.

"Fuck." Rodriguez looked around.

The ship continued to drop as the boat turned. The sound of

grinding machinery came from the aft end as Dinesh slid his now enormous legs into the water and pulled the rudder all the way over. The waves splashed over Dinesh as he dug his heels into the aft end of the boat.

A wave crashed over Lieutenant Henry and he jumped awake. He grabbed Dinesh's shoulder and climbed on his head. He looked down at the water and then back at Rodriguez.

"Life ring," the Lieutenant shouted over the sounds of waves crashing and gears stripping.

"What?" Rodriguez asked.

"*Life. Ring,*" he repeated, pointing to the bridge.

Rodriguez looked over in the small lookout hatch and saw a bright orange life ring stashed in place. He pulled it out, untangling the length of line and coiling it at his feet.

"Throw it," Lieutenant Henry said.

Rodriguez held it over the side and threw it as hard as he could towards the rudder.

Lieutenant Henry jumped off Dinesh's head like it was a diving board. He crashed to the water within a few feet of the life ring. He reached out and grabbed the ring as he was sucked beneath the waves.

Rodriguez stared at the churning water, waiting for a glimpse of bright orange. Finally the life ring surfaced far enough aft to avoid the screw. The Lieutenant was still hanging on. The line at Rodriguez's feet was almost out; he grabbed the end and tied it quickly to a steel eyelet just as the line went taut. It held, but probably not for long.

Rodriguez brought up his pistol. He let out a long, slow breath and aimed for Dinesh's eye. One more breath in and slowly out as he pressed the trigger.

When the gun went off, Dinesh howled in pain. He let go of the rudder and clutched his face. Blood poured from the now empty socket as he fell into the water.

Rodriguez leaned down and yelled to Bone, "All back, reverse your rudder."

"On it," he replied.

Rodriguez held on to the sides of the bridge for support as the boat lunged to the opposite side. He watched Dinesh bounce off the rudder and get sucked down into the screw's vortex.

Rodriguez let out a fist pump and a "*Yessss*" as a fountain of blood shot into the sky.

Dinesh lurched out of the water, flipping in the air and crashing down in a wave of red. The boat reversed into him, the rudder bouncing him back and knocking him down under the water.

Lieutenant Henry was swimming as far away from the aft end as he could. He was at the end of the line and swimming in an arc towards the forward end of the boat.

Rodriguez grabbed his end of the line and started to pull. "Ahead one-third," he shouted to Bone.

"Roger that," Bone replied. The boat shuddered as the gears changed direction.

Rodriguez pulled the Lieutenant closer to the bridge, his eyes never leaving the thrashing, red-tinted whirlpool that swirled aft of the sub. Soon Lieutenant Henry was close enough to the bridge to grab the safety ladder where Harrison still clung.

"Move it, Shirley," Lieutenant Henry said. "I'm coming up."

Harrison shuffled up the ladder, his eyes never leaving the aft end of the boat. When he reached the top, Rodriguez reached out and helped him over.

"Thanks for the help," Rodriguez said.

Harrison looked at him with a blank stare before returning his attention to Dinesh. "He's coming back."

"No way," Rodriguez said. "I doubt he'll be able to swim fast enough, especially after eating our screw."

"He's coming back," Harrison repeated.

"He's right," Lieutenant Henry said as he climbed over the side. "Look."

Rodriguez leaned around Harrison and saw a rush of water approaching the aft end of the sub. The only thing visible was the top of Dinesh's head.

"Fuck this," Rodriguez said. He yelled down to the Control Room, "Bone, all ahead full."

"Roger that," Bone said.

"Harrison, get down there and make Dinesh a contact."

"What if he's not making enough noise?" Harrison asked. "I

need something to track."

"Fuck that, make him a manual contact. Just get me something back there we can shoot." He looked down and grabbed the 9mm from Harrison's hand. "Speaking of which, give me this before you shoot your dick off."

"Uh, sure," Harrison said as he started down the ladder. "On it."

"I told you you've got it in you," Lieutenant Henry said with a smile. "Since you're finally showing your nuts, what have you got in mind?"

"Well Sir," Rodriguez said. "I say we shoot the fucker."

"Kind of close, don't you think?"

"If we can open range, we should be able to throw one over our shoulder."

"Uh-huh," Lieutenant Henry said. "You sure about that?"

"Uh..." Rodriguez glanced behind them and scratched his head.

"Yeah. So instead of feeling like an idiot, how about we figure out how to make this work?"

"Okay Sir," Rodriguez said. "What have *you* got in mind?"

17

Rodriguez sat in the Control Room, his foot propped up on a stool as he sat at the Fire Control display. "I wish I had paid more attention to this shit."

"It's a piece of cake," Lieutenant Henry said from the periscope. He stared at the rush of water that was much farther back but still within sight. "Sonar sends you a contact and you make a bunch of lines. Then we shoot."

"You're not giving me a warm fuzzy," Rodriguez said.

"I'm not giving you a hug. Have you got your contact?"

"Sure I do, not that I have a lot of faith in it," Rodriguez said. "We've basically got a big fucking blob that keeps tracking directly behind us."

"Good enough," the lieutenant said. "I'll pass manual bearings from the scope if we need them. Are we all loaded?"

"Yeah, all four tubes are loaded. You think this will work?"

"Fuck if I know," he said. "Bone, slow to ahead one-third."

"Roger that."

"You got those keys?" Lieutenant Henry asked.

"Yes Sir." Rodriguez grabbed the spool of keys and tossed them to the Lieutenant.

He caught the keys and spun through them until he found one with green tape around the end. He pulled it off the ring and tossed it back to Rodriguez. "Take this to the Torpedo Room."

"You know I'm broke, don't you?" Rodriguez said as he pointed at his leg.

"No choice," Lieutenant Henry said. "It's either you or slap nuts in there." He pointed to Sonar where Harrison sat staring at his screen. His mouth was open wide and he had his finger digging in his ear.

"What about Bone?"

"Oh, sure," Lieutenant Henry said. "And I guess you know how to drive?"

"No..."

"Then quit bitching and get your ass down there."

Rodriguez sighed and looked at the key. "Yes Sir."

Lieutenant Henry turned to Bone. "Left full rudder, bring us to..." he looked over at the compass as it spun wildly out of control. "Aw, hell. Bring us fucking left."

"Fucking left," Bone said. "Got it." The boat leaned to the side as they came around.

Rodriguez stood and grabbed the piping overhead, pulling the weight off his leg as best he could. He slowly made his way through the Command Passageway and down the stairs to the lower level hatch. *Fuck this*, he thought as he lowered his broken leg through the opening and spun his body around the ladder. *I'm gonna be pissed if I kill myself on this damn ladder.*

He slid through the hatch, his broken leg hanging to the side as he gripped the metal railing. He landed on his good leg and hopped around the corner towards the Torpedo Room. He eyed the capsized toolbox nearby, its contents scattered across the floor like metal innards. There were no sounds from the surrounding darkness. From what he could see, nothing moved.

He moved to the control panel and found the override switch. He grabbed a nearby wrench and smashed the plastic safety cover off the key slot as he grabbed the microphone and keyed the Control Room.

"Control, Torpedo Room." He slid the key into the slot and turned. "Key engaged."

"Hey Rodriguez," Lieutenant Henry said over the loudspeaker.

"Yes sir?"

"Eat a dick," he said, followed by a chorus of amplified laughter from the Control Room.

Rodriguez stared at the speaker and resisted the urge to kick it to the floor.

"Relax, guy," the Lieutenant said as he caught his breath. "I think we can dispense with the formalities."

"Roger that, Sir," Rodriguez said. He held his hand over the override button. "Ready to engage override."

"Fucking quit readying yourself and just *do* it."

Rodriguez pressed the button and a glowing red sphere lit up in front of his eyes. It was so bright he had to turn away.

"Fire in the hole," Lieutenant Henry screamed through the

loudspeaker.

Shit, Rodriguez thought as he brought his hands up to cover his ears. He lost his balance and fell to the side, crashing to the deck as an explosion of air rocked the Torpedo Room. The torpedo in tube number one launched.

Asshole, Rodriguez thought as he pulled himself upright, grabbed the overhead pipes, and made his way back to the ladder. He had an easier time pulling himself up, and soon he was wandering up the Command Passageway towards the Control Room.

"You could have given me a warning," Rodriguez said as he drew closer to Lieutenant Henry.

"What?" the Lieutenant said as he stared through the periscope. "I warned you."

"*Fire in the hole* is not exactly a warning," Rodriguez said. "It's something idiots say in the movies."

"Well mom always said I ought to be in movies." He pulled his face away from the periscope and looked into Sonar. "You got a startup?"

"Yes Sir," Harrison said. "Bearing...uh, I don't know. The numbers keep changing. Maybe two-two-zero?"

"Good enough," Lieutenant Henry said. "Bone, steady as she goes."

"Right," Bone said. "Got it."

"Weapon has entered the baffles," Harrison said.

"Perfect," Lieutenant Henry said. He brought his eye back to the periscope and stared.

Rodriguez sat down at the Fire Control console and watched the ripple of water on the periscope display. It headed aft, right towards where Dinesh was moving.

"This is too easy," Lieutenant Henry said.

"Don't say that," Rodriguez said as he looked over at the Lieutenant. "Next thing you know, something fucked up--"

"*Shit*," Lieutenant Henry interrupted.

Rodriguez looked back at the display and saw a giant hand sticking out of the water, the now-impotent torpedo spinning its propellers in the air. "What the hairy ball licking *fuck*?"

"Lieutenant," Harrison said from Sonar. "There's a new

contact masking everything else back there."

"Gee, you fucking think?" Lieutenant Henry asked from the periscope. "That's the Captain back there."

Rodriguez stared at the monitor as the Captain's arm came out of the water, his head and shoulders rising with such force a wave crashed away from him and headed for the ship.

"Shit, Bone, bring us right," Lieutenant Henry screamed. "All ahead full, get us the fuck out of here."

"On it," Bone said as he rang the speed and cut the wheel all the way to the right.

"What the fuck is going on up there?" Lieutenant Jackson asked over the loudspeaker from the Engine Room.

"Not now, fucker," Lieutenant Henry said.

"Harrison," Rodriguez said as he hopped to the Sonar door. "Put a tracker on that thing."

"Why?" Lieutenant Henry asked. "So he can grab another torpedo? Or maybe he can pick us up instead. Play with us like we're a fucking bath toy."

"Dinesh is still out there," Rodriguez said. "And I'm betting the Captain isn't going to play nice."

As if on cue, a great rush of water signaled the arrival of Dinesh. He shot out of the water, one arm waving in the air and reaching for the Captain.

Dinesh's head had been split nearly in two where the submarine's propeller had caught him. His other arm hung limp at his side, holding on by little more than a flap of stretched-out skin. He lunged forward, his one good hand wrapping around the Captain's throat.

The Captain held the torpedo in the air and slammed it down into Dinesh's face. It slid halfway into Dinesh's eye before breaking apart, the tail section falling to the water and sinking into the violent waves. The forward section stuck out of Dinesh's bloody socket, wires hanging free and fuel spraying in all directions.

Dinesh screamed and leaned in close, his fingers still clutched around the Captain's throat. Dinesh lifted the Captain into the air and threw him to the side.

The Captain crashed down into the waves and submerged

for only a moment before bouncing up and rocketing toward Dinesh.

"Now's the time," Lieutenant Henry said as he marked a bearing with the periscope. "Sonar, make that a visual contact."

"On it," Rodriguez said. He tapped Harrison on the shoulder and pointed to the screen. "Do it."

"Contact designated Victor-Six-Nine," Harrison said.

Lieutenant Henry looked up from his periscope and stared at Rodriguez. "Really?"

Rodriguez shrugged and dropped himself onto the bench in front of the Firing Console.

"Fuck it," Lieutenant Henry said. "Rodriguez, fire all three remaining torpedoes."

"I don't have to go back to the Torpedo Room, do I?"

"Not as long as you left the key engaged."

"Perfect." Rodriguez dialed in a firing solution and selected the three remaining torpedo tubes. "Firing in three...two..." He pressed the override button and gave the thumbs-up. "One."

"Fire." Lieutenant Henry pressed the launch switches and the ship rocked with the force of three torpedo tubes going off, one after the other.

In the water, the Captain crashed into Dinesh, his hands balled into fists that crashed into Dinesh's skull. The forward section of the torpedo in his eye broke through the back of his head and plunged into the water below. A stream of blood and brain followed soon after.

"Weapons have started up," Harrison said.

Dinesh reeled back, his hand clutching his face as he swung his limp arm from side to side.

The Captain didn't wait; he dove forward again, his fists raised high as he shot into the air. He came down, each fist slamming into Dinesh's shoulders.

Dinesh's arms dropped to his sides. His head dropped back and he stared up to the sky. His mouth hung open and blood pouring from every orifice.

The Captain hovered over him, a smile spreading across his face.

"They're off," Harrison said. "The weapons are off target."

"Fucking Sonar," Lieutenant Henry said. "Where are my weapons?"

"They're out there," Rodriguez said, "but he's right. We're off target."

"Well here," the Lieutenant screamed. "Here's a fucking bearing." He marked the target on the periscope and it updated the Firing Console. "Want some more? Have some more." He marked five more bearings in quick succession.

Rodriguez watched the bearings appear on the console. They scattered across his display with no real semblance of track. "It's not helping," he said. "The fucking bearings are off, all of them."

"Not my fault," Harrison said.

"Shut the fuck up," Lieutenant Henry said. "Rodriguez, we just shot our entire load, you need to make this happen or we're toast."

"How? You want me to steer the things?"

"Do it."

"That never works," Rodriguez said.

"Well fucking do it anyway," Lieutenant Henry said. "Just get those things on target."

Rodriguez sighed. "Fine. Switching to manual." He keyed a button and grabbed the inch-long joystick on the console in front of him. "Which way?"

"Come left," Harrison said. "Maybe...twenty degrees?"

"Shit." Rodriguez held the stick left and watched the dots track left. "What's our range?"

"I don't know," Harrison said. "Nothing works."

"I *know* nothing works," Rodriguez said. "Can't you guess?"

"We're not gonna make it," Bone said.

"Fuck you," Lieutenant Henry said. "We *are* gonna make it." He looked through the periscope and saw the trails of water where the weapons turned towards the Captain and Dinesh. "We have to."

The Captain was hammering Dinesh over the head, his fists swinging like a windmill as they crushed what remained of his skull. Bits of bone fell away as thick mucus and chunks of brain mixed with the blood that poured into the sea.

Dinesh stood completely still, not even a twitch from his

broken body.

Rodriguez watched through the periscope monitor, waiting for Dinesh to fall, wondering why the hell he hadn't.

"Where are we, Rodriguez?" Lieutenant Henry asked. The plume of water from the torpedoes continued curving towards the two of them, but they weren't moving fast enough.

"Working on it."

"Work harder," the Lieutenant said. "He's almost finished with Dinesh, and I'm sure we're next."

"I'm fucking working on it."

"*Well fucking work harder.*"

"Why don't you drift those things?" Harrison asked.

"Fucking *what*?"

"Seriously, crank the wheel and kick in the speed."

"You're an idiot," Lieutenant Henry said.

"You know we want them to turn," Rodriguez said. "Not go straight."

"Yeah, but once the blades catch they should take off in a straight line," Harrison said. "At least, I think so. Right?"

"You're an idiot," Lieutenant Henry repeated. "This isn't Grand Theft Auto."

"No wait," Rodriguez said. "That might work."

"So now *you're* an idiot."

"No, they're not going to drift. It's not like tires," Rodriguez said. "But if we drop the speed, adjust the heading, then crank it to full speed without going through the steps..." He scratched the stubble on his chin and looked back at the Lieutenant. "It will mess up the gyro, but the propellers should catch."

"Or, they could shut down," Lieutenant Henry said.

"Yeah," Rodriguez said. "That too."

"You know what? I think it might work," Bone said.

"Thanks for your input, wrench monkey," Lieutenant Henry said. "I'm surrounded by idiots." He looked at Rodriguez. "Fuck it. Do it, but if we die I'm blaming you."

Rodriguez looked back at the Fire Control console. The manual steering wasn't going to work. The torpedoes just weren't turning fast enough to make it on their own. "Fuck it." He killed the speed and saw warning lights appear above his head. "I know, I know," he whispered as he turned the torpedoes to the left.

"Lost contact on all weapons," Harrison said.

"No shit," Rodriguez said. "What's your bearing?"

"Uh...two-two-zero? No, wait. Try one-six-zero. Or two-six--"

"Never mind," Rodriguez said. "I'll make it up. He swung around in his chair and pointed one arm towards the front of the sub. With the other, he pointed towards the line of bearing the Lieutenant was looking at through the periscope.

"What the fuck are you doing?" Lieutenant Henry asked.

"Sonar karate," Rodriguez said. "I'm going with one-five zero." He dialed in the new bearing just as the warning lights began to blink.

"You're losing them," the Lieutenant said.

"Not a chance." Rodriguez dialed a new bearing on all three torpedoes and set the speed to max. "Fucking work," he whispered as he waited for something to happen.

"Nothing," Harrison said.

"Give it a minute."

"Talk to me, Rodriguez," Lieutenant Henry said.

"Patience."

"You broke them," Bone said. "Didn't you?"

"Fuck off, Boner."

In the water, the Captain pulled his fist back and punched Dinesh in the chest.

Dinesh's limp body flew out of the water and splashed down a few hundred feet away. Without a sign of life, he sunk beneath the waves.

The Captain turned towards the submarine and smiled.

"That's it, we're toast," Lieutenant Henry said. "Which one of you is sucking my dick before we die?" He reached down and unzipped his pants.

"Not it," Rodriguez said as he touched the tip of his nose.

The Lieutenant turned towards the helm "Bone?"

"Uh--"

"Eew, never mind," Lieutenant Henry said. "You're gross." He turned towards the door to Sonar. "Guess that leaves you,

Harrison."

"Fuck *that*, Sir," Harrison said. "I'm not--wait, multiple contacts bearing...well, somewhere. Sounds like weapon start-up."

"I fucking knew it," Rodriguez said as he slapped the console in front of him. "Now move." On the screen, the dots began appearing once again. They stacked on top of each other, the gyro spinning in circles as they tried to figure out where they were supposed to go. Little by little, they began to track towards the contact.

"Am I pulling my cock out or not?"

"Put your junk away, Lieutenant, we've got movement."

"Are you sure?" Lieutenant Henry asked as he zipped up his pants and went back to the scope.

The Captain was marching through the water, heading for the submarine much faster than Dinesh had been moving.

"Yup," Rodriguez said. "I'm sure."

The Lieutenant stared through the periscope until he saw the ripple of water that was the trio of torpedoes. "I see them. I think they're actually on track."

"What's the range?"

"Not a clue," he said. "I can't even give you a bearing."

Rodriguez looked up at the periscope monitor and tried to judge the distance between the torpedoes and the Captain. "Do we have enough time?"

"Tell you what," Lieutenant Henry said. "You hold your finger over the "blow-the-fuck-up" button and I'll tell you when to press it. Sound good?"

"What?"

The Captain stopped moving and looked down at the water. He held his hands out just above the surface, as if waiting for the torpedoes to get close enough to grab.

"He's going for the weapons," the Lieutenant said. "Stand by."

"Standing by," Rodriguez said. He held his finger over the destruct button and selected the first torpedo.

The three torpedoes ran through the water as the Captain's fingers flexed and clutched the air before opening again. His arms had grown incredibly long; they stretched far away from his body.

"He's gonna grab them," Lieutenant Henry said.

"What?"

"It's not gonna work. He's gonna grab them before they get close enough to do any damage."

"Can you see all three of them?" Rodriguez asked.

"Yeah, they're headed right for him," Lieutenant Henry said.

"No, I mean can you tell that there are three?"

"No, it's just a blob of water rushing towards him."

"Good." Rodriguez selected the second and third torpedoes and killed their engines.

"What the fuck are you doing?" the Lieutenant asked.

"I'm slowing two of them down," Rodriguez said. "We let him grab the first one, then blow it up when he grabs it." He dialed a new course for the second and third torpedoes, each just a few degrees to either side. "That's gotta hurt at least a little, so while he's distracted these two can get right up on him."

"Good idea. It'd better work," Lieutenant Henry said.

"Do we have a choice?" Rodriguez didn't wait for an answer. He cranked the engines on the second and third torpedoes and went back to the first. His finger hovered over the destruct button. "Just let me know as soon as the first one leaves the water."

"Well get ready, because we're almost there." Lieutenant Henry watched the Captain's finger twitch and he plunged his hand into the water. "Wait for it."

The Captain twisted his arm around and pulled it up with the lead torpedo in his hand.

"Now!"

Rodriguez pressed the button and the explosives inside the torpedo went off.

The Captain hurled the burning metal over his head and shook his hand in the air. His mouth opened in a scream as he took a step towards the submarine.

"It's now or never," Lieutenant Henry said. The plumes of water from the second and third torpedo split off towards either side of the Captain.

"Just give me the word," Rodriguez said. He switched over to the second torpedo and waited.

"Now," Lieutenant Henry said as the torpedoes reached their closest point of approach.

Rodriguez pressed the button and switched to the third torpedo.

A cone of water shot up in the air to the left of the Captain. A chunk of his hip tore apart and he fell away from the explosion. His arms went to the water for balance as the third torpedo exploded.

His arms flew through the air, each going in a separate direction. The Captain spun around until he faced away from the submarine. A massive hole had opened up in his back. It was so large that even through the periscope monitor Rodriguez could see the sky beyond.

The Captain swayed back and forth as an ocean of red poured out from his wounds. He let out a final bloody scream as he fell backwards.

Amidst a sea of red foam, the Captain sunk beneath the depths of the Red Sea.

###

"Fucking A," Lieutenant Henry said. "That shit made my dick hard." He turned to Rodriguez. "Guess you guys aren't such idiots after all."

"Well thanks, Sir," Rodriguez said. "Great to know you've got our backs."

"Yeah, thanks," Harrison said before digging into his nose.

"That include me?" Bone asked.

"Don't press your luck," the Lieutenant said.

Rodriguez cleared his display and noticed something had changed. "Hey Lieutenant," he said, "Looks like this shit works again."

"Oh yeah?" He leaned in for a closer look. "Well I'll be damned. Bone, what about you?"

"I've got a solid heading of one-one-four," Bone said.

"No shit?" the Lieutenant glanced through the periscope a

final time before walking over to the GPS. "I wonder if this thing works too." He picked it up turned it on.

"Working just fine, isn't it?" Rodriguez asked.

"Yup," Lieutenant Henry said. "I've got a fix on our position, now let's figure out how to get home." He stepped over to the navigation charts and drew a few lines.

Rodriguez leaned back in his chair and looked at the Sonar display. Everything had returned to normal. Bearings were tracking as they should, and Harrison was falling asleep, just like usual. Rodriguez slapped him in the back of the head.

"Wake up, prick."

"What? I wasn't sleeping," Harrison said as he reached up and rubbed his eyes. "Can someone get me some coffee?"

"Get it yourself," the Lieutenant said. "We're on the surface in the middle of nowhere, and the only other people on board are doing much more important work than you."

"Oh," Harrison said. "Really?" He stood up and retreated towards the forward Sonar Room door, staring at Rodriguez the whole time.

"Fucking go," Rodriguez said. "Just get me a cup while you're at it. Blond and not-too-sweet."

"Black and bitter for me," Lieutenant Henry said.

"Can I have some apple juice?" Bone asked.

"Fucking apple juice?" Lieutenant Henry said. He looked at Harrison. "Get this prick a cup of coffee."

"How do you want it?" Harrison asked.

"Uh, I guess same as you?" Bone said. "I don't drink the stuff."

"Okay," Harrison said. Black with a drop of urine." He disappeared around the corner.

Bone looked at Rodriguez. "Wait, was he serious?"

"You'll have to try it to find out," Rodriguez said. "So Lieutenant, are we really in the middle of nowhere?"

"No, we're right off the coast. Matter of fact, I'm surprised no one has yelled at us yet." He walked over to the periscope, turned it in the opposite direction, and zoomed in. Land appeared in the distance. "That, my friend, is Egypt."

"I don't see any pyramids," Bone said.

"That's because you're an idiot."

"You think someone will come looking for us?" Rodriguez asked. "My leg kind of hurts. I'd like to get it checked out."

"Always thinking about yourself," Lieutenant Henry said. "You know they name street signs after you?"

"Yeah, I know" Rodriguez said. "One way."

"US submarine, this is the USS Nicholas, do you copy?" The voice came from the radio unit at the back of the Control Room.

"Guess you're going to get your leg looked at after all,' Lieutenant Henry said as he walked over to the console. He picked up the handset and responded. "USS Nicholas, this is Alexandria. We read you loud and clear." He turned to Rodriguez and smiled. "Hey fuckhead."

"Yeah, Lieutenant?"

"Just in case I forget to say it, which I will...good job."

EPILOGUE

Rodriguez lay in a hospital bed, in considerably less pain and far more comfort than he'd seen in months. His leg was wrapped in a cast that hung from a hook in the ceiling. He was busy watching re-runs of the Adam West Batman TV series and sipping on a cup of shitty hospital coffee. He took a drink each time *Pow!*, *Bam!*, or *Socko!* flashed across the screen.

He was in his own room so he had free reign over the television. As the credits rolled, he grabbed the remote to change the channel. Before he found something new, the door swung open. A grumpy-looking bald man with four stars on his lapel and a chest full of medals walked in.

"Petty Officer Rodriguez?" he asked.

"Yes Sir," Rodriguez said. He moved to stand but the Admiral waved him down.

"Don't be silly," he said. "You're strung up like a dead cat in a cannibal's kitchen." He walked over to the chair by the window and sat down. "I'm Paul Franks," he said. "Mind if I have a seat?"

"Not at all," Rodriguez said. *Considering your crusty ass already has.*

"That's one hell of a story you boys had to tell."

"Yes Admiral, I imagine it was."

"Do you know why I'm here?"

"Maybe to tell me what an idiot I am?" Rodriguez asked.

The Admiral cocked an eyebrow and stared at Rodriguez.

"Just a guess," Rodriguez said. He cleared his throat. "Uh, no Sir, I don't know why you're here."

"Well, after careful consideration of your story and the corroboration of Lieutenant Henry, I am here to tell you we have a proposition for you."

"We?" Rodriguez asked. "Who's we?"

"The details are above your clearance level, but I *can* tell you that if you sign on under a special reenlistment option you will be put in for a Top Secret S.C.I. clearance and advance promotion."

"A promotion?"

"That's right," the Admiral said. "We can make you a Chief, just like that." He snapped his finger for emphasis.

"Why the hell would I want to do that?" Rodriguez asked.

"Well it certainly isn't mandatory," the Admiral said. "I understand you were running the Sonar department without a Chief, is that right?"

"That's right," Rodriguez said. "But seriously, what exactly are we talking about?"

"We're in need of someone with a certain...type...of experience. You and Lieutenant Henry were both identified as having that kind of experience based on your recent encounter on the Alexandria."

"Wait, you mean you believe us?"

"On the record, your story is a bunch of horseshit," the Admiral said. "Off the record, you're not the first to tell such a story. We may or may not have a team of individuals to handle...*delicate* situations like what you boys found in the Red Sea."

"So you've put together a group of crazy motherfuckers who hunt down the shit that on the record doesn't exist? That's some X-Files shit right there, Sir."

"Something like that, yes."

"And if I don't sign up, I'm basically a crazy motherfucker who's gonna get kicked out of the Navy for making shit up."

"That, and I'll deny ever speaking with you."

"Uh-huh." Rodriguez rubbed the week's-worth of stubble that covered his chin and smiled. "Well hell, I'm already crazy. Do I get a raise out of it?"

"Aside from the potential for promotion, there are various...incentives. They're not all monetary, but I'm sure you'll appreciate them. Plus, Lieutenant Henry...excuse me-- Lieutenant *Commander* Henry--has already requested you on his team."

"Wait, I get to work with the Lieutenant?"

"Lieutenant *Commander*," The Admiral said. "And yes, you do."

Rodriguez looked out the window at the star-filled sky beyond. *Do I really want to go through that shit again? Or maybe worse?* He looked at the Admiral and opened his mouth to speak, but closed it as he wondered, *Or do I want to go back to the same old routine, tracking merchants ships and fishing trawlers across the Atlantic?*

"What do you say, son?" The Admiral asked.

"Okay Admiral," Rodriguez said. "Where do I sign?"